THE BODY IN QUESTION...

"You'd better look," Julia said. "Down there. Down."

Ricky looked through the gap. Water glinted below in the shadows. Trampled mud stank and glistened. Deep scars and slides ploughed the bank. Everything was dead still down there. Particularly the interloper who lay smashed and discarded, face upwards, in the puddled ditch, her limbs all higgledy-piggledy at impossible angles, her mouth awash with muddy water, and her foolish eyes wide open and staring at nothing at all...

"A MASTER OF DIALOGUE
AND CHARACTERIZATION."
—*Los Angeles Herald-Examiner*

"SHE HAS THE GIFT..."
—Erle Stanley Gardner

Also by Ngaio Marsh
from Jove

ARTISTS IN CRIME
BLACK AS HE'S PAINTED
CLUTCH OF CONSTABLES
COLOUR SCHEME
DEAD WATER
DEATH AND THE DANCING FOOTMAN
DEATH AT THE BAR
DEATH IN A WHITE TIE
DEATH IN ECSTASY
DEATH OF A FOOL
DEATH OF A PEER
DIED IN THE WOOL
ENTER A MURDERER
FALSE SCENT
FINAL CURTAIN
GRAVE MISTAKE
HAND IN GLOVE
KILLER DOLPHIN
LIGHT THICKENS
A MAN LAY DEAD
NIGHT AT THE VULCAN
THE NURSING HOME MURDER
OVERTURE TO DEATH
PHOTO FINISH
SCALES OF JUSTICE
SINGING IN THE SHROUDS
SPINSTERS IN JEOPARDY
TIED UP IN TINSEL
VINTAGE MURDER
WHEN IN ROME
A WREATH FOR RIVERA

NGAIO MARSH
Last Ditch

A JOVE BOOK

This Jove book contains the complete
text of the original hardcover edition.
It has been completely reset in a typeface
designed for easy reading and was printed
from new film.

LAST DITCH

A Jove Book / published by arrangement with
Little, Brown and Company, Inc.

PRINTING HISTORY
Little, Brown and Company edition published 1977
Three previous paperback printings
Jove edition / July 1981
Third printing / December 1986

ISBN: 0-515-08798-X

Jove Books are published by The Berkley Publishing Group,
200 Madison Avenue, New York, NY 10016.
The words "A JOVE BOOK" and the "J" with sunburst
are trademarks belonging to Jove Publications, Inc.

PRINTED IN THE UNITED STATES OF AMERICA

Cast of Characters

YOUNG RODERICK ALLEYN (RICKY)

CHIEF SUPERINTENDENT RODERICK ALLEYN: HIS FATHER

TROY ALLEYN: HIS MOTHER

INSPECTOR FOX: HIS GODFATHER

JASPER PHARAMOND

JULIA PHARAMOND: HIS WIFE

SELINA & JULIETTA PHARAMOND: THEIR DAUGHTERS

LOUIS PHARAMOND: THEIR COUSIN

CARLOTTA PHARAMOND: HIS WIFE

BRUNO PHARAMOND: JASPER'S BROTHER

SUSIE DE WAITE

DULCIE HARKNESS: AN EQUESTRIENNE

CUTHBERT HARKNESS: HER UNCLE

GILBERT FERRANT: OF DEEP COVE

MARIE FERRANT: HIS WIFE

LOUIS FERRANT: THEIR SON

SYDNEY JONES: A PAINTER

BOB MAISTRE: LANDLORD OF THE COD-AND-BOTTLE

SERGEANT PLANK: OF DEEP COVE
MRS. PLANK: HIS WIFE
THEIR DAUGHTER

DR. CAREY: POLICE SURGEON, MONTJOY
BOB BLACKER: VETERINARY SURGEON
POLICE CONSTABLES MOSS & CRIBBAGE
JIM LE COMPTE: A SAILOR

SUNDRY FISHERMEN, WAITERS, AND INNKEEPERS.

For
The Family at Walnut Tree Farm

Last Ditch

1

Deep Cove

I

WITH ALL THEIR easygoing behavior there was,
nevertheless, something rarified about the Pharamonds. Or so, on his first encounter with them, it
seemed to Ricky Alleyn.

Even before they came into their drawing room, he
had begun to collect this impression of its owners. It
was a large, eccentric, and attractive room with lemon-
colored walls, polished floor, and exquisite, grubby
Chinese rugs. The two dominant pictures, facing each
other at opposite ends of the room, were of an irritable
gentleman in uniform and a lavishly bosomed
impatient lady, brandishing an implacable fan.

Elsewhere he saw, with surprise, several unframed sketches, drawing-pinned to the walls, one of them being of a free, if not lewd, character.

He had blinked his way around these incompatibles and had turned to the windows and the vastness of sky and sea beyond them when Jasper Pharamond came quickly in.

"Ricky Alleyn!" he stated. "How pleasant. We're all delighted."

He took Ricky's hand, gaily tossed it away and waved him into a chair. "You're like both your parents," he observed. "Clever of you."

Ricky, feeling inadequate, said his parents sent their best remembrances and had talked a great deal about the voyage they had taken with the Pharamonds as fellow passengers.

"They were *so* nice to us," Jasper said. "You can't think. VIPs as they were, and all."

"They don't feel much like VIPs."

"Which is one of the reasons one likes them, of course. But do tell me, exactly why have you come to the island and is the lodging Julia found for you endurable?"

Feeling himself blush, Ricky said that he hoped he had come to work through the Long Vacation, that his accommodation with a family in the village was just what he had hoped for, and that he was very much obliged to Mrs. Pharamond for finding it.

"She adores doing that sort of thing," said her husband. "But aren't you over your academic hurdles with all sorts of firsts and glories? Aren't you a terribly young don?"

Ricky mumbled wildly and Jasper smiled. His small hooked nose dipped and his lip twitched upwards. It was a faunish smile and agreed with his cap of tight curls.

"I know," he said; "you're writing a novel."

"I've scarcely begun."

"And you don't want to talk about it. How wise you are. Here come the others, or some of them."

Two persons came in, a young woman and a youth of about thirteen years whose likeness to Jasper established him as a Pharamond.

"Julia," Jasper said, "and Bruno. My wife and my brother."

Julia was beautiful. She greeted Ricky with great politeness and a ravishing smile, made inquiries about his accommodation, and then turned to her husband.

"Darling," she said. "A surprise for you. A girl."

"What do you mean, Julia? Where?"

"With the children in the garden. She's going to have a baby."

"Immediately?"

"Of course not." Julia began to laugh. Her whole face broke into laughter. She made a noise like a soda-water syphon and spluttered indistinguishable words. Her husband watched her apprehensively. The boy, Bruno, began to giggle.

"Who is this girl?" Jasper asked. And to Ricky: "You must excuse Julia. Her life is full of drama."

Julia addressed herself warmly to Ricky. "It's just that we do seem to get ourselves let in for rather peculiar situations. If Jasper stops interrupting I'll explain."

"I have stopped interrupting," Jasper said.

"Bruno and the children and I," Julia explained to Ricky, "drove to a place called Leathers to see about hiring horses from the stable people. Harness, they're called."

"Harkness," said Jasper.

"Harkness. Mr. and Miss. Uncle and niece. So they weren't in their office and they weren't in their stables. We were going to look in the horse paddock when we heard someone howling. And I mean *really* howling. Bawling. And being roared back at. In the harness room, it transpired, with the door shut. Something about Mr. Harkness threatening to have somebody called Mungo shot because he'd kicked the sorrel mare. I think perhaps Mungo was a horse. But while we stood helpless it turned into Mr. H. calling Miss H. a Whore of Babylon. Too awkward. Well, what would you have done?"

Jasper said: "Gone away."

"Out of tact or fear?"

"Fear."

Julia turned enormous eyes on Ricky.

"So would I," he said hurriedly.

"Well, so might I, too, because of the children, but before I could make up my mind there came the sound of a really hard slap and a yell, and the tack-room door burst open. Out flew Miss Harness."

"Harkness."

"Well, anyway out she flew and bolted past us and round the house and away. And there in the doorway stood Mr. Harkness with a strap in his hand, roaring out Old Testament anathemas."

"What action did you take?" asked her husband.

"I turned into a sort of policewoman and said, 'What seems to be the trouble, Mr. Harkness?' and he strode away."

"And then?"

"We left. We couldn't go running after Mr. Harkness when he was in that sort of mood."

"He might have hit *us,*" Bruno pointed out. His voice had the unpredictable intervals of adolescence.

"Could we get back to the girl in the garden with the children? A sense of impending disaster seems to tell me she is Miss Harkness."

"But none other. We came upon her on our way home. She was standing near the edge of the cliffs with a very odd look on her face, so I stopped the car and talked to her and she's nine weeks gone. My guess is that she won't tell Mr. Harkness who the man is, which is why he set about her with the strap."

"Did she tell you who the man is?"

"Not yet. One mustn't nag, don't you feel?" asked Julia, appealing to Ricky. "All in good time. Come and meet her. She's not howling now."

Before he could reply two more Pharamonds came in: an older man and a young woman, each looking very like Bruno and Jasper. They were introduced as "our cousins, Louis and Carlotta." Ricky supposed them to be brother and sister until Louis put his arms around Carlotta from behind and kissed her neck. He then noticed that she wore a wedding ring.

"Who," she asked Julia, "is the girl in the garden with the children? Isn't she the riding-school girl?"

"Yes, but I can't wade through it all again now, darling. We're going out to meet her, and you can come too."

"We have met her already," Carlotta said. "On that narrow path, one could hardly shove by without uttering. We passed the time of day."

"Perhaps it would be kinder to bring her indoors," Julia suggested. "Bruno, darling, be an angel and ask Miss Harkness to come in."

Bruno strolled away. Julia called after him: "And bring the children, darling, for Ricky to meet." She gave Ricky a brilliant smile: "You *have* come in for a tricky luncheon haven't you?" she said.

"I expect I can manage," he replied, and the Pharamonds looked approvingly at him. Julia turned to Carlotta. "Would you say you were about the same size?" she asked.

"As who?"

"Darling, as Miss Harkness. Her present size, I mean, of course. Sufficient unto the day is the evil thereof."

"What is all this?" Carlotta demanded in a rising voice. "What's Julia up to?"

"No good, you may depend upon it," Jasper muttered. And to his wife: "Have you asked Miss

Harkness to stay? Have you dared?"

"But where else is there for her to go? She can't return to Mr. Harkness and be beaten up. In her condition. Face it."

"They are coming," said Louis, who was looking out the windows. "I don't understand any of this. Is she lunching?"

"And staying, apparently," said Carlotta. "And Julia wants me to give her my clothes."

"Lend, not give, and only something for the night," Julia urged. "Tomorrow there will be other arrangements."

Children's voices sounded in the hall. Bruno opened the door and two little girls rushed noisily in. They were aged about five and seven and wore nothing but denim trousers with crossover straps. They flung themselves upon their mother, who greeted them in a voice fraught with emotion.

"*Dar*-lings!" cried Julia, tenderly embracing them.

Then came Miss Harkness.

She was a well-developed girl with a weather-beaten complexion and hands so horny that Ricky was reminded of hooves. A marked puffiness around the eyes bore evidence to her recent emotional contretemps. She wore jodhpurs and a checked shirt.

Julia introduced her all around. Miss Harkness changed her weight from foot to foot, nodded and sometimes said "Uh." The Pharamonds all set up a conversational breeze while Jasper produced a tray of drinks. Ricky and Bruno drank beer and the family either sherry or white wine. Miss Harkness in a hoarse voice asked for Scotch and soda and downed it in three noisy gulps. Louis Pharamond began to talk to her about horses, and Ricky heard him say he had played polo badly in Brazil.

How pale they all were, Ricky thought. Really, they looked as if they had been forced, like vegetables under covers, and had come out severely bleached. Even

Julia, a Pharamond only by marriage, was without
color. Hers was a lovely pallor, a dramatic setting for
her impertinent eyes and mouth. She was rather like an
Aubrey Beardsley lady.

At luncheon, Ricky sat on her right and had
Carlotta for his other neighbor. Diagonally opposite,
by Jasper, and with Louis on her right, sat Miss
Harkness with another whiskey and soda, and
opposite her, on their father's left, the little girls who
were called Selina and Julietta. Louis was the darkest
and much the most *mondain* of all the Pharamonds.
He wore a threadlike black moustache and a silken
jumper and was smoothly groomed. He continued to
make one-sided conversation with Miss Harkness,
bending his head towards her and laughing in a
flirtatious manner into her baleful face. Ricky noticed
that Carlotta, who, he gathered, was Louis's cousin as
well as his wife, glanced at him from time to time with
amusement.

"Have you spotted our 'Troy'?" Julia asked Ricky,
and pointed to a picture above Jasper's head. He had,
but had been too shy to say so. It was a conversation
piece—a man and a woman seated in the foreground,
and behind them a row of wind-blown promenaders,
dashingly indicated against a lively sky.

"Jasper and me," Julia said, "on board the *Oriana*.
We adore it. Do you paint?"

"Luckily, I don't even try."

"A policeman, perhaps?"

"Not even that, I'm afraid. An unnatural son."

"Jasper," said his wife, "is a mathematician and is
writing a book about the binomial theorem but you
mustn't say I said so because he doesn't care to have
it known. Selina, darling, one more face like that and
out you go before the pudding which is strawberries
and cream."

Selina, with the aid of her fingers, had dragged
down the corners of her mouth, slitted her eyes, and

leered across the table at Miss Harkness. She let her
face snap back into normality, and then lounged in her
chair, sinking her chin on her chest and rolling her eyes.
Her sister, Julietta, was consumed with laughter.

"Aren't children awful," Julia asked, "when they set
out to be witty? Yesterday at luncheon Julietta said,
'My pud's made of mud,' and they both laughed
themselves sick. Jasper and I were made quite
miserable by it."

"It won't last," Ricky assured her.

"It had better not." She leaned toward him. He
caught a whiff of her scent, became startlingly aware of
her thick immaculate skin, and felt an extraordinary
stillness come over him.

"So far, so good, wouldn't you say?" she breathed.
"I mean—at least she's not cutting up rough."

"She's eating quite well," Ricky muttered.

Julia gave him a look of radiant approval. He was
uplifted. "Gosh!" he thought. "Oh, gosh, what is all
this?"

It was with a sensation of having been launched
upon uncharted seas that he took his leave of the
Pharamonds and returned to his lodging in the village.

"That's an upsetting lady," thought Ricky. "A very
lovely and upsetting lady."

II

The fishing village of Deep Cove was on the north
coast of the island: a knot of cottages clustered around
an unremarkable bay. There was a general store and
post office, a church and a pub—the Cod-and-Bottle.
A van drove over to Montjoy on the south coast with
the catch of fish when there was one. Montjoy, the only
town on the island, was a tourist resort with three
smart hotels. The cove was eight miles away, but not

many Montjoy tourists came to see it because there were no "attractions," and it lay off the main road. Tourists did, however, patronize Leathers, the riding school and horse-hiring establishment run by the Harknesses. This was situated a mile out of Deep Cove and lay between it and the Pharamonds' house, which was called L'Esperance and had been in the possession of the family, Jasper had told Ricky, since the mid-eighteenth century. It stood high above the cliffs and could be seen for miles around on a clear day.

Ricky had hired a bicycle and had left it inside the drive gates. He jolted back down the lane, spun along the main road in grand style with salt air tingling up his nose, and turned into the steep descent to the cove.

Mr. and Mrs. Ferrant's stone cottage was on the waterfront; Ricky had an upstairs front bedroom and the use of a suffocating parlor. He preferred to work in his bedroom. He sat at a table at the window, which commanded a view of the harbor, a strip of sand, a jetty, and the little fishing fleet when it was at anchor. Seagulls mewed with the devoted persistence of their species in marine radio-drama.

When he came into the passage he heard the thump of Mrs. Ferrant's iron in the kitchen and caught the smell of hot cloth. She came out, a handsome dark woman of about thirty-five with black hair drawn into a knot, black eyes, and a full figure. In common with most of the islanders, she showed her Gallic heritage.

"You're back then," she said. "Do you fancy a cup of tea?"

"No, thank you very much, Mrs. Ferrant. I had an awfully late luncheon."

"Up above at L'Esperance?"

"That's right."

"That would be a great spread, and grandly served?"

There was no defining her style of speech. The choice of words had the positive character almost of the West Country, but her accent carried the

swallowed r's of France. "They live well, up there," she
said.

"It was all very nice," Ricky murmured. She passed
her working-woman's hand across her mouth. "And
they would all be there. All the family?"

"Well, I think so, but I'm not really sure what the
whole family consists of."

"Mr. and Mrs. Jasper and the children. Young
Bruno, when he's not at his schooling."

"That's right," he agreed. "He was there."

"Would that be all the company?"

"No," Ricky said, feeling cornered, "there were Mr.
and Mrs. Louis Pharamond, too."

"Ah," she said after a pause. "Them."

Ricky started to move away but she said: "That
would be all, then?"

He found her insistence unpleasant.

"Oh no," he said, over his shoulder, "there was
another visitor," and he began to walk down the
passage.

"Who might that have been, then?" she persisted.

"A Miss Harkness," he said shortly.

"What was *she* doing there?" demanded Mrs.
Ferrant.

"She was lunching," Ricky said very coldly and ran
upstairs two steps at a time. He heard her slam the
kitchen door.

He tried to settle down to work but was unable to do
so. The afternoon was a bad time in any case, and he'd
had two glasses of beer. Julia Pharamond's magnolia
face stooped out of his thoughts and came close to him,
talking about a pregnant young woman who might as
well have been a horse. Louis Pharamond was making
a pass at her and the little half-naked Selina pulled
faces at all of them. And there, suddenly, like some
bucolic fury, was Mrs. Ferrant: "You're back, then"
she mouthed. She's going to scream, he thought, and
before she could do it, woke up.

He rose, shook himself, and looked out of the window. The afternoon sun made sequined patterns on the harbor and enriched the colors of boats and the garments of such people as were abroad in the village. Among them, in a group near the jetty, he recognized his landlord, Mr. Ferrant.

Mr. Ferrant was the local plumber and general handyman. He possessed a good-looking car and a little sailing boat with an auxiliary engine in which, Ricky gathered, he was wont to putter around the harbor and occasionally venture quite far out to sea, fishing. Altogether the Ferrants seemed to be very comfortably off. He was a big fellow with a lusty, rather sly look about him but handsome enough with his high color and clustering curls. Ricky thought that he was probably younger than his wife and wondered if she had to keep an eye on him.

He was telling some story to the other men in the group. They listened with half smiles, looking at each other out of the corners of their eyes. When he reached his point they broke into laughter and stamped about, doubled in two, with their hands in their trouser pockets. The group broke up. Mr. Ferrant turned toward the house, saw Ricky in the window and gave him the slight, sideways jerk of the head which served as a greeting in the cove. Ricky lifted his hand in return. He watched his landlord approach the house, heard the front door bang and boots going down the passage.

Ricky thought he would now give himself the pleasure of writing a bread-and-butter letter to Julia Pharamond. He made several shots at it but they all looked either affected or labored. In the end he wrote:

Dear Mrs. Pharamond,
    It was so kind of you to have me and I did enjoy myself so *very* much.

                                    With many thanks,

                    RICKY

P.S. I do hope your other visitor has settled in nicely.

He decided to go out and post it. He had arrived only last evening in the village and had yet to explore it properly.

There wasn't a great deal to explore. The main street ran along the front and steep little cobbled lanes led off it through ranks of cottages of which the one on the corner, next door to the Ferrants', turned out to be the local police station. The one shop there was, Mercer's Drapery and General Suppliers, combined the functions of post office, grocery, hardware, clothing, stationery, and toy shops. Outside hung ranks of duffel coats, pea jackets, oilskins and sweaters, all strung above secretive windows beyond which one could make out further offerings set out in a dark interior. Ricky was filled with an urge to buy. He turned in at the door and sustained a sharp jab below the ribs.

He swung round to find himself face to face with a wild luxuriance of hair, dark spectacles, a floral shirt, beads and fringes.

"Yow!" said Ricky and clapped a hand to his waist. "What's that for?"

A voice behind the hair said something indistinguishable. A gesture was made, indicating a box slung from the shoulder, a box of a kind very familiar to Ricky.

"I was turning round, wasn't I," the voice mumbled.

"OK," said Ricky. "No bones broken. I hope."

"Hurr," said the voice, laughing dismally.

Its owner lurched past Ricky and slouched off down the street, the paint box swinging from his shoulder.

"Very careless, that was," said Mr. Mercer, the solitary shopman, emerging from the shadows. "I don't care for that type of behavior. Can I interest you in anything?"

Ricky, though still in pain, could be interested in a

dark blue polo-necked sweater that carried a label "Hand-knitted locally. Very special offer."

"That looks a good kind of sweater," he said.

"Beautiful piece of work, sir. Mrs. Ferrant is in a class by herself."

"Mrs. Ferrant?"

"Quite so, sir. You are accommodated there, I believe. The pullover," Mr. Mercer continued, "would be your size, I'm sure. Would you care to try?"

Ricky did try and not only bought the sweater but also a short blue coat of a nautical cut that went very well with it. He decided to wear his purchases.

He walked along the main street, which stopped abruptly at a flight of steps leading down to the strand. At the foot of these steps, with an easel set up before him, a palette on his arm, and his paint box open at his feet, stood the man he had encountered in the shop.

He had his back toward Ricky and was laying swaths of color across a large canvas. These did not appear to bear any relation to the prospect before him. As Ricky watched, the painter began to superimpose, in heavy black outline, a female nude with minuscule legs, a vast rump, and no head. Having done this he fell back a step or two, paused, and then made a dart at his canvas and slashed down a giant fowl taking a peck at the nude. Leda, Ricky decided, and, therefore, the swan.

He was vividly reminded of the sketches pinned to the drawing-room wall at L'Esperance. He wondered what his mother, whose work was very far from being academic, would have had to say about this picture. He thought that it lacked integrity.

The painter seemed to decide that it was completed. He scraped his palette and returned it and his brushes to the box. He then fished out a packet of cigarettes and a matchbox, turned his back to the sea breeze, and saw Ricky.

For a second or two he seemed to glower menacingly but the growth of facial hair was so luxuriant that it hid all expression. Dark glasses gave him the look of some dubious character on the Côte d'Azur.

Ricky said: "Hullo, again. I hope you don't mind my looking on for a moment."

There was movement in the whiskers and a dull sound. The painter had opened his matchbox and found it empty.

"Got a light?" Ricky thought must have been said.

He descended the steps and offered his lighter. The painter used it and returned to packing up his gear.

"Do you find," Ricky asked, fishing for something to say that wouldn't be utterly despised, "do you find this place stimulating? For painting, I mean."

"At least," the voice said, "it isn't bloody picturesque. I get power from it. It works for me."

"Could I have seen some of your things up at L'Esperance—the Pharamonds' house?"

He seemed to take another long stare at Ricky and then said: "I sold a few things to some woman the other day. Street show in Montjoy. A white sort of woman with black hair. Talked a lot of balls, of course. They always do. But she wasn't bad, figuratively speaking. Worth the odd grope."

Ricky suddenly felt inclined to kick him.

"Oh, well," he said. "I'll be moving on."

"You staying here?"

"Yes."

"For long?"

"I don't know," he said, turning away.

The painter seemed to be one of those people whose friendliness increases in inverse ratio to the warmth of its reception.

"What's your hurry?" he asked.

"I've got some work to do," Ricky said.

"Work?"

"That's right. Good evening to you."

"You write, don't you?"

"Try to," he said over his shoulder.

The young man raised his voice. "That's what Gil Ferrant makes out, anyway. He reckons you write."

Ricky walked on without further comment.

On the way back he reflected that it was highly possible every person in the village knew by this time that he lodged with the Ferrants—and tried to write.

So he returned to the cottage and tried.

He had his group of characters. He knew how to involve them, one with the other, but so far he didn't know where to put them: they hovered, they floated. He found himself moved to introduce among them a woman with a white magnolia face, black hair and eyes, and a spluttering laugh.

Mrs. Ferrant gave him his evening meal on a tray in the parlor. He asked her about the painter and she replied in an offhand, slighting manner that he was called Sydney Jones and had a "terrible old place up to back of Fishermen's Steps."

"He lives here, then?" said Ricky.

"He's a foreigner," she said, dismissing him, "but he's been in the Cove a while."

"Do you like his paintings?"

"My Louis can do better." Her Louis was a threatening child of about ten.

As she walked out with his tray she said: "That's a queer old sweater you're wearing."

"I think it's a jolly good one," he called after her. He heard her give a little grunt and thought she added something in French.

Visited by a sense of well-being, he lit his pipe and strolled down to the Cod-and-Bottle.

Nobody had ever tried to tart up the Cod-and-Bottle. It was unadulterated pub. In the bar the only decor was a series of faded photographs of local worthies and a map of the island. A heavily pocked dartboard hung on the wall and there was a shove-ha'penny at the far end of the bar. In an enormous fireplace, a pile of driftwood blazed a good-smelling welcome.

The bar was full of men, tobacco smoke, and the fumes of beer. A conglomerate of male voices, with their overtones of local dialect, engulfed Ricky as he walked in. Ferrant was there, his back propped against the bar, one elbow resting on it, his body curved in a classic pose that was sexually explicit and, Ricky felt, deliberately contrived. When he saw Ricky he raised his pint-pot and gave him that sidelong wag of his head. He had a coterie of friends about him.

The barman, who, as Ricky was to learn, was called Bob Maistre, was the landlord of the Cod-and-Bottle. He served Ricky's pint of bitter with a flourish.

There was an empty chair in the corner and Ricky made his way to it. From here he was able to maintain the sensation of being an onlooker.

A group of dart players finished their game and moved over to the bar, revealing to Ricky's unenthusiastic gaze Sydney Jones, the painter, slumped at a table in a far corner of the room with his drink before him. Ricky looked away quickly, hoping that he had not been spotted.

A group of fresh arrivals came between them: fishermen, by their conversation. Ferrant detached himself from the bar and lounged over to them. There followed a jumble of talk, most of it incomprehensible. Ricky was to learn that the remnants of a patois that had grown out of a Norman dialect, itself long vanished, could still be heard among the older islanders.

Ferrant left the group and strolled over to Ricky.

"Evening, Mr. Alleyn," he said. "Getting to know us?"

"Hoping to, Mr. Ferrant," Ricky said.

"Quiet enough for you?"

"That's what I like."

"Fancy that now, what you like, eh?"

His manner was half bantering, half indifferent. He stayed a minute or so longer, took one or two showy pulls at his beer, said, "Enjoy yourself, then," turned and came face to face with Mr. Sydney Jones.

"Look what's come up in my catch," he said. He fetched Mr. Jones a shattering clap on the back and returned to his friends.

Mr. Jones evidently eschewed all conventional civilities. He sat down at the table, extended his legs, and seemed to gaze at nothing in particular. A shout of laughter greeted Ferrant's return to the bar and drowned any observation that, by a movement of his head, Mr. Jones would seem to have offered.

"Sorry," Ricky said. "I can't hear you."

He slouched across the table and the voice came through, still faintly antipodean and uneasy in its choice of outdated slang.

"Care to come up to my pad?" it invited.

There was nothing, at the moment, that Ricky fancied less.

"That's very kind of you," he said. "One of these days I'd like to see some of your work, if I may."

The voice said, with what seemed to be an imitation of Ricky's accent, "Not 'one of these days.' Now."

"Oh," Ricky said, temporizing, "now? Well—"

"You won't catch anything," Mr. Jones sneered loudly. "If that's what you're afraid of."

"Oh God!" Ricky thought. "Now he's insulted. What a bloody bore."

He said: "My dear man, I don't for a moment suppose anything of the sort."

Jones emptied his pint-pot and got to his feet.

"Fair enough," he said. "We'll push off, then."

And without another glance at Ricky he walked out of the bar.

It was dark outside and chilly with a sea nip in the air and misty halos round the few street lamps along the front. The high tide slapped against the seawall.

They walked in silence as far as the place where Ricky had seen Mr. Jones painting in the afternoon. Here they turned left into deep shadow and began to climb what seemed to be an interminable flight of wet, broken-down steps, between cottages that grew farther apart and finally petered out altogether.

Ricky's right foot slid under him; he lurched forward and snatched at wet grass on a muddy bank.

"Too rough for you?" sneered—or seemed to sneer—Mr. Jones.

"Not a bit of it," Ricky jauntily replied.

"Watch it. I'll go first."

They were on some kind of very wet and very rough path. Ricky could only just see his host, outlined against the dim glow of what seemed to be dirty windows.

He was startled by a prodigious snort followed by squelching footsteps close at hand.

"What the hell's that?" Ricky exclaimed.

"It's a horse," Mr. Jones tossed off.

The invisible horse blew down its nostrils.

They arrived at the windows and at a door. Mr. Jones gave the door a kick and it ground noisily open. It had a dirty parody of a portiere on the inside.

Without an invitation or, indeed, any kind of comment, he went in, leaving Ricky to follow.

He did so, and was astonished to find himself face to face with Miss Harkness.

2

Syd Jones's Pad and Montjoy

I

RICKY HEARD A voice that might have been anybody's but his saying, "Oh, hullo. Good evening. We meet again. Ha-ha."

She looked at him with contempt. He said to Mr. Jones: "We met at luncheon up at L'Esperance."

"Oh Christ!" Mr. Jones said in a tone of utter disgust. And to Miss Harkness, "What the hell were you doing up there?"

"Nothing," she mumbled. "I came away."

"So I should bloody hope. Had they got some things of mine up there?"

"Yes."

He grunted and disappeared through a door at the far end of the room. Ricky attempted a conversation with Miss Harkness but got nowhere with it. She said something inaudible and retired upon a stereo system where she made a choice and released a cacophony.

Mr. Jones returned. He dropped onto a sort of divan bed covered with what looked like a horse rug. He seemed to be inexplicably excited.

"Take a chair," he yelled at Ricky.

Ricky took an armchair, misjudging the distance between his person and the seat, which, having lost its springs, thudded heavily on the floor. He landed in a ludicrous position, his knees level with his ears. Mr. Jones and Miss Harkness burst into raucous laughter. Ricky painfully joined in—and they immediately stopped.

He stretched out his legs and began to look about him. Syd's place was a "pad," all right.

As far as he could make out in the restricted lighting provided by two naked and dirty bulbs, he was in the front of a dilapidated cottage whose rooms had been knocked together. The end where he found himself was occupied by a bench bearing a conglomeration of painter's materials. Canvases were ranged along the walls, including a work which seemed to have been inspired by Miss Harkness herself or at least by her breeches, which were represented with unexpected realism.

The rest of the room was occupied by the divan bed, chairs, a filthy sink, a color television, and the stereo components. A certain creeping smell as of defective drainage was overlaid by the familiar pungency of turpentine, oil, and lead.

Ricky began to ask himself a series of unanswerable questions. Why had Miss Harkness decided against L'Esperance? Was Mr. Jones the father of her child? How did Mr. Jones contrive to support an existence combining extremes of squalor with color television and highly sophisticated stereo equipment? How good or how bad was Mr. Jones's painting?

As if in answer to this last conundrum, Mr. Jones got up and began to put a succession of canvases on the easel, presumably for Ricky to look at.

This was a familiar procedure for Ricky. For as long as he could remember, young painters, fortified by an introduction or propelled by their own hardihood, would bring their works to his mother and prop them up for her astringent consideration. Ricky hoped he had learned to look at pictures in the right way but he had never learned to talk easily about them, and in his experience the painters themselves, good or bad, were as a rule extremely inarticulate. Perhaps, in this respect, Mr. Jones's formidable silences were merely occupational characteristics.

But what would Troy, Ricky's mother, have said about the paintings? Mr. Jones had skipped through a tidy sequence of styles. As representation retired before abstraction and abstraction yielded to collage and collage to surrealism, Ricky fancied he could hear her crisp dismissal: "Not much cop, I'm afraid, poor chap."

The exhibition and the pop music came to an end and Mr. Jones's high spirits seemed to die with them. In the deafening silence that followed Ricky felt he had to speak. He said, "Thank you very much for letting me see them."

"Don't give me that," said Mr. Jones yawning hideously. "Obviously you haven't understood what I'm doing."

"I'm sorry."

"Stuff it. You smoke?"

"If you mean what I think you mean, no, I don't."

"I didn't mean anything."

"My mistake," Ricky said.

"You ever take a trip?"

"No."

"Bloody smug, aren't we?"

"Think so?" Ricky said and not without difficulty struggled to his feet. Miss Harkness was fully extended on the divan bed and was possibly asleep.

Mr. Jones said, "I suppose you think you know what you like."

"Why not? Anyway that's a pretty crummy old crack, isn't it?"

"Do you ever look at anything that's not in the pretty peep department?"

"Such as?"

"Oh, you wouldn't know," Mr. Jones said. "Such as Troy. *Does* the name Troy mean anything to you, by the way?"

"Look," Ricky said, "it really is bad luck for you and I can't answer without making it sound like a payoff line. But, yes, the name Troy does mean quite a lot to me. She's—I feel I ought to say 'wait for it, wait for it'— she's my mother."

Mr. Jones's jaw dropped. This much could be distinguished by a change of direction in his beard. There were, too, involuntary movements of the legs and arms. He picked up a large tube of paint, which he appeared to scrutinize closely. Presently he said in a voice pitched unnaturally high: "I couldn't be expected to know that, could I?"

"Indeed, you couldn't."

"As a matter of fact, I've really gone through my Troy phase. You won't agree, of course, but I'm afraid I feel she's painted herself out."

"Are you?"

Mr. Jones dropped the tube of paint on the floor. Ricky picked it up.

"Jerome et Cie," he said. "They're a new firm, aren't they? I think they sent my Mum some specimens to try. Do you get it direct from France?"

Jones took it from him.

"I generally use acrylic," he said.

"Well," Ricky said, "I think I'll seek my virtuous couch. It was nice of you to ask me in."

They faced each other as two divergent species in a menagerie might do.

"Anyway," Ricky said, "we do both speak English, don't we?"

"You reckon?" said Mr. Jones. And after a further silence: "Oh Christ, forget the lot and have a beer."

"I'll do that thing," said Ricky.

II

To say that after this exchange all went swimmingly at Mr. Jones's Pad would not be an accurate account of that evening's strange entertainment, but at least the tone became less acrimonious. Indeed, Mr. Jones developed high spirits of a sort and instructed Ricky to call him Syd. He was devoured by curiosity about Ricky's mother, her approach to her work and—this was a tricky one—whether she took pupils. Ricky found this behavioral change both touching and painful.

Miss Harkness took no part in the conversation but moodily produced bottled beer of which she consumed rather a lot. It emerged that the horse Ricky had shrunk from in the dark was her mount. So, he supposed, she would not spend the night at Syd's Pad, but would ride, darkling, to the stables or—was it possible?—all the way to L'Esperance and the protection (scarcely, it seemed, called for) of the Pharamonds.

By midnight Ricky knew that Syd was a New Zealander by birth, which accounted for certain habits of speech. He had left his native soil at the age of seventeen and had lived in his Pad for a year. He did some sort of casual labor at Leathers, the family riding

stables to which Miss Harkness was attached but from
which she seemed to have been evicted.

"He mucks out," said Miss Harkness in a solitary
burst of conversation and, for no reason that Ricky
could divine, gave a hoarse laugh.

It transpired that Syd occasionally visited Saint
Pierre-des-Roches, the nearest port on the Normandy
coast to which there was a weekly ferry service.

At a quarter to one Ricky left the Pad, took six
paces into the night, and fell flat on his face in the mud.
He could hear Miss Harkness's horse giving signs of
equine consternation.

The village was fast asleep under a starry sky, the
sound of the night tide rose and fell uninterrupted by
Ricky's rubber-shod steps on the cobbled front.
Somewhere out on the harbor a solitary light bobbed
and he wondered if Mr. Ferrant was engaged in his
hobby of night fishing. He paused to watch it and
realized that it was nearer inshore than he had
imagined and coming closer. He could hear the
rhythmic dip of oars.

There was an old bench facing the front. Ricky
thought he would wait there and join Mr. Ferrant, if
indeed it was he, when he landed.

The light vanished around the far side of the jetty.
Ricky heard the gentle thump of the boat against the
pier, followed by irregular sounds of oars being stowed
and objects shifted. A man with a lantern rose into view
and made fast the mooring lines. He carried a pack on
his back and began to walk down the jetty. He was too
far away to be identified.

Ricky was about to get up and go to meet him when,
as if by some illusionist's trick, there was suddenly a
second figure beside the first. Ricky remained where he
was, in shadow.

The man with the lantern raised it to the level of his
face and Ricky saw that he was indeed Ferrant, caught
in a Rembrandt-like golden effulgence. Ricky kept

very still, feeling that to approach them would be an intrusion. They came toward him. Ferrant said something indistinguishable and the other replied in a voice that was not that of the locals: "OK, but watch it. Good night." They separated. The newcomer walked rapidly away toward the turning that led up to the main road and Ferrant crossed the street to his own house.

Ricky ran lightly and soundlessly after him. Ferrant was fitting his key in the lock and had his back turned.

"Good morning, Mr. Ferrant," Ricky said.

He spun around with an oath.

"I'm sorry," Ricky stammered, himself jolted by this violent reaction. "I didn't mean to startle you."

Ferrant said something, in French, Ricky thought, and laughed, a little breathlessly.

"Have you been making a night of it, then?" he said. "Not much chance of that in the Cove."

"I've been up at Syd Jones's."

"Have you now," said Ferrant. "Fancy that." He pushed the door open and stood back for Ricky to enter.

"Good night then, Mr. Alleyn," said Ferrant.

As Ricky entered he heard in the distance the sound of a car starting. It seemed to climb the steep lane out of Deep Cove, and at that moment he realized that the second man on the wharf had been Louis Pharamond.

The house was in darkness. Ricky crept upstairs making very little noise. Just before he shut his bedroom door he heard another door close, quite near at hand.

For a time he lay awake, listening to the sound of the tide and thinking what a long time it seemed since he arrived in Deep Cove. He drifted into a doze and found the scarcely formed persons of the book he hoped to write taking upon themselves characteristics of the Pharamonds, of Sydney Jones, of Miss Harkness and the Ferrants, so that he scarcely knew which was which.

The next morning was cold and brilliant, with a March wind blowing through a clear sky. Mrs. Ferrant gave Ricky a gray mullet for his breakfast: the reward, it emerged, of her husband's night excursion.

By ten o'clock he had settled down to a determined attack on his work.

He wrote in longhand, word after painful word. He wondered why on earth he couldn't set about this job with something resembling a design. Once or twice he thought possibilities—the ghosts of promise—began to show themselves. There was one character, a woman, who had stepped forward and presented herself to be written about. An appreciable time went by before he realized he was dealing with Julia Pharamond.

It came as quite a surprise to find that he had been writing for two hours. He eased his fingers and filled his pipe. "I'm feeling better," he thought.

Something spattered against the windowpane. He looked out and down and there, with his face turned up, was Jasper Pharamond.

"Good morning to you," Jasper called in his alto voice, "are you incommunicado? Is this a liberty?"

"Of course not. Come up."

"Only for a moment."

He heard Mrs. Ferrant go down the passage, the door open, and Jasper's voice on the stairs, "It's all right, thank you, Marie. I'll find my way."

Ricky went out to the landing and watched Jasper come upstairs. He pretended to make heavy weather of the ascent, rocking his shoulders from side to side and thumping his feet.

"Really!" he panted when he arrived. "This is the authentic setting. Attic stairs and the author embattled at the top. You must be sure to eat enough. May I come in?"

He came in, sat on Ricky's bed with a pleasant air of familiarity, and waved his hand at the table and papers.

"The signs are propitious," he said.

"The place is propitious," Ricky said warmly. "And I'm very much obliged to you for finding it. Did you go tramping about the village and climbing interminable stairs?"

"No, no. Julia plumped for Marie Ferrant."

"You knew her already?"

"She was in service up at L'Esperance before she married. We're old friends," said Jasper lightly.

Ricky thought that might explain Mrs. Ferrant's curiosity.

"I've come with an invitation," Jasper said. "It's just that we thought we'd go over to Montjoy to dine and trip a measure on Saturday and we wondered if it would amuse you to come."

Ricky said, "I ought to say no, but I won't. I'd love to."

"We must find somebody nice for you."

"It won't by any chance be Miss Harkness?"

"My dear!" exclaimed Jasper excitedly. "A propos! The Harkness! Great drama! Well, great drama in a negative sense. She's gone!"

"When?"

"Last night. Before dinner. She prowled down the drive, disappeared and never came back. Bruno wonders if she jumped over the cliff—too awful to contemplate."

"You may set your minds at rest," said Ricky. "She didn't do that." And he told Jasper all about his evening with Syd Jones and Miss Harkness.

"Well!" said Jasper, "there you are. What a very *farouche* sort of girl. No doubt the painter is the partner of her shame and the father of her unborn babe. What's he like? His work, for instance?"

"You ought to be the best judge of that. You've got some of it pinned on your drawing-room walls."

"I might have known it!" Jasper cried dramatically. "Another of Julia's finds! She bought them in the street

in Montjoy on Market Day. I can't wait to tell her,"
Jasper said rising energetically. "What fun! No. We
must both tell her."

"Where is she?"

"Down below, in the car. Come and see her, do."

Ricky couldn't resist the thought of Julia so near at
hand. He followed Jasper down the stairs, his heart
thumping as violently as if he had run up them.

It was a dashing sports car and Julia looked dashing
and expensive to match it. She was in the driver's seat,
her gloved hands drooping on the wheel with their
gauntlets turned back so that her wrists shone
delicately. Jasper at once began to tell about Miss
Harkness, inviting Ricky to join in. Ricky thought how
brilliantly she seemed to listen and how this air of being
tuned-in invested all the Pharamonds. He wondered if
they lost interest as suddenly as they acquired it.

When he had answered her questions she said
briskly: "A case, no doubt of like calling to like. Both of
them naturally speechless. No doubt she's gone into
residence at the Pad."

"I'm not so sure," Ricky said. "Her horse was there,
don't forget. It seemed to be floundering about in the
dark."

Jasper said, "She would hardly leave it like that all
night. Perhaps it was only a social call after all."

"How very odd," Julia said, "to think of Miss
Harkness in the small hours of the morning, riding
through the cove. I wonder she didn't wake you up."

"She may not have passed by my window."

"Well," Julia said, "I'm beginning all of a sudden to
weary of Miss Harkness. It was very boring of her to be
so rude, walking out on us like that."

"It'd have been a sight more boring if she'd stayed,
however," Jasper pointed out.

There was a clatter of shoes on the cobblestones and
the Ferrant son, Louis, came running by on his way
home from school. He slowed up when he saw the car

and dragged his feet, staring at it and walking
backwards.

"Hullo, young Louis," Ricky said.

He didn't answer. His sloe eyes looked out of a pale
face under a dark thatch of hair. He backed slowly
away, turned, and suddenly ran off down the street.

"That's Master Ferrant, that was," said Ricky.

Neither of the Pharamonds seemed to have heard
him. For a second or two they looked after the little
boy and then Jasper said lightly: "Dear me! It seems
only the other day that his Mum was a bouncing
tweeny or parlormaid, or whatever it was she bounced
at."

"Before my time," said Julia. "She's a marvelous
laundress and still operates for us. Darling, we're
keeping Ricky out here. Who can tell what golden
phrase we may have aborted. Super that you can come
on Saturday, Ricky."

"Pick you up at eightish," cried Jasper, bustling into
the car. They were off, and Ricky went back to his
room.

But not, at first, to work. He seemed to have taken
the Pharamonds upstairs, and with them little Louis
Ferrant, so that the room was quite crowded with
white faces, black hair, and brilliant pitch-ball eyes.

III

Montjoy might have been on another island from
the cove and in a different sea. Once a predominantly
French fishing village, it was now a fashionable *plage*
with marinas, a yacht club, surfing, striped umbrellas,
and, above all, the celebrated Hotel Montjoy itself with
its Stardust Ballroom whose plate glass dome and
multiple windows could be seen, airily glowing, from
far out at sea. Here, one dined and danced expensively

to a famous band, and here, on Saturday night, at a window table, sat the Pharamonds, Ricky, and a girl called Susie de Waite.

They ate lobster salad and drank champagne. Ricky talked to and danced with Susie de Waite as was expected of him and tried not to look too long and too often at Julia Pharamond.

Julia was in great form, every now and then letting off the spluttering firework of her laughter. As he had noticed at luncheon, she had uninhibited table manners and ate very quickly. Occasionally she sucked her finger. Once when he had watched her doing this he found Jasper looking at him with amusement.

"Julia's eating habits," he remarked, "are those of a partially trained marmoset."

"Darling," said Julia, waggling the sucked fingers at him, "I love you better than life itself."

"If only," Ricky thought, "she would look at me like that," and immediately she did, causing his unsophisticated heart to bang at his ribs and the blood to mount to the roots of his hair.

Ricky considered himself pretty well adjusted to the contemporary scene. But, he thought, every adventure that he had experienced so far had been like a bit of fill-in dialogue leading to the entry of the star. And here, beyond all question, she was.

She waltzed now with her cousin Louis. He was an accomplished dancer and Julia followed him effortlessly. They didn't talk to each other, Ricky noticed. They just floated together—beautifully.

Ricky decided that he didn't perhaps quite like Louis Pharamond. He was too smooth. And anyway, what had he been up to in the cove at one o'clock in the morning?

The lights were dimmed to a blackout. From somewhere in the dome, balloons, treated to respond to ultraviolet light, were released in hundreds and jostled uncannily together, filling the ballroom with luminous bubbles. The band reduced itself to the whispering shish-shish of waves on the beach below. The dancers, scarcely moving, resembled those shadows that seem to bob and pulse behind the screen of an inactive television set.

"May we?" Ricky asked Susie de Waite.

He had once heard his mother say that a great deal of his father's success as an investigating officer stemmed from his gift for getting people to talk about themselves. "It's surprising," she had said, "how few of them can resist him."

"Did you?" her son asked.

"Yes," Troy said, and after a pause, "but not for long."

So Ricky asked Susie de Waite about herself and it was indeed surprising how readily she responded. It was also surprising how unstimulating he found her self-revelations.

And then, abruptly, the evening was set on fire. They came alongside Julia and Louis and Julia called to Ricky.

"Ricky, if you don't dance with me again at once I shall take umbrage." And then to Louis. "Good-bye, darling. I'm off."

And she was in Ricky's arms. The stars in the sky had come reeling down into the ballroom and the sea had got into his eardrums and bliss had taken up its abode in him for the duration of a waltz.

They left at two o'clock in the large car that belonged, it seemed, to the Louis Pharamonds. Louis drove with Susie de Waite next to him and Bruno on her far side. Ricky found himself at the back between Julia and Carlotta and Jasper was on the tip-up seat facing them.

When they were clear of Montjoy on the straight road to the cove, Louis asked Susie if she'd like to steer and on her rapturously accepting, put his arm round her. She took the wheel.

"Is this all right?" Carlotta asked at large. "Is she safe?"

"It's fantastic," gabbled Susie. "Safe as houses. Promise! Ow! Is this right?"

"She really is rather an ass of a girl," Ricky thought.

Julia picked up Ricky's hand and then Carlotta's. "Was it a pleasant party?" she asked, gently tapping their knuckles together. "Have you liked it?"

Ricky said he'd adored it. Julia's hand was still in his. He wondered whether it would be all right to kiss it under, as it were, her husband's nose but felt he lacked the style. She gave his hand a little squeeze, dropped it, leaned forward and kissed her husband.

"Sweetie," Julia cried extravagantly, "you *are* such heaven! Do look, Ricky, that's Leathers up there where Miss Harkness does her stuff. We really must all go riding with her before it's too late."

"What do you mean," her husband asked, "by your 'too late'?"

"Too late for Miss Harkness, of course. Unless, of course, she does it on purpose, but that would be very silly of her. Too silly for words," said Julia severely.

Susie de Waite let out a scream that modulated into a giggle. The car shot across the road and back again.

Carlotta said sharply: "Louis, do keep your techniques for another setting."

Louis gave what Ricky thought of as a bedroom laugh, cuddled Susie up, and closed his hand over hers on the wheel.

"Behave," he said. "Bad girl."

They arrived at the lane that descended precipitously into the cove. Louis took charge, drove pretty rapidly down it and pulled up in front of the Ferrant cottage.

"Here we are," he said. "Abode of the dark yet passing-fair Marie. Is she still dark and passing-fair, by the way?"

Nobody answered.

Louis said very loudly: "Any progeny? Oh, but of course. I forgot."

"Shut up," Jasper said, in a tone of voice that Ricky hadn't heard from him before.

He and Julia and Carlotta together said goodnight to Ricky, who by this time was outside the car. He shut the door as quietly as he could and stood back. Louis reversed noisily and much too fast. He called out something that sounded like "Give her my love." The car shot away in low gear and roared up the lane.

Upstairs on the dark landing Ricky could hear Ferrant snoring prodigiously and pictured him with his red hair and high color and his mouth wide open. Evidently he had not gone fishing that night.

IV

In her studio in Chelsea, Troy shoved her son's letter into the pocket of her painting smock and said: "He's fallen for Julia Pharamond."

"Has he, now?" said Alleyn. "Does he announce it in so many words?"

"No, but he manages to drag her into every other sentence of his letter. Take a look."

Alleyn read his son's letter with a lifted eyebrow. "I see what you mean," he said presently.

"Oh well," Troy muttered. "It'll be one girl and then another, I suppose, and then, with any luck, just one and that a nice one. In the meantime, she's very attractive, isn't she?"

"A change from dirty feet, jeans, and beads in the soup, at least."

"She's beautiful," said Troy.

"He may tire of her heavenly inconsequence."

"You think so?"

"Well, I would. They seem to be taking quite a lot of

trouble over him. Kind of them."

"He's a jolly nice young man," Troy said firmly.

Alleyn chuckled and read on in silence.

"Why," Troy asked presently, "do you suppose they live on that island?"

"Dodging taxation. They're clearly a very clannish lot. The other two are there."

"The cousins that came on board at Acapulco?"

"Yes," Alleyn said. "It was a sort of enclave of cousins."

"The Louises seem to live with the Jaspers, don't they?"

"Looks like it." Alleyn turned a page of the letter. "Well," he said, "besotted or not, he seems to be writing quite steadily."

"I wonder if his stuff's any good, Rory? Do you wonder?"

"Of course I do," he said and went to her.

"It can be tough going, though, can't it?"

"Didn't you swan through a similar stage?"

"Now I come to think of it," Troy said, squeezing a dollop of flake white on her palette, "I did. I wouldn't tell my parents anything about my young men and I wouldn't show them anything I painted. I can't imagine why."

"You gave me the full treatment when I first saw you, didn't you? About your painting?"

"Did I? No, I didn't. Shut up," said Troy, laughing. She began to paint.

"That's the new brand of color, isn't it? Jerome et Cie?" said Alleyn and picked up a tube.

"They sent it for free. Hoping I'd talk about it, I suppose. The white and the earth colors are all right but the primaries aren't too hot. Rather odd, isn't it, that Rick should mention them?"

"Rick? Where?"

"You haven't got to the bit about his new painting chum and the pregnant equestrienne."

"For the love of Mike!" Alleyn grunted and read on. "I must say," he said when he'd finished, "he *can* write, you know, darling. He can indeed."

Troy put down her palette, flung her arm around him and pushed her head into his shoulder. "He'll do us nicely," she said, "won't he? But it was quite a coincidence, wasn't it? About Jerome et Cie and their paint?"

"In a way," said Alleyn, "I suppose it was."

V

On the morning after the party, Ricky apologized to Mrs. Ferrant for the noisy return in the small hours, and although Mr. Ferrant's snores were loud in his memory, said he was afraid he had been disturbed.

"It'd take more than that to rouse *him*," she said. She never referred to her husband by name. "*I* heard you. Not *you* but him. Pharamond. The older one."

She gave Ricky a sideways look that he couldn't fathom. Derisive? Defiant? Sly? Whatever lay behind her manner, it was certainly not that of an ex-domestic, however emancipated. She left him with the feeling that the corner of a curtain had been lifted and dropped before he could see what lay beyond it.

During the week he saw nothing of the Pharamonds except in one rather curious incident on the Thursday evening. Feeling the need of a change of scene, he had wheeled his bicycle up the steep lane, pedaled along the road to Montjoy, and at a point not far from L'Esperance had left his machine by the wayside and walked toward the cliff edge.

The evening was brilliant and the Channel, for once, blue with patches of bedazzlement. He sat down with his back to a warm rock at a place where the cliff opened into a ravine through which a rough path led between clumps of wild broom down to the sea. The air was heady and a salt breeze felt for his lips. A lark sang and Ricky would have liked a girl—any girl—to come up through the broom from the sea with a reckless face and the sun in her eyes.

Instead, Louis Pharamond came up the path. He was below Ricky, who looked at the top of his head. He leaned forward, climbing, swinging his arms, his chin down.

Ricky didn't want to encounter Louis. He shuffled quickly around the rock and lay on his face. He heard Louis pass by on the other side. Ricky waited until the footsteps died away, wondering at his own behavior.

He was about to get up when he heard a displaced stone roll down the path. The crown of a head and the top of a pair of shoulders appeared below him. Grossly foreshortened though they were, there was no mistaking whom they belonged to. Ricky sank down behind his rock and let Miss Harkness, in her turn, pass him by.

He rode back to the cottage.

He was gradually becoming *persona grata* at the pub. He was given a good evening when he came in and warmed up to when, his work having prospered that day, he celebrated by standing drinks all around. Bill Prentice, the fish-truck driver, offered to give him a lift into Montjoy if ever he fancied it. They settled for the coming morning. It was now that Miss Harkness came into the bar, alone.

Her entrance was followed by a shuffling of feet and by the exchange of furtive smiles. She ordered a glass of port. Ferrant, leaning back against the bar in his favorite pose, looked her over. He said something that Ricky couldn't hear that raised a guffaw. She smiled slightly. Ricky realized that with her entrance the atmosphere in the Cod-and-Bottle had become that of the stud. And that not a man there was unaware of it. So this, he thought, is what Miss Harkness is about.

The next morning, very early, Ricky tied his bicycle to the roof of the fish truck and himself climbed into the front seat.

He was taken aback to find that Syd Jones was to be a fellow passenger. Here he came, hunched up in a dismal mackintosh with his paint box slung over his shoulder, a plastic carrier-bag, and a large and superior suitcase which seemed to be unconscionably heavy.

"Hullo," Ricky said. "Are you moving into the Hotel Montjoy, with your grand suitcase?"

"Why the hell would I do that?"

"All right, all right, let it pass. Sorry."

"I'm afraid I don't fall about at upper-middle-class humor."

"My mistake," said Ricky. "I do better in the evenings."

"I haven't noticed it."

"You may be right. Here comes Bill. Where are you going to put your case? On the roof with my upper-middle-class bike?"

"In front. Shift your feet. Watch it."

He heaved the case up, obviously with an effort, pushed it along the floor under Ricky's legs, and climbed up. Bill Prentice, redolent of fish, mounted the driver's seat, Syd nursed his paint box, and Ricky was crammed in between them.

It was a sparkling morning. The truck rattled up the steep lane; they came out into sunshine at the top and banged along the main road to Montjoy. Ricky was in good spirits.

They passed the entry into Leathers with its signboard: "Riding Stables. Hacks and Ponies for hire. Qualified instructors." He wondered if Miss Harkness was up and about. He shouted above the engine to Syd: "You don't go there every day, then?"

"Definitely bloody not," Syd shouted back. It was the first time Ricky had heard him raise his voice.

The road made a blind turn round a dense copse.

Bill took it on the wrong side at forty miles an hour.

The windscreen was filled with Miss Harkness on a plunging bay horse, all teeth and eyes and flying hooves. An underbelly and straining girth reared into sight. The brakes shrieked, the truck skidded, the world turned sideways, and the passenger's door flew open. Syd Jones, his paint box, and his suitcase shot out. The van rocked and sickeningly righted itself on the verge in a cloud of dust. The horse could be seen struggling on the ground and its rider on her feet with the reins still in her hands. The engine had stopped and the air was shattered by imprecations—a three-part disharmony of oaths from Bill, Syd, and, predominantly, Miss Harkness.

Bill turned off the ignition, dragged his hand brake on, got out, and approached Miss Harkness, who told him with oaths to keep off. Without a pause in her stream of abuse she encouraged her mount to clamber to its feet, checked its impulse to bolt, and began gently to examine it, her great horny hand passing with infinite delicacy down its trembling legs and heaving barrel. It was, Ricky saw, a wall-eyed horse.

"Keep the hell out of it," she said softly. "You'll hear about this."

She led the horse along the far side of the road and past the truck. It snorted and plunged but she calmed it. When they had gone some distance, she mounted. The sound of its hooves, walking, diminished. Bill began to swear again.

Ricky slid out of the truck on the passenger's side. The paint box had burst open and its contents were scattered about the grass. The catches on the suitcase had been sprung and the lid had flown back. Ricky saw that it was full of unopened cartons of Jerome et Cie's paints. Syd Jones squatted on the verge, collecting tubes and fitting them back into their compartments.

Ricky stooped to help him.

"Cut that out!" he snarled.

"Very well, you dear little man," Ricky said, with a strong inclination to throw one at his head. He took a step backwards, felt something give under his heel and looked down. He had trodden on a tube of vermillion and burst the end open. Paint had spurted over his shoe.

"Oh damn, I'm sorry," he said. "I'm most awfully sorry."

He reached for the depleted tube. It was snatched from under his hand. Syd, on his knees, the tube in his grasp and his fingers reddened, mouthed at him. What he said was short and unprintable.

"Look," Ricky said. "I've said I'm sorry. I'll pay for the paint and if you feel like a fight you've only to say so and we'll shape up and make fools of ourselves here and now. How about it?"

Syd was crouched over his task. He mumbled something that might have been "Forget it." Ricky, feeling silly, walked round to the other side of the truck. It was being inspected by Bill Prentice with much the same intensity that Miss Harkness had displayed when she examined her horse. The smell of petrol now mingled with the smell of fish.

"She's OK," Bill said at last and climbed into the driver's seat. "Silly bitch," he added, referring to Miss Harkness, and started up the engine.

Syd loomed up on the far side with his suitcase, around which he had buckled his belt. His jeans drooped from his hip bones as if from a coat hanger.

"Hang on a sec," Bill shouted.

He engaged his gear and the truck lurched back on the road. Syd waited. Ricky walked around to the passenger's side. To his astonishment, Syd observed on what sounded like a placatory note: "Bike's OK, then?"

They climbed on board and the journey continued. Bill's strictures upon Miss Harkness were severe and modified only, Ricky felt, out of consideration for Syd's supposed feelings. The burden of his plaint was that horse traffic should be forbidden on the roads.

"What was she on about?" he complained. "The horse was OK."

"It was Mungo," Syd offered. "She's crazy about it. Savage brute of a thing."

"That so?"

"Bit me. Kicked the old man. He wants to have it destroyed."

"Is it all right with her?" asked Ricky.

"So she reckons. It's an outlaw with everyone else."

They arrived at the only petrol station between the cove and Montjoy. Bill pulled into it for fuel and oil and held the attendant rapt with an exhaustive coverage of the incident.

Syd complained in his dull voice: "I've got a bloody boat to catch, haven't I?"

Ricky who was determined not to make advances looked at his watch and said that there was time in hand.

After an uncomfortable silence Syd said, "I'm funny about my painting gear. You know? I can't do with anyone else handling it. You know? If anyone else scrounges my paint, you know, borrows some, I can't use that tube again. It's kind of contaminated. Get what I mean?"

Ricky thought that what he seemed to mean was a load of highfalutin balls, but he gave a tolerant grunt and after a moment or two Syd began to talk. Ricky could only suppose that he was trying to make amends. His discourse was obscure but it transpired that he had been given some kind of agency by Jerome et Cie. He was to leave free samples of their paints at certain shops and with a number of well-known painters in return for which he was given his fare, as much of their products for his own use as he cared to ask for, and a small commission on sales. He produced their business card with a note "Introducing Mr. Sydney Jones" written on it. He showed Ricky the list of painters they had given him. Ricky was not altogether surprised to find his mother's name at the top.

With as ill a grace as could be imagined, he said he supposed Ricky "wouldn't come at putting the arm on her," which Ricky interpreted as a suggestion that he should give Syd an introduction to his mother.

"When are you going to pay your calls?" Ricky asked.

The next day, it seemed. And it turned out that Syd was spending the night with friends who shared a place in Battersea. Jerome et Cie had expressed the wish that he would modify his personal appearance.

"Bloody commercial shit," he said violently. "Make you vomit, wouldn't it?"

They arrived at the wharves in Montjoy at half-past eight. Ricky watched the crates of fish being loaded into the ferry and saw Syd Jones go up the gangplank. He waited until the ferry sailed. Syd had vanished, but at the last moment he reappeared on deck wearing his awful raincoat, with his paint box still slung over his shoulder.

Ricky spent a pleasant day in Montjoy and bicycled back to the cove in the late afternoon.

Rather surprisingly, the Ferrants had a telephone. That evening Ricky put a call through to his parents, advising them of the approach of Sydney Jones.

3

The Gap

I

"AS FAR AS I can see," Alleyn said, "he's landing us with a sort of monster."

"He thinks it might amuse us to meet him after all we've heard."

"It had better," Alleyn said mildly.

"It's only for a minute or two."

"When do you expect him?"

"Sometime in the morning, I imagine."

"What's the betting he stays for luncheon?"

Troy stood before her husband in the attitude that he particularly enjoyed, with her back straight, her hands in the pockets of her painting smock, and her chin down rather like a chidden little boy.

"And what's the betting," he went on, "my own true love, that before you can say Flake White, he's showing you a little something he's done himself."

"That," said Troy grandly, "would be altogether another pair of boots and I should know how to deal with them. And anyway, he told Rick he thinks I've painted myself out."

"He grows more attractive every second."

"It was funny about the way he behaved when Rick trod on his vermillion."

Alleyn didn't answer at once. "It was, rather," he said at last. "Considering he gets the stuff free."

"Trembling with rage, Rick said, and his beard twitching."

"Delicious."

"Oh well," said Troy, suddenly brisk. "We can but see."

"That's the stuff. I must be off." He kissed her. "Don't let this Jones fellow make a nuisance of himself," he said. "As usual, my patient Penny-lope, there's no telling when I'll be home. Perhaps for lunch or perhaps I'll be in Paris. It's that narcotics case. I'll get them to telephone. Bless you."

"And you," said Troy cheerfully.

She was painting a tree in their garden from within the studio. At the heart of her picture was an exquisite little silver birch just starting to burgeon, treated with delicate and detailed realism. But this tree was at the core of its own diffusion into a larger and much more stylized version of itself and that, in turn, melted into an abstract of the two trees it enclosed. Alleyn said it was like the unwinding of a difficult case with the abstractions on the outside and the implacable "thing itself" at the hard center. He had begged her to stop before she went too far.

She hadn't gone any distance at all when Mr. Sydney Jones presented himself.

There was nothing very remarkable, Troy thought,

about his appearance. He had a beard, close cropped, revealing a full, vaguely sensual but indeterminate mouth. His hair was of a medium length and looked clean. He wore a sweater over jeans. Indeed, all that remained of the Syd Jones Ricky had described was his huge silly-sinister pair of black spectacles. He carried a suitcase and a newspaper parcel.

"Hullo," Troy said, offering her hand. "You're Sydney Jones, aren't you? Ricky rang up and told us you were coming. Do sit down, won't you?"

"It doesn't matter," he mumbled, and sniffed loudly. He was sweating.

Troy sat on the arm of a chair. "Do you smoke?" she said. "I'm sorry I haven't got any cigarettes but do if you'd like to."

He put his suitcase and the newspaper parcel down and lit a cigarette. He then picked up his parcel.

"I gather it's about Jerome et Cie's paints, isn't it?" Troy suggested. "I'd better say that I wouldn't want to change to them and I can't honestly give you a blurb. Anyway I don't do that sort of thing. Sorry." She waited for a response but he said nothing. "Rick tells us," she said, "that you paint."

With a gesture so abrupt that it made her jump, he thrust his parcel at her. The newspaper fell away and three canvases tied together with string were exposed.

"Is that," Troy asked, "some of your work?"

He nodded.

"Do you want me to look at it?"

He muttered.

Made cross by having been startled, Troy said: "My dear boy, do for pity's sake speak out. You make me feel as if I were giving an imitation of a woman talking to herself. Stick them up there where I can see them."

With unsteady hands he put them up, one by one, changing them when she nodded. The first was the large painting Ricky had decided was an abstraction of Leda and the swan. The second was a kaleidoscopic arrangement of shapes in hot browns and raucous blues. The third was a landscape, more nearly representational than the others. Rows of perceptible houses with black, staring windows stood above dark water. There was some suggestion of tactile awareness but no real respect, Troy thought, for the medium.

She said: "I think I know where we are with this one. Is it Saint Pierre-des-Roches on the coast of Normandy?"

"Yar," he said.

"It's the nearest French port to your island, isn't it? Do you often go across?"

"Aw—yar," he said, fidgeting. "It turns me on. Or did. I've worked that vein out, as a matter of fact."

"Really," said Troy. There was a longish pause. "Do you mind putting up the first one again. The Leda."

He did so. Another silence. "Well," she said, "do you want me to say what I think? Or not?"

"I don't mind," he mumbled and yawned extensively.

"Here goes, then. I find it impossible to say whether I think you'll develop into a good painter or not. These three things are all derivative. That doesn't matter while you're young: if you've got something of your own, with great pain and infinite determination you will finally prove it. I don't think you've done that so far. I do get something from the Leda thing—a suggestion that you've got a strong sense of rhythm but it's no more than a suggestion. I don't think you're very self-critical." She looked hard at him. "You don't fool about with drugs do you?" asked Troy.

There was a very long pause before he answered quite loudly, "No."

"Good. I only asked because your hands are unsteady and your behavior erratic, and—" She broke off. "Look here," she said, "you're *not* well, are you? Sit down. No, don't be silly, sit down."

He did sit down. He was shaking, sweat had started

out under the line of his hair, and he was the color of a peeled banana. He gaped and ran a dreadful tongue round his mouth. She fetched him a glass of water. The dark glasses were askew. He put up his trembling hand to them and they fell off, disclosing a pair of pale ineffectual eyes. Gone was the mysterious Mr. Jones.

"I'm all right," he said.

"I don't think you are."

"Party. Last night."

"What sort of party?"

"Aw. A fun thing."

"I see."

"I'll be OK."

Troy made some black coffee and left him to drink it while she returned to her work. The spirit trees began to enclose their absolute inner tree more firmly.

When, at a quarter-past one, Alleyn walked into the studio, it was to find his wife at work and an enfeebled young man avidly watching her from an armchair.

"Oh," said Troy, grandly waving her brush and staring fixedly at Alleyn. "Hullo, darling. Syd, this is my husband. This is Rick's friend Syd Jones, Rory. He's shown me some of his work and he's going to stay for luncheon."

"Well!" Alleyn said, shaking hands, "this *is* an unexpected pleasure. How are you?"

II

Three days after Ricky's jaunt to Montjoy Julia Pharamond rang him up at lunchtime. He had some difficulty in pulling himself together and attending to what she said.

"You do ride, don't you?" she asked.

"Not at all well."

"At least you don't fall off?"

"Not very often."

"There you are, then. Super. All settled."

"What," he asked, "is settled?"

"My plan for tomorrow. We get some Harkness hacks and ride to Bon Accord."

"I haven't any riding things."

"No problem. Jasper will lend you any amount. I'm ringing you up while he's out because he'd say I was seducing you away from your book. But I'm not, am I?"

"Yes," said Ricky, "you are, and it's lovely," and heard her splutter.

"Well, anyway," she said, "it's all settled. You must leap on your *bicyclette* and pedal up to L'Esperance for breakfast and then we'll all sweep up to the stables. Such fun."

"Is Miss Harkness coming?"

"No. How can you ask! Before we knew where we were she'd miscarry."

"If horse exercise was going to make her do that it would have done so already, I fancy," said Ricky and told her about the mishap on the road to Montjoy. Julia was full of exclamations and excitement. "How," she said, "you dared not to ring up and tell us immediately!"

"I thought you'd said she was beginning to be a bore."

"She's suddenly got interesting again. So she's back at Leathers and reconciled to Mr. Harkness?"

"I've no idea."

"But couldn't you *tell?* Couldn't you *sense* it?"

"How?"

"Well, from her conversation."

"It consisted exclusively of oaths."

"I can't wait to survey the scene at Leathers. Will Mr. Jones be there, mucking out?"

"He was in London, quite recently."

"In London! Doing what?"

"Lunching with my parents among other things."

"You really are *too* provoking. I can see that all sorts of curious things are happening and you're being furtive and sly about them."

"I promise to disclose all. I'm not even fully persuaded, by the way, that she and Syd Jones *are* lovers."

"I shall be the judge of that. Here comes Jasper; I'll have to tell him I've seduced you. Goodbye."

"Which is no more than God's truth," Ricky shouted fervently. He heard her laugh and hang up the receiver.

The next morning dawned brilliantly and at half-past nine Ricky, dressed in Jasper's spare jodhpurs and boots and his own Ferrant sweater, proposed to take a photograph of the Pharamonds, including the two little girls produced for the purpose. They assembled in a group on the patio. The Pharamonds evidently adored being photographed, especially Louis who looked almost embarrassingly smooth in breeches, boots, sharp hacking jacket, and gloves.

"Louis, darling," Julia said, surveying him, "*Très snob—presque cad!* You lack only the polo stick!"

"I don't understand how it is," Carlotta said, "but nothing Louis wears ever looks even a day old."

Ricky thought that this assessment didn't work if applied to Louis's face. His very slight tan looked almost as if it had been laid on, imposing a spurious air of health over a rather dissipated foundation.

"I bought this lot in Acapulco eight years ago," said Louis.

"I remember. From a dethroned prince who'd lost his all at the green baize tables," said Julia.

"My recollection," Carlotta said, "is of a déclassé gangster, but I may be wrong."

Selina, who had been going through a short repertoire of exhibitionist antics ignored by her seniors, suddenly flung herself at Louis and hung from his wrist, doubling up her legs and shrieking affectedly.

"You little monster," he said, "you've nearly torn off a button," and examined his sleeve.

Selina walked away with a blank face.

Bruno said, "Do let's get posed-up for Ricky and then take off for the stables."

"Let's be ultramondains," Julia decided. She sank into a swinging chaise longue, dangled an elegantly breeched leg, and raised a drooping hand above her head.

Jasper raised it to his lips. "Madame is enchanting—nay irresistible—*ce matin,*" he said.

Selina stuck out her tongue.

Bruno, looking impatient, merely stood.

"Thank you," said Ricky.

They piled into Louis's car and drove to Leathers.

The avenue, a longish one, led to an ugly Victorian house and continued around the back into the stable yard, and beyond this to a barn at some distance from the other buildings. They followed the extension.

"Hush!" Julia said dramatically. "Listen! Louis, stop."

"Why?" asked Louis, but stopped nevertheless.

Somewhere around the corner of the house a man was shouting.

"My dears!" said Julia. "Mr. Harkness in a rage again. How too awkward."

"What should we do about it?" Carlotta asked. "Slink away or what?"

"Oh, nonsense," Jasper said. "He may be ticking off a horse or even Mr. Jones for all we know."

"Ricky says Mr. Jones is in London."

"Was," Ricky amended.

"Anyway, I refuse to be done out of our riding treat," said Bruno. "Press on, Louis."

"Be quiet, Bruno. Listen."

Louis wound down the window. A female voice could be clearly heard.

"And if I want to bloody jump the bloody hedge, by God I'll bloody jump it, I'll jump it on Mungo, by God."

"Anathema! Blasphemy!"

"Don't you lay a hand on me: I'm pregnant," bellowed Miss Harkness.

"Harlot!"

"Shut up."

"Strumpet!"

"Stuff it."

"Oh, do drive on, Louis," said Carlotta crossly. "They'll stop when they see us. It's so boring, all this."

Louis said, "It would be nice if people made up their minds."

"We have. Press on."

He drove into the stable yard.

The picture that presented itself was of a row of six loose-boxes, each with a horse's bridled head looking out of the upper half, and flanked at one end by a tack room and at the other by an open coach house containing a small car, coils of old wire, discarded gear, tools, and empty sacks—all forming a background for a large red man with profuse whiskers towering over Miss Harkness, who faced him with a scowl of defiance.

"Lay a hand on me and I'll call the police," she threatened.

Mr. Harkness, for undoubtedly it was he, had his back to the car. Arrested, no doubt, by a sudden glaze that overspread his niece's face, he turned and was transfixed.

His recovery was almost instantaneous. He strode toward them, all smiles.

"Morning, morning. All ready for you. Six of the best," shouted Mr. Harkness. He opened car doors, offered a large freckled hand with ginger bristles, helped out the ladies, and, laughing merrily, piloted them across the yard.

"Dulcie's got 'em lined up," he said.

Julia beamed upon Mr. Harkness and, to his obvious bewilderment, gaily chided Miss Harkness for deserting them. He shouted: "Jones!"

Syd Jones slid out of the tack-room door and, with a sidelong scowl at Ricky, approached the loose-boxes.

Julia advanced upon him with extended hand. She explained to Mr. Harkness that she and Syd were old friends. It would be difficult to say which of the two men was the more embarrassed.

Syd led out the first horse, a sixteen-hand bay, and Mr. Harkness said he would give Jasper a handsome ride. Jasper mounted, collecting the bay and walking it around the yard. The others followed, Julia on a nice-looking gray mare. It was clear to Ricky that the Pharamonds were accomplished horse people. He himself was given an aged chestnut gelding who, Mr. Harkness said, still had plenty of go in him if handled sympathetically. Ricky walked and then jogged him around the yard in what he trusted was a sympathetic manner.

Bruno was mounted on a lively, fidgeting sorrel mare and was told she would carry twelve stone very prettily over the sticks. "You asked for a lively ride," Mr. Harkness said to Bruno, "and you'll get it. Think you'll be up to her?"

Bruno said with dignity that he did think so. Clearly not averse to showing off a little, he rode out into the horse paddock where three hurdles had been set up. He put the sorrel at them and flew over very elegantly. Ricky, with misgivings, felt his mount tittupping under him. "You shut up," he muttered to it. Julia, who had come alongside, leaned toward him, her face alive with entertainment.

"Ricky!" she said, "are you feeling precarious?"

"Precarious!" he shouted, "I'm terror-stricken. And now you're going to laugh at me," he added, hearing the preliminary splutter.

"If you fall off, I'll try not to. But you're sitting him like a rock."

"Not true, alas."

"Nearly true. Good God! He's at it again!"

Mr. Harkness had broken out into the familiar roar, but this time his target was Bruno. The horse paddock sloped downhill toward a field from which it was separated by a dense and pretty high blackthorn hedge. Bruno had turned the sorrel to face a gap in the hedge and the creature, Ricky saw, was going through the mettlesome antics that manifest an equine desire to jump over something.

"No, stop! You can't! Here! Come back!" Mr. Harkness roared. And to Jasper: "Call that kid back. He'll break his neck. He'll ruin the mare. Stop him!"

The Pharamonds shouted but Bruno dug in his heels and put the sorrel at the gap. It rose, its quarters flashed up, it was gone and there was no time, or a lifetime, before they heard an earthy thump and a diminishing thud of hooves.

Mr. Harkness was running down the horse paddock. Jasper had ridden past him when, on the slope beyond the hedge, Bruno appeared, checking his dancing mount. Farther away, on the hillside, a solitary horse reared, plunged, and galloped idiotically up and down a distant hedge. Ricky thought he recognized the wall-eyed Mungo.

Bruno waved, vaingloriously.

Julia had ridden alongside Ricky. "Horrid, showing-off little brute," said Julia. "Wait till I get at him." And she began shakily to laugh.

Mr. Harkness bawled infuriated directions to Bruno about how to rejoin them by way of gates and a lane. The Pharamonds collected round Julia and Ricky.

"I am ashamed of Bruno," said Jasper.

"What's it like," Carlotta asked, "on the other side?"

"A sheer drop to an extremely deep and impossibly

wide ditch. The mare's all Harkness said she was to clear it."

"Bruno's good, though," said Julia.

"He's given you a fright and he's shown like a mountebank."

Julia said: "Never mind!" and leaned along her horse's neck to touch her husband's hand. Ricky suddenly felt quite desolate.

The Pharamonds waited ominously for the return of the errant Bruno while Mr. Harkness enlarged upon the prowess of Sorrel Lass, which was the stable name of the talented mare. He also issued a number of dark hints as to what steps he would have taken if she had broken a leg and had to be destroyed.

In the middle of all this, and just as Bruno, smiling uneasily, rode his mount into the stable yard, Miss Harkness, forgotten by all, burst into eloquence.

She was "discovered" leering over the lower half-door of an empty loose-box. With the riding crop, from which she appeared never to be parted, she beat on the half-door and screamed in triumph.

"Yar! Yar! Yar!" Miss Harkness screamed, "Old Bloody Unk! She's bloody done it, so sucks boo to rotten old you."

Her uncle glared at her but made no reply. Jasper, Carlotta, and Louis were administering a severe if inaudible wigging to Bruno, who had unwillingly dismounted. Syd Jones had disappeared.

Julia said to Ricky: "We ought to bring Bruno and Dulcie together, they seem to have something in common, don't you feel? What have you lot been saying to him?" she asked her husband who had come across to her.

"I've asked for another mount for him."

"Darling!"

"He's got to learn, sweetie. And in any case Harkness doesn't like the idea of him riding her. After that performance."

"But he rode her beautifully. We must admit."

"He was told not to put her at the hedge."

Syd Jones came out and led away the sorrel. Presently he reappeared with something that looked like an elderly polo pony upon which Bruno gazed with evident disgust.

The scene petered out. Miss Harkness emerged from the loose-box, strode past her uncle, shook hands violently with the sulking Bruno, and continued into the house, banging the door behind her.

Mr. Harkness said: "Dulcie gets a bit excitable."

Julia said: "She's a high-spirited girl, isn't she? Carlotta, darling, don't you think we ought to hit the trail? Come along, boys. We're off."

There was, however, one more surprise to come. Mr. Harkness approached Julia with a curious, almost sheepish smile and handed up an envelope.

"Just a little thing of my own," he said. "See you this evening. Have a good day."

When they reached the end of the drive Julia said, "What can it be?"

"Not the bill," Carlotta said. "Not when he introduced it like that."

"Oh, I don't know. The bill, after all, would be a little thing of his own."

Julia had drawn what appeared to be a pamphlet from the envelope. She began to read. "Not true!" she said, and looked up, wide-eyed, at her audience. "Not true," she repeated.

"What isn't?" Carlotta asked crossly. "Don't go on like that, Julia."

Julia handed the pamphlet to Ricky. "You read it," she said. "Aloud."

"DO YOU KNOW," Ricky read, "that you are in danger of HELLFIRE?

"DO YOU KNOW, that the DAY of JUDGMENT is *AT HAND*?

"WOE! WOE! WOE!!! cries the Prophet—"

"Obviously," Julia interrupted, "Mr. Harkness is the author."

"Why?"

"Such very horsey language. "Whoa! Whoa! Whoa!"

"He seems to run on in the same vein for a long time," Ricky said, turning the page. "It's all about the last trump and one's sins lying bitter in one's belly. Wait a bit. Listen."

"What?"

"Regular gatherings of the Inner Brethren at Leathers on Sunday evenings at 7:30 to which you are Cordially Invited. Bro. Cuthbert (Cuth) Harkness will lead. Discourse and Discussion. Light Supper. Gents 50p. Ladies a basket. All welcome."

"Well," said Jasper after a pause, "that explains everything. Or does it?"

"I *suppose* it does," said Julia doubtfully. "Mr. Harkness, whom we must learn to call Cuth, even if it sounds as if one had lost a tooth—"

"How do you mean, Julia?"

"Don't interrupt. 'Cuspid,'" Julia said hurriedly. "Clearly, he's a religious fanatic and that's why he's taken Miss Harkness's pregnancy so hard."

"Of course. Evidently they're extremely strict," Jasper agreed.

"I wonder what they do at their parties. Would it be fun—"

"No, Julia," said Louis, "It would not be fun, ladies a basket or no."

Carlotta said: "Do let's move on. We can discuss Mr. Harkness later. There's a perfect green lane round the corner."

So all the Pharamonds and Ricky rode up the hill. They showed for some moments on the skyline, elegant against important clouds. Then the lane dipped into a valley and they followed it and disappeared.

III

The little pub at Bon Accord on the extreme northern tip of the island proved to be satisfactory. It was called the Fisherman's Rest and was indeed full of guernseys, gumboots, and the smell of fish. The landlord turned out to be a cousin of Bob Maistre at the Cod-and-Bottle.

Jasper stood drinks all around and Julia captivated the men by asking about the finer points of deep-sea fishing. From here she led the conversation to Mr. Harkness, evoking a good deal of what Louis afterwards referred to as bucolic merriment.

"Cuth Harkness," the landlord said, "was a sensible enough chap when he first came. A riding instructor or some such in the army, he were. Then he took queer with religion."

"He were all right till he got cranky-holy," someone said. "Druv himself silly brooding on hellfire, I reckon."

"Is Miss Harkness a member of the group?" Louis asked and Ricky saw that mention of Miss Harkness evoked loose-mouthed grins and sidelong looks.

"Dulce?" somebody blurted out as if the name itself was explicit. "Her?" And there was a general outbreak of smothered laughter.

"Reckon her's got better things to do," the landlord said. This evoked a further round of stifled merriment.

"Quite a girl, our Dulcie, isn't she?" Louis said easily. He passed a white hand over the back of his patent-leather head. "Mind you," he added, "I wouldn't know," and he called for another round. Carlotta and Julia walked out into the fresh air where Ricky joined them.

"I wish he wouldn't," Carlotta said.

"Louis?" Julia asked.

"Yes," said Carlotta. "That's right. Louis. My husband, you know. Shouldn't we be moving on?" She smiled at Ricky. "But we're an ever-so-jolly family, of course," she said. "Aren't we, Julia?"

"Come on," Julia said. "Let's get the fiery steeds. Where's Bruno?"

"With them, I expect. Still a bit huffy."

But Bruno left off being huffy when they all rode a fine race across a stretch of open turf. Ricky's blood tingled in his ears and his bottom began to be sore.

When they had pulled up Louis gave a cry. He dismounted and hopped about on his elegant left foot.

"Cramp?" asked Jasper.

"What do you suppose it is, love, hopscotch? Blast and hell, I'll have to get this boot off," groaned Louis. "Here. Bruno!"

Bruno very efficiently pulled off the boot. Louis wrenched at his foot, hissing with pain. He stood up, stamped, and limped.

"It's no good," he said. "I'll have to go back."

"I'll come with you, darling," his wife offered.

"No, you won't, damn it," he said. He mounted, holding the boot in his right hand. He flexed his right foot, keeping it out of the iron, and checked his horse's obvious desire to break away.

"Will you be OK?" asked Jasper.

"I will if you'll all be good enough to move off," he said. He turned his horse and began to walk it back along the turf.

"Leave it," Carlotta said. "He'll be cross if we don't. He knows what he's doing."

In spite of a marked increase in his saddle-soreness, Ricky enjoyed the rest of the day's outing. They took roundabout lanes back to the cove, and the sun was far in the west when, over a rise in the road, L'Esperance came unexpectedly into view, a romantic silhouette, distant and very lonely against a glowing sky.

"Look at our lovely house!" cried Julia. She began to sing a Spanish song and the other Pharamonds joined in. They sang, off and on, all the way to Leathers and up the drive.

"Will Louis have taken the car or is he waiting for us?" Bruno wondered.

"It'd be a hell of a long wait," said Jasper.

"I fancy he'll be walking home," Carlotta said. "It's good for his cramp to walk."

As they turned at the corner of the house into the stable yard, they saw the car where Louis had left it. It was unoccupied.

"Yes, he's walking," said Jasper. "We'll catch up with him."

There was nobody about in the yard. Everything seemed very quiet.

"I'll dig someone up," Jasper said. He turned his hack into a loose-box and walked off.

Bruno, who had recovered from the effects of his wigging and showed signs of wanting to brag about his exploit, said: "Julia, come down and look at my jump. Ricky, will you come? Carlotta, come look. Come on."

"If we do, it doesn't mean to say we approve," Julia said sternly. "Shall we?" she asked Ricky and Carlotta. "I'd rather like to."

They rode their bored horses into the paddock and down the hill. A long shadow from the blackthorn hedge reached toward them and the air struck cold as they entered it.

Ricky felt his horse's barrel expand between his knees. It lifted its head, neighed, and reared on its hind legs.

"Here!" he exclaimed, "what's all this!" It dropped back on its forefeet and danced. From far beyond the hedge, on the distant hillside, there came an answering scream.

Julia crammed her own now-agitated mount up to the gap in the hedge where Bruno had jumped. Ricky watched her bring the horse around and heard it snort. It stood and trembled. Julia leaned forward in the saddle and patted its neck. She looked over the gap and down. Ricky saw her gloved hand clench. For a moment she was perfectly still. Then she turned toward him and he thought he had never seen absolute pallor in a face until now.

Behind him Carlotta said: "What's possessing the animals?" And then: "Julia, what is it?"

"Ricky," Julia said in somebody else's voice, "let Bruno take your horse and come here. Bruno, take Carlotta and the horses back to the yard and stay there. Do what I tell you, Carlotta. Do it at once. And find Jasper. Send him down here."

They did what she told them. Ricky walked down the slope to Julia, who dismounted.

"You'd better look," she said. "Down there. Down."

Ricky looked through the gap. Water glinted below in the shadows. Trampled mud stank and glistened. Deep scars and slides ploughed the bank. Everything was dead still down there. Particularly the interloper who lay smashed and discarded, face upwards, in the puddled ditch, her limbs all higgledy-piggledy at impossible angles, her mouth awash with muddy water, and her foolish eyes wide open and staring at nothing at all. On the hillside the sorrel mare—saddled, bridled, and dead lame—limped here and there, snatching inconsequently at the short grass. Sometimes she threw up her head and whinnied. She was answered from the hilltop by Mungo, the wall-eyed bay.

IV

"I told her," Mr. Harkness sobbed. "I told her over and over again not to. I reasoned with her. I even chastised her for her soul's sake but she would! She was consumed with pride and she would do it and the Lord has smitten her down in the midst of her sin." He knuckled his eyes like a child, gazed balefully about him, and suddenly roared out: "Where's Jones?"

"Not here, it seems," Julia ventured.

"I'll have the hide off him. He's responsible. He's as good as murdered her."

"Jones?" Carlotta exclaimed. "Murdered?"

"Orders! He was ordered to take her to the smith. To be reshod on the off-fore. If he'd done that she wouldn't have been here. I ordered him on purpose to get her out of the way."

Julia and Carlotta made helpless noises. Bruno kicked at a loose-box door. Ricky felt sick. Inside the house Jasper could be heard talking on the telephone.

"What's he doing?" Mr. Harkness demanded hopelessly. "Who's he talking to? What's he saying?"

"He's getting a doctor," Julia said, "and an ambulance."

"And the vet?" Mr. Harkness demanded. "Is he getting the vet? Is he getting Bob Blacker, the vet? She may have broken her leg, you know. She may have to be destroyed. Have you thought of that? And there she lies looking so awful. Somebody ought to close the eyes. I can't, but somebody ought to."

Ricky, to his great horror, felt hysteria rise in his throat. Mr. Harkness rambled on, his voice clotted with tears. It was almost impossible to determine when he spoke of his niece and when of his sorrel mare. "And what about the hacks?" he asked. "They ought to be unsaddled and rubbed down and fed. She ought to be seeing to them. She sinned. She sinned in the sight of the Lord! It may have led to hellfire. More than probable. What about the hacks?"

"Bruno," Julia said, "could you?"

Bruno, with evident relief, went into the nearest loose-box. Characteristic sounds—snorts, occasional stamping, the clump of a saddle dumped across the half-door and the bang of an iron against wood—lent an air of normality to the stable yard.

Mr. Harkness dived into the next-door box so

suddenly that he raised a clatter of hooves.

He could be heard soothing the gray hack: "Steady girl. Stand over," and interrupting himself with an occasional sob.

"This is too awful," Julia breathed. "What can one do?"

Carlotta said: "Nothing."

Ricky said: "Shall I see if I can get him a drink?"

"Brandy? Or something?"

"He may have given it up because of hellfire," Julia suggested. "It might send him completely bonkers."

"I can but try."

He went into the house by the back door and, following the sound of Jasper's voice, found him at the telephone in an office where Mr. Harkness evidently did his bookkeeping.

Jasper said: "Yes. Thank you. As quick as you can, won't you?" and hung up the receiver. "What now?" he asked. "How is he?"

"As near as damn it off his head. But he's doing stables at the moment. The girls thought perhaps a drink."

"I doubt if we'll find any."

"Should we look?"

"I don't know. Should we? Might it send him utterly cuckoo?"

"That's what we wondered," said Ricky.

Jasper looked around the room and spotted a little corner cupboard. After a moment's hesitation he opened the door and was confronted with a skull and crossbones badly drawn in red ink and supported by a legend:

BEWARE!!!
This Way Lies Damnation!!!

The card on which this information was inscribed had been hung around the neck of a whisky bottle.

"In the face of that," Ricky said, "what should we do?"

"I've no idea. But I know what I'm going to do," said Jasper warmly. He unscrewed the cap and took a fairly generous pull at the bottle. "I needed that," he gasped and offered it to Ricky.

"No thanks," Ricky said. "I feel sick already."

"It takes all sorts," Jasper observed, wiping his mouth and returning the bottle to the cupboard. "The doctor's coming," he said. "And so's the vet." He indicated a list of numbers above the telephone. "And the ambulance."

"Good," said Ricky.

"They all said: 'Don't move her.'"

"Good."

"The vet meant the mare."

"Naturally."

"God," said Jasper. "This is awful."

"Yes. Awful."

"Shall we go out?"

"Yes."

They returned to the stable yard. Bruno and Mr. Harkness were still in the loose-boxes. There was a sound of munching and an occasional snort.

Jasper put his arm round his wife. "OK?" he asked.

"Yes. You've been drinking."

"Do you want some?"

"No."

"Where's Bruno?"

Julia jerked her head at the loose-boxes. "Come over here," she said and drew the two men toward the car. Carlotta was in the driver's seat, smoking.

"Listen," Julia said. "About Bruno. You know what he's thinking, of course?"

"What?"

"He's thinking it's his fault. Because he jumped the gap first. So she thought she could."

"Not his fault if she did."

"That's what I say," said Carlotta.

"Try and persuade Bruno of it! He was told not to and now see what's come of it. That's the way he's thinking."

"Silly little bastard," said his brother uneasily.

Ricky said: "She'd made up her mind to do it before we got here. She'd have done it if Bruno had never appeared on the scene."

"Yes, Ricky," Julia said eagerly. "That's just it. That's the line we must take with Bruno. Do say all that to him, won't you? How right you are."

"There'll be an inquest, of course, and it'll come out," Jasper said. "Bruno's bit'll come out."

"Hell," said Carlotta.

A car appeared, rounded the corner of the house and pulled up. The driver, a man in a tweed suit carrying a professional bag, got out.

"Doctor Carey?" Jasper asked.

"Blacker's the name. I'm the vet. Where's Cuth? What's up, anyway?"

"I should explain," Jasper said and was doing so when a second car arrived with a second man in a tweed suit carrying a professional bag. This was Dr. Carey. Jasper began again. When he had finished Dr. Carey said: "Where is she then?" and being told walked off down the horse paddock. "When the ambulance comes," he threw over his shoulder, "will you show them where? I'll see her uncle when I get back."

"I'd better talk to Cuth," said the vet. "This is a terrible thing. Where is he?"

As if in answer to a summons, Mr. Harkness appeared, like a woebegone Mr. Punch, over the half-door of a loose-box.

"Bob," he said. "Bob, she's dead lame. The sorrel mare, Bob. Bob, she's dead lame and she's killed Dulcie."

And then the ambulance arrived.

Ricky stood in a corner of the yard, feeling

extraneous to the scenes that followed. He saw the vet move off and Mr. Harkness, talking pretty wildly, make a distracted attempt to follow him and then stand wiping his mouth and looking from one to the other of the two retreating figures, each with its professional bag, rather like items in a surrealistic landscape.

Then Mr. Harkness ran across the yard and stopped the two ambulance men who were taking out a stretcher and canvas cover. Lamentations rolled out of him like sludge. The men seemed to calm him after a fashion and they listened to Jasper when he pointed the way. But Mr. Harkness kept interrupting and issuing his own instructions. "You can't miss it," he kept saying. "Straight across there. Where there's the gap in the hedge. I'll show you. You can't miss it."

"We've got it, thank you, sir," they said. Don't trouble yourself. Take it easy."

They walked away, carrying the stretcher between them. He watched them and pulled at his underlip and gabbled under his breath. Julia went to him. She was still very white and Ricky saw that her hand trembled. She spoke with her usual quick incisiveness.

"Mr. Harkness," Julia said. "I'm going to take you indoors and give you some very strong black coffee and you're going to sit down and drink it. Please don't interrupt because it won't make the smallest difference. Come along."

She put her hand under his elbow and, still talking, he suffered himself to be led indoors.

Carlotta remained in the car. Jasper went over to talk to her. Bruno was nowhere to be seen.

It occurred to Ricky that this was a situation with which his father was entirely familiar. It would be at about this stage, he supposed, that the police car would arrive and his father would stoop over death in the form it had taken with Miss Harkness and would dwell upon that which Ricky turned sick to remember. Alleyn did not discuss his cases with his family, but

Ricky, who loved him, often wondered how so
fastidious a man could have chosen such work. And
here he pulled up. "I must be barmy," he told himself,
"I'm thinking about it as if it were not a bloody
accident but a crime."

Presently Julia came out of the house.

"He's sitting in his parlor," she said, "drinking
instant coffee with a good dollop of Scotch in it. I don't
know whether he's spotted the Scotch and is pretend-
ing he hasn't or whether he's too bonkers to know."

There was the sound of light wheels on gravel and
around the corner of the house came a policeman on a
bicycle.

"Good evening, all," said the policeman dismount-
ing. "What seems to be the trouble?"

Julia walked up to him with outstretched hand.

"You say it!" she cried. "You really do say it! How
perfectly super."

"Beg pardon, madam?" said the policeman, sizing
her up.

"I thought it was only a joke thing about policemen
asking what seemed to be the trouble and saying
'Evening, all.'"

"It's as good a thing to say as anything else,"
reasoned the policeman.

"Of *course* it is," she agreed warmly. "It's a splendid
thing to say."

Jasper intervened. "My wife's had a very bad shock.
She made the discovery."

"That's right," Julia said in a trembling voice. "My
name's Julia Pharamond and I made the discovery and
I'm not quite myself."

The policeman—he was a sergeant—had removed
his bicycle clips and produced his notebook. He made a
brief entry.

"Is that the case?" he said. "Mrs. J. Pharamond of
L'Esperance, that would be, wouldn't it? I'm sure I'm
very sorry. It was you that rang the station, sir, was it?"

"No. I expect it was Dr. Carey. I rang him. Or perhaps it was the ambulance."

"I see, sir. And I understand it's a fatality. A horse-riding accident?" They made noises of assent. "Very sad, I'm sure," said the sergeant. "Yes. So if I might just take a wee look-see."

Once more Jasper pointed the way. The sergeant in his turn tramped down the horse paddock to the blackthorn hedge.

"You could do with some of that coffee and grog yourself, darling," Jasper said.

"I did take a sly gulp. I can't think why I rushed at Sergeant Dixon like that."

"He's not Sergeant Dixon."

"There! You see! I'll be calling him that to his face if I'm not careful. Too rude. I suppose you're right. I suppose I'm like this on account of my taking a wee look-see." She burst into sobbing laughter and Jasper took her in his arms.

He looked from Ricky to Carlotta. "We ought to get her out of this," he said.

"Why don't we all just go? We can't do any good hanging about here," said Carlotta.

"We can't leave Mr. Harness," Julia sobbed into her husband's coat. "We don't know what he mightn't get up to. Besides Sergeant Thing will want me to make a statement and Ricky, too, I expect. That's very important, isn't it, Ricky? Taking statements on the scene of the crime."

"What crime!" Carlotta exclaimed. "Have you gone dotty, Julia?"

"Where's Bruno got to now?" Jasper asked.

"He went away to be sick," said Carlotta. "I expect he'll be back in a minute."

Jasper put Julia into the back of the car and stayed beside her for some time. Bruno returned, looking ghastly and saying nothing. At last the empty landscape became reinhabited. First, along a lane beyond a distant hedge, appeared the vet leading the sorrel mare. They could see her head, pecking up and down, and the top of the vet's tweed hat. Then, beyond the gap in the blackthorn hedge, partly obscured by leafy twigs, some sort of activity was seen to be taking place. Something was being half lifted, half hauled up the bank on the far side. It was Miss Harkness on the stretcher, decently covered.

4

Intermission

I

MISS HARKNESS, parcelled in canvas, lay in the
ambulance, her uncle was in his office with the doctor,
and Julia and Bruno had been driven home to
L'Esperance by Carlotta. Ricky and Jasper still waited
in the stable yard because they didn't quite like to go
away. Ricky wandered about in a desultory fashion,
half looking at what there was to be seen but unable to
dismiss his memory of Dulcie Harkness. He drifted
into the old coach house. Beside the car, a broken-
down gig, pieces of perished harness, and a heap of
sacks, a coil of old and discarded wire hung from a peg.
Ricky idly examined it and found that the end had
recently been cut.

He could hear the sorrel mare blowing through her nostrils—she was in a loose-box with her leg bandaged, having a feed. The vet came out.

"It's a hell of a sprain, in her near fore," said the vet. "And a bad cut in front, halfway down the splint bone. I can't quite understand the cut. There must have been *something* in the gap to cause it. I think I'll go down and have a look at the terrain. Now they've taken away—now—er—it's all clear."

"The police sergeant's there," Ricky said. "He went back after he'd seen Mr. Harkness."

"Old Joey Plank?" said the vet. "He's all right. I'd be obliged if you'd come down with me, though. I'd like to see just where this young hopeful of yours took off when he cleared the jump. I don't like being puzzled. Of course, anything can happen. For one thing, he'll be very much lighter than Dulcie. She's a big girl but all the same it's a pretty good bet Dulcie Harkness wouldn't go wrong over the same sticks on the same mount as a kid of thirteen. She's—she would have been in the top class if she'd liked to go in for it. Be glad if you'd stroll down. OK?"

In one way, there was nothing in the wide world Ricky wanted to do less, and he fancied Jasper felt much the same, but they could hardly refuse and at least they would get away from the yard and the ambulance with its two men sitting in front and its closed doors with Miss Harkness behind them. Jasper did point out that they were the width of the paddock away when Bruno jumped, but Mr. Blacker paid no attention and led the way downhill.

The turf was fairly soft and copiously indented with hoof prints. When they got to within a few feet of the gap the vet held up his hand and they all stopped.

"Here you are, then," he said. "Here's where they took off and here's the mark of the hind hooves, the first lot with the boy up being underneath, with the second overlapping at the edges and well dug in.

Tremendous thrust, you know, when the horse takes off. See the difference between these and the prints left by the forefeet."

Sergeant Plank, in his shirtsleeves and red with exertion, loomed up in the gap.

"This is a nasty business, Joey," said the vet.

"Ah. Very. And a bit of a puzzle, at that. Very glad these two gentlemen have come down. If it's all the same I'll just get a wee statement about how the body was found, like. We have to do these things in the prescribed order, don't we? Half a mo'."

He didn't climb through the gap but edged his way down the hedge to where he'd hung his tunic. From this he extracted his notebook and pencil. He joined them and fixed his gaze—his eyes were china-blue and very bright—upon Ricky.

"I understand you was the first to see deceased, sir," he said.

Ricky experienced an assortment of *frissons*.

"Mrs. Pharamond was the first," he said. "Then me."

"Pardon me. So I understood. Could I have the name, if you please, sir?"

"Roderick Alleyn."

A longish silence followed.

"Oh yes?" said the sergeant. "How is that spelt, if you please?"

Ricky spelled it.

"You wouldn't," Sergeant Plank austerely suggested, "be trying to take the Micky, would you, sir?"

"Me? Why? Oh!" said Ricky, blushing. "No, sergeant, I wouldn't dream of it. I'm his son."

A further silence.

"I had the pleasure," said Sergeant Plank, clearing his throat, "of working under the Chief Superintendent on a case in the West Country. In a very minor capacity. Guard duty. He wouldn't remember, of course."

"I'll tell him," said Ricky.

"He still wouldn't remember," said Sergeant Plank, "but it *was* a pleasure, all the same."

Yet another silence was broken by Mr. Blacker. "Quite a coincidence," he said.

"It is that," Sergeant Plank said warmly. And to Ricky: "Well then, sir, even if it seems a bit funny, perhaps you'll give me a few items of information."

"If I can, Mr. Plank, of course."

So he gave, at dictation speed, his account of what he saw when Julia called him down to the gap. He watched the sergeant laboriously begin every line of his notes close to the edge of the page and fill in to the opposite edge in the regulation manner. When that was over he took a statement from Jasper. He then said that he was sure they realized that he would, as a matter of routine, have to get statements from Julia and Bruno.

"There'll be an inquest, sir, as I'm sure you'll realize, and no doubt your wife will be called to give formal evidence, being the first to sight the body. And your young brother may be asked to say something about the nature of his own performance. Purely a matter of routine."

"I suppose so," said Jasper. "I wish it wasn't, however. The boy's very upset. He's got the idea, we think, that she wouldn't have tried to jump the gap if he hadn't done it first. She seemed to be very excited about him doing it."

"Is that so? Excited?"

Mr. Blacker said: "She would be. From what I can make out from Cuth Harkness, it'd been a bit of a bone of contention between them. He told her she shouldn't try it on and she kind of defied him. Or that's what I made out. Cuth's in a queer sort of state."

"Shock," said the sergeant still writing. "I wouldn't be surprised. Who broke the news?"

"My wife and I did," said Jasper. "He insisted on coming down here to look for himself."

"He's fussed. One minute it's the mare and the next it's the niece. He didn't seem," Sergeant Plank said, "to be able to tell the difference, if you can understand."

"Only too well."

The vet had moved away. He was peering through the gap at the ditch and the far bank. The remains of a post-and-rail fence ran through the blackthorn hedge and was partly exposed. He put his foot on the lower rail as if to test whether it would take his weight.

"I'd be obliged, Mr. Blacker," said the sergeant raising his china-blue gaze from his notes, "if you didn't. Just a formality, but it's what we're instructed. No offense."

"What? Oh. Oh, all right," said Blacker. "Sorry, I'm sure."

"That's quite all right, sir. I wonder," said the sergeant to Ricky, "if you'd just indicate where you and Mrs. Pharamond were when you noticed the body."

For the life of him, Ricky could not imagine why this should be of interest but he described how Julia had called him to her and how he had dismounted, giving his horse to Bruno, and had gone to her, and how she, too, had dismounted and he had peered through the gap. He parted some branches near the end of the gap.

"Like that," he said.

He noticed that the post at his left hand was loose in the ground. Near the top on the outer side and almost obscured by brambles was a fine scar that cut through the mossy surface and bit into the wood. The opposite post at the other end of the gap was overgrown with blackthorn. He crossed and saw broken twigs and what seemed to be a scrape up the surface of the post.

"Would you have noticed," Sergeant Plank said behind him, making him jump, "anything about the gap, sir?"

Ricky turned to meet the sergeant's blue regard.

"I was too rattled," he said, "to notice anything."

"Very natural," Plank said, still writing. Without looking up he pointed his pencil at the vet. "And would you have formed an opinion, Mr. Blacker, as to how, exactly, the accident took place? Like—would you think that what went wrong went wrong on this side after the horse took off? Or would you say it cleared the gap and crashed on the far bank?"

"If you'd let me go and take a look," Blacker said a trifle sourly, "I'd be better able to form an opinion, wouldn't I?"

"Absolutely correct," said the disconcerting sergeant. "I agree with every word of it. And if you can notice the far bank—it's nice and clear from here—I've used pegs to mark out the position of the body, which was, generally speaking, eccentric, owing to the breakage of limbs, et cetera, et cetera. Not but what the impression in the mud doesn't speak for itself quite strong. I daresay you can see the various other indications—they stand out, don't they? Can be read like a book, I daresay, by somebody as up in the subject as yourself, Mr. Blacker."

"I wouldn't go as far as all that," Blacker said, mollified. "What I *would* say is that the mare came down on the far bank—you can see a clear impression of a stirrup iron in the mud—and seems to have rolled on Dulcie. Whether Dulcie pitched forward over the mare's head or fell with her isn't so clear."

"Very well put. And borne out by the nature of the injuries. I don't think you've seen the body, have you, Mr. Blacker?"

"No."

"No. Quite so. The head's in a nasty mess. Kicked. Shocking state, really. You'll have remarked the state of the face, I daresay, Mr. Alleyn."

Ricky nodded. His mouth went dry. He had indeed remarked it.

"Yes. Well, now, I'd better go up and have a wee chat with the uncle," said Sergeant Plank.

"You won't find that any too easy," Jasper said.

Sergeant Plank made clucking noises. He struggled into his tunic, buttoned up his notebook, and led the way back to the house. "Very understandable, I'm sure," he threw out rather vaguely. "There'll be the little matter of identification. By the next of kin, you know."

"Oh God!" Ricky said. "You can't do that to him."

"We'll make it as comfortable as we can."

"Comfortable!"

"I'll just have a wee chat with him first."

"You don't want us any more, do you?" Jasper asked him.

"No, no, no," he said. "We know where to find you, don't we? I'll drop in at L'Esperance if you don't object, sir, and just pick up a little signed statement from your good lady and maybe have a word with this young show-jumper of yours. Later on, this evening, if it suits."

"It'll have to, won't it, sergeant? But I can't pretend," Jasper said with great charm, "that I hadn't hoped that they'd be let off any more upsets for today at least."

"That's right," said Sergeant Plank cordially. "You would, too. We can't help it, though, can we, sir! So if you'll excuse me, I ought to give Superintendent Curie at Montjoy a tinkle about this. It's been a pleasure, Mr. Alleyn. Quite a coincidence. *A ce soir,*" added the sergeant.

He smiled upon them, crossed over to the ambulance and spoke to the men, one of whom got out and went around to the rear doors. He opened them and disappeared inside. The doors clicked to. Sergeant Plank nodded in a reassuring manner to Jasper and Ricky and walked into the house.

"Would you say," Jasper asked Ricky, "that Sergeant Plankses abound in our police force?"

"Not as prolifically as they used to, I fancy."

"Well, my dear Ricky, I suppose we now take our bracing walk to L'Esperance."

"You don't think—"

"What?"

"We ought to stay until he's—done it? Looked."

"The doctor's with him."

"Yes. So he is."

"Well, then—"

But as if the ambulance and its passenger had laid some kind of compulsion on them, they still hesitated. Jasper lit a cigarette. Ricky produced his pipe but did nothing with it.

"The day," said Jasper, "has not been without incident."

"No."

They began to move away.

"I'm afraid you have been distressed by it," said Jasper. "Like my poorest Julia and, for a different reason, my tiresome baby brother."

"Haven't *you?*" Ricky asked. Jasper came to a halt.

"Been distressed? Not profoundly, I'm afraid. I didn't see her, you know. I have a theory that the full shock and horror of a death is only experienced when it has been seen. I must, however, confess to a reaction in myself at one point of which I daresay I should be ashamed. I don't know that I am, however."

"Am I to hear what it was?"

"Why not? It happened when the ambulance men came into the yard here, carrying Miss Harkness on their covered stretcher. I had been thinking: thank God I wasn't the one to find them. The remains, as of course they will be labeled. And then, without warning, there came upon me a—really a quite horribly strong impulse to go up to the stretcher and uncover it. I almost believe that if it could have been accomplished in a flash with a single flourish I would have done it— like Antony revealing Caesar's body to the Romans. But of course the cover was fastened down and it would have been a fiddling, silly business and they would have stopped me. But why on earth should such a notion come upon me? Really, we do *not* know ourselves, do we?"

"It looks like it."

"Confession may be good for the soul," Jasper said lightly, "but I must say I find it a profoundly embarrassing exercise."

"He's coming."

Mr. Harkness came out of the house under escort, like the victim of an accident. Doctor Carey and Sergeant Plank had him between them, their hands under his arms. The driver got down and opened the rear doors. His colleague looked out.

"It'll only take a moment," they heard Dr. Carey say.

On one impulse they turned and walked away, around the house and down the drive, not speaking to each other. A motorcycle roared down the cliff road, turned in at the gates, and, with little or no diminution of speed, bore down upon them.

"Look who's here," said Jasper.

It was Syd Jones. At first it seemed that he was going to ignore them but at the last moment he cut down his engine and skidded to a halt.

"G' day," he said morosely and exclusively to Jasper. "How's tricks?"

They looked wildly at each other.

"Seen Dulce?" asked Syd.

II

Any number of distracted reactions tumbled about in Ricky's head. For an infinitesimal moment he actually thought Syd wanted to know if he'd seen dead Dulce with the broken body. Then he thought "we've got to tell him" and then that dead Dulce might be carrying Syd's baby (this was the first time he'd remembered about what would doubtless be referred to as her "condition"). He had no idea how long this state of muddled thinking persisted, but their silence or their manner must have been strange because Syd said, "What's wrong?" He spoke directly to Jasper and had not looked at Ricky.

Jasper said: "There's been an accident. I'm afraid this is going to be a shock."

"It's bad news, Syd," Ricky said. Because he thought he ought to and because he was unexpectedly filled with a warmth of compassion for Syd, he laid a hand on his arm and was much discomforted when Syd shook him off without a glance.

"It's about Dulcie Harkness," Jasper said.

"What about her? Did you say an accident? Here!" Syd demanded. "What are you on about? Is she dead? Or what?"

"I'm afraid she is, Syd," Ricky ventured.

After a considerable pause he said, "Poor old Dulce." And then to Jasper: "What happened?"

Jasper told him. Syd was, Ricky knew, a quite remarkably inexpressive person and allowances had to be made for that. He seemed to be sobered, taken aback, even perturbed, but, quite clearly, not shattered. And still he would not look at Ricky.

"You can hardly credit it," he mumbled.

He seemed to turn the information over in his mind and after doing so for some time said: "She was pregnant. Did you know that?"

"Well, yes," Jasper said. "Yes, we did."

"They'll find that out, won't they?"

"Yes, I expect they will."

"Too bad," he said.

Jasper caught Ricky's eye and made a slight face at him.

"Who," he asked, "is the father?"

"I dunno," said Syd, almost cheerfully. "And I reckon she didn't. She was quite a girl."

Somebody else had used the phrase about her. Recently. It was Louis, Ricky remembered, Louis Pharamond in the Fisherman's Rest at Bon Accord.

"Where's the old man?" Syd asked Jasper.

"In the house. The doctor's there. And a police sergeant."

"What's *he* want?" Syd demanded.

"They have to make a formal appearance at fatal accidents," Ricky said and was ignored.

"He's very much upset," said Jasper.

"Who is?"

"Mr. Harkness."

"He warned her, didn't he? You heard him."

"Of course he did."

"Fair enough, then. What's he got to worry about?"

"Good God!" Jasper burst out and then checked himself.

"My dear Jones," he urged. "The man's had a monstrous shock. His niece has been killed. He's had to identify her body. He's—"

"Aw," said Syd. "That, yeah."

And to Ricky's bewilderment he actually turned pale.

"That's different again," he said. "That could be grotty, all right."

He stood for a moment or two with his head down, looking at his boots. Then he hitched his shoulder, settled himself on his seat, and revved up his engine.

"Where are you going?" Jasper shouted.

"Back," he said. "No sense going on, is there? It was her I wanted to see."

They stood and watched him. He kicked the ground, turned his machine, and roared off the way he had come.

"That creature's a monster," said Jasper.

"He may be a monster," Ricky said, "but there's one

thing we can be sure he's not."

"Really? Oh, I see what you mean. Yes, I suppose we can."

The sound of the motorcycle faded.

"That's a bloody expensive machine," Ricky said.

"Oh?"

"New."

"Really?" said Jasper without interest. "Shall we shog?"

It was an opulent evening, as if gold dust had been shaken out of some heavenly sifter, laying a spell over an unspectacular landscape. Even the effects of chiaroscuro were changed so that details, normally close at hand, were set at a golden remove. L'Esperance itself was enskied by inconsequent drifts of cloud at its base. The transformation would have been a bit too much of a good thing, Ricky thought, if its impermanence had not lent it a sort of austerity. Even as they saw the glow on each other's face, it faded and the evening was cold.

"Ricky," Jasper said, "come up and have a drink and supper with us. We would like you to come."

But Ricky thought it best to say no and they parted at the entrance to the drive. He mounted his bicycle and was sharply reminded of his saddle-soreness.

When he got back to the cove it was to find that news of the accident was already broadcast. Mrs. Ferrant met him in the passage.

"This is a terrible business, then," she said without any preliminaries and stared at Ricky out of her stewed-prune eyes. He had no mind to discuss it with her, anticipating a series of greedy questions. He remembered Mrs. Ferrant's former reactions to mention of Dulcie Harkness.

"They're saying it was a horse-riding accident," she probed. "That's correct, is it? They're saying there was arguments with the uncle, upalong, over her being too bold with her jumping. Is it true, then, what they're saying, that you was a witness to the accident? Was it you that found her, then? There's a terrible retribution for you, isn't it, whatever she may have been in the past?"

Ricky staved her off as best he could but she served his supper—one of her excellent omelets—with a new batch of questions at each reappearance, and he fought a losing battle. In the end he was obliged to give an account of the accident.

While this was going on he became aware of sundry bumps and shufflings in the passage outside.

"That's him," Mrs. Ferrant threw out. "He's going on one of his holidays over to Saint Pierre-des-Roches by the morning boat."

"I didn't know there was one."

"The *Island Belle*. She calls once a week on her way from Montjoy."

"Really?" said Ricky, glad to steer Mrs. Ferrant herself into different waters. "I might take the trip one of these days."

"It's an early start. Five A.M."

She had left the door ajar. From close on the other side, but without showing himself, Ferrant called peremptorily: "Marie! Hé!"

"Yes," she said quickly and went out, shutting the door.

Ricky heard them walk down the passage.

He finished his supper and climbed up to his room, suddenly very tired. Too tired and too sore and becoming too stiff to go along to the Cod-and-Bottle, where in any case he would be avidly questioned about the accident. And much too tired to write. He had a hot bath, restraining a yelp when he got into it, applied with difficulty first aid plasters to the raw discs on his bottom, and went to bed, where he fell at once into a heavy sleep.

He woke to find his window pallid in the dawn light. He was aware of muted sounds in the downstairs passage. The heavy front door was shut. Footsteps sounded on the outside path.

Wide awake, he got out of bed, went to his open window, and looked down.

Mr. Ferrant, with two suitcases, walked toward the jetty where the *Island Belle* was coming in. There was something unexpected, unreal even, about her, sliding alongside in the dawn light. Quiet voices sounded, and the slap of rope on the wet jetty. Mr. Ferrant was a solitary figure with his baggage and his purposeful tread. But what very grand suitcases they were: soft hide, surely, not plastic, and coming, Ricky was sure, from some very smart shop. As for Mr. Ferrant, one could hardly believe it was he, in a camel's hair overcoat, porkpie hat, suede shoes, and beautiful gloves. He turned his head and Ricky saw that he wore dark glasses.

He watched Mr. Ferrant, the only embarking passenger, go up the gangplank and disappear. Some packages and a mailbag were taken aboard and then the *Island Belle,* with a slight commotion from her propeller, pulled out, her lights wan in the growing morning.

Ricky returned to bed and to sleep. When he finally awoke at nine o'clock, Mr. Ferrant's departure seemed unreal as a dream, enclosed, like a dream, between sleep and sleep.

Three days later the inquest was held in the Cove village hall. The coroner came out from Montjoy. The jury was made up of local characters, some of whom were known to Ricky as patrons of the Cod-and-Bottle.

Julia and Ricky were called to give formal evidence as to sighting the body, and Mr. Harkness as to its identity. He was subdued and shaky and extremely lugubrious, answering in a low, uneven voice. He tried to say something about the dangerous nature of the jump and about the warnings he had given his niece and the rows this had led to.

"I allowed anger to take hold on me," he said and looked around the assembly with washed-out eyes. "I went too far and I said too much. I may have driven her to it." He broke down and was allowed to leave the room.

Doctor Carey gave evidence as to the nature of the injuries, which were multiple and extensive. Some of the external ones could be seen to have been caused by a horse's hoof, others were breakages. The internal ones might have been brought about by the mare rolling on her rider. It was impossible, on the evidence, to arrive at a more precise conclusion. She was some eight or nine weeks pregnant, Dr. Carey added, and a little eddy of attention seemed to wash through the court. Superintendent Curie, from Montjoy, nominally in charge of the police investigation, was ill in hospital but, to the obvious surprise of the jury, applied through Sergeant Plank for an adjournment, which was agreed to.

Outside in the sunshine, Ricky talked to Julia and Jasper. It was his first meeting with them since the accident, although they had spoken on the telephone. Nobody could have been more simply dressed than Julia and nobody could have looked more exquisite, he thought, or more exotic in that homespun setting.

"I don't in the least understand all this," Julia said. "Why an adjournment? Ricky, you're the one to explain to us."

"Why me?"

"Because your gorgeous papa is a copper. Is he perpetually asking for adjournments when everybody longs for the whole thing to be—" She stopped, looked for a moment into his eyes, and then said rapidly, "—to be dead, buried and forgotten."

"Honestly, I don't know anything at all about police goings-on. He never speaks of his cases. We've so much else to talk about," Ricky said simply. "I imagine they have to be almost insanely thorough and exhaustive."

"I can't think that it makes any difference to anyone, not even Mr. Harkness in all his righteous anguish, whether poor Dulcie fell forwards, sideways, or over the horse's tail. Oh God, Jasper, darling, why does everything I say always have to sound so perfectly heartless and beastly!"

"Because you're a realist, my love, and anyway it doesn't," said Jasper. "You'd be the most ghastly fake if you pretended to be heartbroken over the wretched girl. You had a beastly shock because you saw her. If you'd only *heard* she'd been killed you'd have said, 'How awful for poor Cuth,' and sent flowers to the funeral. Which, by the way, we ought perhaps to do. What do you think?"

But Julia paid no attention.

"Ricky," she said. "It couldn't be, or could it? That the police—what is it that's always said in the papers—don't rule out the possibility of 'foul play'? Could it be that, Ricky?"

"I don't know. Truly I don't know," Ricky said. And then, acutely conscious of their fixed regard, he blurted out what he had in fact been thinking.

"I had wondered," said Ricky.

III

"'So I thought,'" Alleyn read aloud, "'I'd ask you if the idea's just plain silly. And if you don't think it's silly, whether you think I ought to say anything to Sergeant Plank or whether that would be behaving like the typical idiot layman. Or, finally, whether it's a guinea to a gooseberry Sergeant Plank will have thought of it for himself.' Which," Alleyn said looking up from the letter, "will certainly be the case if Sergeant Plank's worth his stripes."

"Wouldn't we much rather Rick kept out of it, whatever it may be, and got on with his book?" asked Ricky's mother.

"Very much rather. Drat the boy, why does he want to go and get himself involved?" Alleyn rubbed his nose and looked sideways at his wife. "Quite neat of him to spot that bit, though, wasn't it? 'Obviously recent,' he says."

"Should we suggest he come home?" Troy wondered and then: "No. Silly of me. Why on earth, after all?"

"He may be called when the inquest is reopened, in which case he'd have to go trundling back. No, I shouldn't worry. It's odds on there's nothing in it and he's perfectly well able to cope, after all, with anything that may turn up." Alleyn returned to the letter. "I see," he said, "that Julia was dreadfully upset but rallied gallantly and gave her evidence quite beautifully. So that's still on the tapis, one gathers."

"I hope she's not finding him a bore."

"Does a woman ever dislike the admiration of a reasonably presentable young chap?"

"True."

"He really does seem to have struck a rum setup one way or another," said Alleyn, still reading. "What with his odd-jobbing plumber of a landlord dressed up like a con man at the crack of dawn and going on holiday to Saint Pierre-des-Roches."

"It's a pretty little peep of a place. I painted it when I was a student. The egregious Syd has made a regrettable slosh at it. But it's hardly the spot for camel's hair coats and zoot suits."

"Perhaps Ferrant uses it as a jumping-off place for the sophisticated south."

"And then there's Louis Pharamond," said Troy, pursuing her own thoughts, "having had some sort of affair with poor Miss Harkness, doesn't it seem? Or does it?"

"In company with your visitor with the free paints and the dizzy spell. And listen to this," said Alleyn. "'My Mrs. Ferrant reacts very acidly to mention of Dulcie Harkness, even though she does make obligatory 'non nisi' noises. I can't help wondering if Mr. Ferrant's roving eye has lit sometime or another on Miss Harkness.' Really!" said Alleyn, "The island jollities seem to be of a markedly uninhibited kind. And Miss Harkness of an unusually obliging disposition."

"Bother!" said Troy.

"I know. And then, why should the egregious Jones scream with rage when Ricky trod on his vermillion? There's plenty more where that came from, it seems. For free. And if it comes to that, why should Jones take it into his head to cut Rick? Apparently he would neither look at, nor speak to him. Not a word about having taken a luncheon off us, it appears."

"He's a compulsive boor, of course. Mightn't we be making far too much of a series of unrelated and insignificant little happenings?"

"Of course we might," Alleyn agreed warmly. He finished reading his son's letter, folded it, and put it down. "He's taken pains over that," he said. "Very long and very detailed. He even goes to the trouble of describing the contents of the old coach house."

"The whole thing's on his mind and he thinks writing it all out may help him to get shot of it."

"He's looking for a line. It's rather like those hidden-picture games they used to put in kids' books. A collection of numbered dots and you joined them up in the given order and found you'd got a pussycat or something. Only Rick's dots aren't numbered and he can't find the line."

"If there is one."

"Yes. There may be no pussycat."

"It's the sort of thing you're doing all the time, isn't it?"

"More or less, my treasure. More or less."

"Oh!" Troy exclaimed, "I do *hope* there isn't a line and I do hope Miss Harkness wasn't—"

"What?"

"Murdered," said Troy. "That, really, is what the letter's all about, isn't it?"

"Oh, yes," Alleyn agreed. "That's what it's all about."

The telephone rang and he answered it. It was his Assistant Commissioner. Being a polite man he made his usual token apology.

"Oh, Rory," he said. "Sorry to disturb you at home. Did I hear you mention your boy was staying on that island where Sunniday Enterprises, if that's what they call themsleves, have set up a holiday resort of sorts?"

It pleased the A.C., nobody knew why, when engaged in preliminaries, to affect a totally false vagueness about names, places, and activities.

Alleyn said: "Yes, sir, he's there," and wondered why he was not surprised. It was as if he had been waiting for this development, an absurd notion to entertain.

"Staying at this place of theirs? What's it called? Mount something?"

"Hotel Montjoy. Lord no. He's putting up at a plumber's cottage on the non-u side of the island."

"The Bay. Or Deep Bay, would that be?"

"Deep Cove," Alleyn said, beginning to feel exasperated as well as apprehensive.

"To be sure, yes. I remember, now, you did say something about a plumber and Deep Cove," said the bland A.C.

Alleyn thought: "You devious old devil, what *are* you up to?" and waited.

"Well," said the A.C., "the thing is I wondered if he might be helpful. You remember the dope case you tidied up in Rome? Some of the Ziegfeldt group?"

"Oh *that*," Alleyn said, greatly relieved. "Yes."

"Well, as we all know to our discomfort, Ziegfeldt himself still operates in a very big way."

"Quite. I understand," said Alleyn, "there have been extensive improvements to his phony castle in the Lebanon. Loos on every landing."

"Maddening, isn't it?" said the A.C. "Well, my dear Rory, the latest intelligence through Interpol and from chaps in our appropriate branch is that the route has been altered. From Izmir to Marseilles it still rings the changes between the Italian ports, and the morphine-heroin transformation is still effected in laboratories outside Marseilles. But from there on there's a difference. Some of the heroin now gets away through a number of French seaports, some of them quite small. You can guess what I'm coming to, I daresay."

"Not to Saint Pierre-des-Roches, by any chance?"

"And from there to this island of yours—"

"It's not mine. With respect," said Alleyn.

"—from where it finds its way to the English market. We don't *know* any of this," said the A.C., "but it's been suggested. There are pointers! There's a character with a bit of a record who shows signs of unexpected affluence. That kind of thing."

"May I ask, sir," Alleyn said, "the name of the character who shows signs of unexpected affluence?"

"Of course you may. He's a plumber and odd-job man living in Deep Cove and he is called Ferrant."

"Fancy that," Alleyn said tonelessly.

"Quite a coincidence, isn't it?"

"Life is full of them."

"So I just wondered if your young man had noticed anything."

"He's noticed his landlord, who is called Ferrant and is a plumber, leaving at dawn by a channel packet, if that's what it is, dressed up to kill with suede suitcases and bound for Saint Pierre-des-Roches."

"There now!" cried the A.C. "Splendid fellow your son. Jolly good! Super!" He occasionally adopted the mannerisms of an effusive scoutmaster.

"Has anything been said by the appropriate branch about a painter called Jones?" Alleyn asked.

"A house painter?"

"No, though you might make the mistake. A picture painter."

"Jones. Jones. Jones. No. No Joneses. Why?"

"He travels in artists' materials for a firm called Jerome et Cie with a factory in Saint Pierre-des-Roches. Makes frequent visits to London."

"Artists' materials?"

"In tubes. Oil colors. Big ones."

There was a longish silence.

"Oh, yes?" said the A.C. in a new voice. The strange preliminaries evidently were over and they were down to the hard stuff.

"First name?" snapped the A.C.

"Sydney."

"Living?"

"In Deep Cove. The firm's handing out free color to one or two leading painters, including Troy. He called on us, here, with an introduction from Rick. I'd say he was getting over a hangover."

"They don't like that. The bosses. It doesn't work out—pusher into customer."

"Of course not. But I wouldn't think he was a habitual. There'd been a party the night before. My guess would be that he was suffering from withdrawal symptoms but from what Ricky says of him, he doesn't seem to be hooked. Yet. It may amount to nothing."

"Anything else about him?"

Alleyn told him about the roadside incident when Ricky trod on the vermillion.

"Got into a stink, did he?"

"Apparently."

"It's worth watching."

"I wondered."

"We haven't got anyone on the island so far. The lead on Saint Pierre's only just come through. What's the young chap doing there, Rory?"

Alleyn said very firmly: "He's writing a book, sir. He went over there to put himself out of the way of distraction and has set himself a time limit."

"Writing!" repeated the A.C. discontentedly. "A book!" And he added: "Extraordinary what they get up to nowadays, isn't it? One of mine runs a discotheque."

Alleyn was silent.

"Nothing official, of course, but you might suggest he keep his eyes open," said the A.C.

"They'll be down on his book, I hope."

"All right. All right. Oh, by the way, there's something else come through. About an hour ago. Another coincidence in a way, I suppose one might call it. From this island of yours."

"Oh?"

"Yes. The Super at Montjoy rang up. Superintendent Curie, he is. There's been a riding fatality. A fortnight ago. Looked like a straightforward accident but they're not satisfied. Inquest adjourned. Thing is: the super's been inconsiderate enough to perforate his appendix and they want us to move in. Did you say anything?"

"No."

"There's a funny noise."

"It may be my teeth. Grinding."

The A.C. gave a high whinnying laugh.

"You can take Fox with you, of course," he said. "And while you're at it you may find—"

His voice, edgy and decisive, continued to issue unpalatable instructions.

IV

After posting his long letter to his parents, Ricky thought that now, perhaps, he could push the whole business of Dulcie Harkness into the background and get on with his work. The answer couldn't reach him for at least three days and when it came it might well give half-a-dozen good suggestions why there should be fresh scars, as of wire, on the posts of the broken-down fence and why the wire that might have made them had been removed and why there was a gash that the vet couldn't explain on a sorrel mare's near foreleg and why there was a new-looking cut end to a coil of old wire in the coach house. And perhaps his father would advise him to refrain from teaching his grandmother, in the unlikely person of Sergeant Plank, to suck eggs.

Tomorrow was the day when the *Island Belle* made her dawn call at the cove. There was a three-day-a-week air service but Ricky liked the idea of the little ship. He came to a sudden decision. If the day was fine he would go to Saint Pierre-des-Roches, return in the evening to Montjoy, and either walk the eight miles or so to the Cove or stand himself a taxi. The break might help him to get things into perspective. He wondered if he were merely concocting an elaborate excuse for not getting on with his work.

"I may run into Mr. Ferrant," he thought, "taking his ease at his inn. I might even have a look at Jerome et Cie's factory. Anyway, I'll go."

He told Mrs. Ferrant of his intention and that disconcerting woman bestowed one of her protracted stares upon him and then said she'd give him something to eat at half-past four in the morning. He implored her to do no such thing but merely fill his thermos flask overnight with her excellent coffee and allow him to cut himself a "piece."

She said, "I don't know why you want to go over there; it's no great masterpiece, that place."

"Mr. Ferrant likes it, doesn't he?"

"Him."

"If there's anything you want to send him, Mrs. Ferrant, I'll take it with pleasure."

She gave a short laugh that might as well have been a snort.

"He's got everything *he* wants," she said and turned away. Ricky thought that on her way downstairs she said something about the unlikelihood of his encountering Mr. Ferrant but he couldn't be sure of this.

He woke himself up at four to a clear sky and a waning moon. The harbor was stretched like silk between its confines with the inverted village for a pattern. A party of gulls sat motionless on their upside-down images, and the jetty was deserted.

When he was dressed and shaved he stole down to the kitchen. It was much the biggest room in the house and the Ferrants used it as a living room. It had television and radio, armchairs, and a hideous dresser with a great array of china. Holy oleographs abounded. The stove and refrigerator looked brand new and so did an array of pots and pans. Ricky felt as if he had disturbed the kitchen in a nightlife of its own.

It was warm and smelled of recent cooking. His thermos stood in the middle of the table and, beside it, a message on the back of an envelope.

Mr. Allen.
                    Food in warm drawer.

When he opened the drawer he found a dish of toasted bacon sandwiches. She must have come down and prepared them while he was getting up. They were delicious. When he had finished them and drunk his coffee, he washed up in a gingerly fashion. It was now twenty to five. Ricky felt adventurous. He wondered if perhaps he would want to stay in Saint Pierre-des-Roches, and on an impulse returned to his room and pushed overnight gear and an extra shirt and jeans into his rucksack.

And now, there was the *Island Belle* coming quietly into harbor with not a living soul to see her, it seemed, but Ricky.

He went downstairs and wrote on the envelope.

Thank you. Delicious. May stay a day or two but
more likely back tonight.

Then he let himself out and walked down the empty
street to the jetty. The sleeping houses in the Cove
looked pallid and withdrawn. He felt as if he saw them
for the first time.

The *Island Belle* was already alongside. Two local
men, known to Ricky at the pub, were putting a few
crates on board. He exchanged a word with them and
then followed them up the gangway. A sailor took
charge of the crates and wished him good morning.

The *Belle* was a small craft, not more than five
hundred tons. She did not make regular trips to the
Devon and Cornwall coast but generally confined
herself to trading between the islands and nearby
French ports. The captain was on the bridge, an elderly
bearded man, who gave Ricky an informal salute. A
bell rang. The gangway was hauled up, and one of the
cove men freed the mooring ropes. The *Belle* slid out
into the harbor.

Ricky watched the village shift back, rearrange
itself, and become a picture rather than a reality. He
went indoors and found a little box of a purser's office
where a man in a peaked cap sold him a return ticket.
He looked into the empty saloon with its three tables,
wall benches, and shuttered miniature bar.

When he returned on deck they were already outside
the heads and responding, he found with misgiving, to
a considerable swell. The chilly dawn breeze caught
him and he began to walk briskly along the starboard
side, past the wheelhouse and toward the forward
hatch.

Crates of fish covered with tarpaulins were lashed
together on the deck. Ricky stopped short. Someone
was standing motionless on the far side of the crates

with his back turned. This person wore a magenta woolen cap pulled down over his ears, with the collar of his coat turned up to meet it. A sailor, Ricky supposed.

Conscious of a feeling of inward uneasiness, he moved forward, seeking a passageway around the cargo, and had found one when the man in the magenta cap turned. It was Sydney Jones.

Ricky hadn't seen him since they met in the drive to Leathers on the day of the accident. On that occasion, Syd's inexplicable refusal to speak to or look at him seemed to put a stop to any further exchanges. Ricky's mother had written a brief account of his visit. "When he dropped to it that your poor papa was a policeman," she wrote, "which was just before he went back to the Yard, Jones lost not a second in shaking our dust off his sandals. Truly we *were* nice to him. Daddy thinks he was suffering from a hangover. I'm afraid his work isn't much cop, poor chap. Sorry, darling."

And here they were, confronted. Not for long, however. Syd, gray in the face, jerked away and Ricky was left staring at his back across a crate of fish.

"Ah, to hell with it," he thought and walked around the cargo.

"Look here," he said. "What *is* all this? What've I done?"

Syd made a plunge, an attempt, it seemed, to dodge around him, but they were both caught by an ample roll of the *Island Belle* and executed an involuntary pas de deux that landed them nose to nose across the fish crate as if in earnest and loving colloquy. Syd's dark glasses slid away from his washed-out eyes.

In spite of growing queasiness Ricky burst out laughing. Syd mouthed at him. He was regrowing his beard.

"Come on," Ricky said. "Let's know the worst. You can't insult me! Tell me all." He was beginning to be cold. Quite definitely all was not well within. Syd contemplated him with unconcealed disgust.

"Come on," Ricky repeated with an awful attempt at jauntiness. "What's it all about, for God's sake?"

Clinging to the fish crate and exhibiting intense venom, Syd almost shrieked at him: "It's about me wanting to be on my bloody pat, that's what it's about. Get it? It's about I can't take you crawling round after me. It's about I'm not one of those. It's not my scene, see? No way. See? *No way.* So do me a favor and—"

Another lurch from the *Island Belle* coincided with a final piece of obscene advice.

"You unspeakable—" Ricky shouted and pulled himself up. "I was wrong," he said. "You can insult me, can't you, or have a bloody good try, and if I thought you meant what you said I'd knock your bloody little block off. 'Crawl round after *you*,'" quoted Ricky, failing to control a belch. "I'd rather crawl after a caterpillar. You make me sick," he said. He attempted a dismissive gesture and, impelled by the ship's motion, broke into an involuntary canter down the sloping deck. He fetched up clinging to the taffrail where, to his fury, he was indeed very sick. When it was over, he looked back at Syd. He too, had retired to the taffrail where he was similarly engaged.

Ricky moved as far aft as he was able and for the remainder of the short voyage divided his time between a bench and the side.

Saint Pierre-des-Roches lay in a shallow bay between two nondescript headlands. Rows of white houses stared out to sea through blank windows. A church spire stood over them, and behind it on a hillside appeared buildings of a commercial character.

As the ship drew nearer some half-dozen small hotels sorted themselves out along the front. Little streets appeared and shop fronts with titles that became readable: "Dupont Frères," "Occasions," "Chatte Noire," and then, giving Ricky—wan and shaky but improving—quite a little thrill: "Jerome et Cie" above a long roof on the hillside.

Determined to avoid another encounter, Ricky watched Syd Jones go ashore, gave him a five-minute start, and then himself went down the gangway. He passed through the duanes and a *bureau-de-change* and presently was walking up a cobbled street in Saint Pierre-des-Roches.

Into one of the best smells in all the world: the smell of fresh-brewed coffee and fresh-baked brioches and croissants. His seasickness was as if it had never been. There was "La Chatte Noire" with an open door through which a gust of warm air conveyed these delectable aromas, and inside were workpeople having their breakfasts; perhaps coming off night shift. Suddenly Ricky was ravenous.

The little bistro was rather dark. Its lamps were out and the early morning light was still tentative. A blue drift of tobacco smoke hung on the air. Although the room was almost full of customers, there was not much conversation.

Ricky went to the counter and gave his order in careful French to the *patronne,* a large lady with an implacable bosom. He was vaguely conscious, as he did so, that another customer had come in behind him.

He took the only remaining single seat, facing the street door, and was given his *petit déjeuner.* No coffee is ever quite as good as it smells, but this came close to it. The butter and confitures in little pots were exquisite and he slapped sumptuous dollops of them on his warm brioches. This was adventure.

He had almost finished when there was a grand exodus from the bistro, with much scraping of chair legs, clearing of throats, and exchanging of pleasantries with the *patronne.* Ricky was left with only three other customers in view.

Or were there only three? Was there perhaps not someone still there in the corner of the room behind his back? He had the feeling that there was and that it would be better not to turn around and look.

Instead he raised his eyes to the wall facing him and looked straight into the disembodied face of Sydney Jones.

The shock was so disconcerting that seconds passed before he realized that what he saw was Syd's reflection, dark glasses and all, in a shabby looking glass, and that it was Syd who sat in the corner behind his back and had been watching him.

There is always something a little odd, a little uncomfortable, about meeting another person's eyes in a glass: it is as if the watchers had simultaneously caught each other out in a furtive exercise. In this case the sensation was much exaggerated. For a moment Ricky and Syd stared at each other's image with something like horror and then Ricky scrambled to his feet, paid his bill, and left in a hurry.

As he walked up the street with his rucksack on his back, he wondered if Syd was going to ruin his visit to Saint Pierre-des-Roches by cropping up like a malignant being in a Hans Christian Andersen tale. Since Dulcie Harkness's death he hadn't thought much about Syd's peculiar behavior, being preoccupied with misgivings of another kind concerning freshly cut wire scars on wooden posts and a gash on a sorrel mare's leg. He thought how boring it was of Syd to be like that. If they were on friendly terms he could have asked him about the wire. And then he thought, with a nasty jolt, that perhaps it mightn't be a good idea to ask Syd about the wire.

He passed several shops and an estaminet and arrived at a square with an hôtel-de-ville, central gardens, a frock-coated statue of a portentous gentleman with whiskers, a public lavatory, a cylindrical billboard, and a newsagent. There were also several blocks of offices, a consequential house or two, and L'Hôtel des Roches, which Ricky liked the look of.

The morning was now well established, the sun shone prettily on the Place Centrale, as the little square was called, and Ricky thought it would be fun to stay overnight in Saint Pierre and perhaps not too extravagant to put up at L'Hôtel des Roches. He went in and found it to be a decorous hostelry, very provincial in tone and smelling of beeswax. In a parlor opening off the entrance hall, a bourgeois family sat like caricatures of themselves and read their morning papers. A dim clerk said they could accommodate Monsieur and an elderly porter escorted him by way of a cautious old lift to a room with a double bed, a wash-hand-stand, an armchair, a huge wardrobe, and not much else. Left alone he took the opportunity to wash the legacy of the fish crate from his hands and then looked down from his lattice window at a scene that might have been painted by a French Grandmère Moses. Figures, dressed mostly in black, walked briskly about the Place Centrale, gentlemen removed hats, ladies inclined their heads, children in smocks, bow ties, and berets skittered in the central gardens, housewives in shawls marched steadfastly to market. And behind all this activity was the harbor with the *Island Belle* at her moorings.

This didn't look like Syd Jones's scene, Ricky thought, still less like Mr. Ferrant's, with his camel's hair coat and porkpie hat. Days rather than hours might have passed since he sailed away from the Cove: it was a new world.

He changed into jeans and a T-shirt, left his rucksack in his room, and went out to explore. First, he would go uphill. The little town soon petered out. Some precipitous gardens, a flight of steps and a road to a cemetery led to the church, not surprisingly dedicated to Saint Pierre-des-Roches. It turned out to be rather commonplace except perhaps for a statue of the saint himself in pastel colors, wearing his custodial keys and stationed precariously on an unconvincing rock. *"Tu es Pierre,"* said a legend, *"et sur cette pierre Je bâtirai Mon église."*

One could, for a small sum, climb the tower. Ricky
did so and was rewarded by a panorama of the town, its
environs, the sparkling sea, and a fragile shadow that
was his own island out there in the Channel.

And, quite near at hand, were the premises of
Jerome et Cie with their own legend in electric lights
garnished with the image of a tube from which erupted
a sausage of paint. At night, by a quaint device this
would seem to gush busily. It reminded Ricky of the
morning when he trod on Syd's vermillion. Perhaps
Syd had come over to Saint Pierre to renew his stock of
samples and to this end would be calling on Messrs.
Jerome et Cie. Ricky rested his arms on the balustrade
and watched the humanoids moving about in the street
below: all heads and shoulders. A funeral crawled up
the road. He looked down into a wreath of lilies on top
of the hearse. The cortège turned into the cemetery and
presently there was a procession with a priest, a boy
swinging a censer, and a following of black midgets. He
imagined he could catch a whiff of incense. The cortège
disappeared behind a large monument.

Ricky, caught in a kind of indolence, couldn't make
up his mind to leave the balcony. He still lounged on
the balustrade and stared down at the scene below.
Into a straggle of pedestrians there emerged from
beneath him someone who seemed to have come out of
the church itself, a figure with a purplish-red cap. It
wore a belted coat and something square hung from its
shoulder.

Ricky was not really at all surprised.

A frightful rumpus outraged his eardrums and
upheaved his diaphragm. The church clock, under his
feet, was striking ten.

5

Intermezzo with Storm

I

THE LAST STROKE of ten still rumbled on the air as Ricky
watched the midget that was Syd walk up the street
and, sure enough, turn in at the gateway to Jerome et
Cie's factory. Had he come out of the church? Had he
already been lurking in some dark corner when Ricky
came in? Or had he followed Ricky? Why had he gone
there? To say his prayers? To look for something to
paint? To rest his legs? The box, loaded as it always
seemed to be with large tubes of paint, must be
extremely heavy. And yet he had shifted it casually
from one shoulder to the other and there was nothing
in the movement to suggest weight. Perhaps it was

empty and he was going to get a load of free paints from Jerome et Cie.

Ricky was visited by a sequence of disturbing notions. Did Sydney Jones really think that he, Ricky, was following him around, spying on him or—unspeakable thought—lustfully pursuing him? Or was the boot on the other foot? Was Syd, in fact, keeping Ricky under observation? Had Syd, for some unguessable reason, followed him on board the *Island Belle?* Into the bistro? Up the hill to the church? When cornered, were the abuse and insults a shambling attempt to throw him off the scent? Which was the hunter and which the hunted?

It had been after Syd's return from London and after Dulcie's death that he had, definitively, turned hostile. Why? Had anything happened when he lunched with Ricky's parents to make him so peculiar? Was it because Troy had not thought well of his paintings? Or had asked if he was messing about with drugs?

And here Ricky suddenly remembered Syd's face, six inches from his own when they were vis-à-vis across the fish crate and Syd's dark glasses had slid down his nose. Were his eyes not pin-pupilled? And did he not habitually snuffle and sweat? And what about the night at Syd's Pad when he asked if Ricky had ever taken a trip? And behaved very much as if he'd taken something or another himself? Could drugs in fact be the explanation? Of everything? The scene he made when vermillion paint burst out of the wrong end of the tube? The sulks? The silly violence? Everything?

A squalid, boring explanation, he thought, and one that didn't really satisfy him. There was something else. It came to him that he would very much like to rake the whole thing over with his father.

He descended the church tower and went out to the street. Which way? On up the hill to Jerome et Cie or back to the town? Without consciously coming to a decision he found he had turned to the right and was approaching the entrance to the factory.

Opposite it was a café with chairs and tables set out under an awning. The day was beginning to be hot. He had walked quite a long way and climbed a tower. He chose a table beside a potted rubber plant whose leaves shielded him from the factory entrance but were not dense enough to prevent him watching it. He ordered beer and a roll and began to feel like a character in a *roman policier*. He supposed his father had often done this sort of thing and tried to imagine him, with his air of casual elegance, "keeping observation" hour after hour with a pile of saucers mounting on the table. "At a certain little café in the suburbs of Saint Pierre-des-Roches...," thought Ricky. That was how they began *roman policiers* in the salad days of the genre.

The beer was cold and delicious. It was fun to be keeping his own spot of observation, however pointless it might turn out to be.

Someone had left a copy of *Le Monde* on the table. He picked it up and began laboriously to read it, maintaining through the rubber plant leaves a pretty constant watch on the factory gates.

Feeling as if the waiters and every customer in the café observed him with astonishment, he contrived to make a hole in the paper which might be useful if, by some freakish chance, Syd should take it into his head to refresh himself when he emerged from the factory. Time went by slowly. It really was getting awfully hot. The newspaper tipped forward. He gave a galvanic jerk, opened his eyes and found himself looking through the rubber plant leaves at Syd Jones, crossing the street toward him.

Ricky whipped the paper up in front of his face and found that the peephole he had made was virtually useless. He stole a quick look over the top and there was Syd, sure enough, seating himself at a distant table with his back to Ricky. He dumped his paint box on the unoccupied seat. There was no doubt that now it was extremely heavy.

Ricky asked himself what the devil he thought he was up to and why it had become so important to find a reason for Syd Jones's taking a scunner to him. And why was he so concerned to find out if Syd doped himself? Was it because there were details in a pattern that refused to emerge and somehow or another—yes, that, absurdly, was it—could be associated with the death of Dulcie Harkness?

Having arrived at this preposterous conclusion, what was he going to do about it? Waste his little holiday by playing an inane game of hide-and-seek with Syd Jones and return to the island no wiser than when he left it?

There were no looking glasses in this café, and Syd had his back to Ricky, who had widened the hole in *Le Monde*. He was assured that his legs were unrecognizable since he had changed into jeans and espadrilles.

The waiter took an order from Syd and came back with *café-nature* and a glass of water.

And now Ricky became riveted to the hole in his paper. Syd looked round furtively. There were only four other people including Ricky in the café and he had chosen a table far removed from any of them. Suddenly, as far as Ricky could make out, he put the glass on the seat of his chair, between his thighs. He then appeared to take something out of the breast pocket of his shirt. His head was sunk on his chest, and he leaned forward as if to rest his left forearm on his knee and seemed intent on some hidden object. He became very still. After a few seconds his right arm jerked slightly, there was a further manipulation of some sort, he raised his head, and his body seemed to relax as if in the gift of the sun.

"That settles the drug question, poor sod," thought Ricky.

But he didn't think it settled anything else.

Syd began to tap the ground with his foot as though keeping time with an invisible band. With the fingers of his right hand he beat a tattoo on the lid of his paint box. Ricky heard him laugh contentedly. The waiter walked over to his table and looked at him. Syd groped in his pocket and dropped quite a little handful of coins on the table. The waiter picked up what was owing and waited for his tip. Syd made a wide extravagant gesture. "Help yourself," Ricky heard him say. *"Servez-vous, mon vieux,"* in execrable French. *"Prenez le tout."* The man bowed and swept up the coins. He turned away and, for the benefit of his fellow waiter, lifted his shoulders and rolled his head. Syd had not touched his coffee.

"Good morning, Mr. Alleyn."

Every nerve in Ricky's body seemed to leap. He let out an exclamation, dropped the newspaper and turned to find Mr. Ferrant smiling down at him.

II

After the initial shock, Ricky's reaction was one of hideous embarrassment joined to fury. He sat there with a flaming face knowing himself to look the last word in abysmal foolishness. How long, oh God, how long had Mr. Ferrant stood behind him and watched him squint with screwed up countenance through a hole in a newspaper at Syd Jones? Mr. Ferrant, togged out in skintight, modishly flared white trousers, a pink striped T-shirt, white buckskin sandals, and a medallion on a silver chain. Mr. Ferrant of the clustering curls and impertinent smile. Mr. Ferrant, incongruously enough, the plumber and odd-job man.

"You made me jump," Ricky said. "Hullo. Mrs. Ferrant said you might be here."

Mr. Ferrant snapped his fingers at the waiter.

"Mind if I join you?" he asked Ricky.

"No. Please. Do. What," Ricky invited in a strange voice, "will you have?"

He would have beer. Ricky ordered two beers and felt that he himself would be awash with it.

Ferrant, whose every move seemed to Ricky to express a veiled insolence, slid into a chair and stretched himself. "When did you come over, then?" he asked.

"This morning."

"Is that right?" he said easily. "So did *he*," and nodded across at Syd who now fidgeted and looked at his watch. At any moment, Ricky thought, he might turn round and see them and what could that not lead to?

The waiter brought their beer. Ferrant lit a cigarette. He blew out smoke and wafted it away with a workman's hand. "And what brought you over, anyway?" he asked.

"Curiosity," said Ricky and then, hurriedly, "To make a change from work."

"Work? That'd be writing, wouldn't it?" he said as if there was something suspect in the notion. "Where're you staying?" Ricky told him.

"That's a crummy little old place, that is," he said. "I go to Le Beau Rivage myself."

He took the copy of *Le Monde* out of Ricky's nerveless grasp and stuck his blunt forefinger through the hole. "Quite fascinating what you was reading, seemingly. Couldn't take your eyes off of it, could you, Mr. Alleyn?"

"Look here," Ricky said. He put his hand up to his face and felt its heat. "I expect you think there was something a bit off about—about—my looking—about. But there wasn't. I can't explain but—"

"Me!" said Ferrant. "Think! I don't think nothing."

He drained his glass and clapped it down on the table. "We all get our little fancies, like," he said.

"Right? And why not? Nice drop of ale, that." He was on his feet. "Reckon I'll have a word with Syd," he said. "Quite a coincidence. He come in the morning boat, too. Lovely weather, isn't it? Might turn to thunder later on."

He strolled across between the empty tables with slight but ineffable shifts of his vulgar little stern. Ricky could have kicked him but he could have kicked himself still harder.

It seemed an eternity before Ferrant reached Syd, who appeared to have dozed off. Ricky, held in a nightmarish inertia, could not take his eyes off them. Ferrant laid his hand on Syd's head and rocked it, not very gently, to and fro.

Syd opened his eyes. Ferrant twisted the head towards Ricky. He said something that didn't seem to register. Syd blinked and frowned as if unable to focus his eyes, but he made a feeble attempt to shake Ferrant off. Ferrant released him with a bully's playful buffet. Ricky saw awareness dawn on Syd's face and a mounting anger.

Ferrant shifted the paint box to the ground and sat down. He put his hand on Syd's knee and leaned toward him. He might have been giving him some important advice. The waiter strolled toward Ricky, who paid and tipped him. He said something about *"un drôle de type, celui-là,"* meaning Ferrant.

Ricky left the café. On his way out Ferrant waved to him.

He walked back into the town, chastened.

Perhaps the circumstance that most mortified him was the certainty that Ferrant by this time had told Syd about the hole in the newspaper.

The day had turned into a scorcher and the soles of his feet were cobbled with red-hot marbles. He reached the front and sought the shade of a wooden pavillion facing the sea. He shuffled out of his espadrilles, lit his pipe, and began to feel a little better.

The *Island Belle* was still at her berth. After the upset with Syd Jones on the way over Ricky hadn't thought of finding out when she sailed for Montjoy. He wondered whether he should call it a day, sail with her, and retire to his proper occupation of writing a book and perhaps licking the wounds in his self-esteem.

He was unable to make up his mind. French holiday-makers came and went; with the approach of noon the day grew hotter and the little pavillion less endurable. Ricky left it and walked painfully along the front to a group of three hotels, each of which had private access to a beach. He went into the first, Le Beau Rivage, hired bathing drawers and a towel, and swam about among the decorous bourgeoisie, hoping to become refreshed and in better heart.

What he did become was hungry. Unable to face the walk along scorching pavements, he took a taxi to his hotel, lunched there in a dark little *salle à manger,* and retired to his room where he fell into a very heavy sleep.

He woke, feeling awful, at three o'clock. The room had darkened. When he looked out his window it was to the ominous rumble of thunder and at steely clouds rolling in from the north. The harbor had turned gray and choppy and the *Island Belle* jaunced at her moorings. There were very few people about in the town and those that were to be seen walked quickly, seeking shelter.

Ricky was one of those beings who respond uncomfortably to electric storms. They produced a nervous tingling in his arms and legs and a sense of impending disaster. As a small boy they had aroused a febrile excitement so that at one moment he wanted to hide and at the next to stand at the window or even go out of doors for the sheer terror of doing so. Although he had learned to control these reactions and to give little outward sign of them, the restlessness they induced even now was almost unbearable.

The room flashed up and out. Ricky counted the

seconds automatically, scarcely knowing that he did so. "One-a-b, two-a-b," up to seven, when the thunder broke. That meant, or so he had always believed, that the core of the storm was seven miles away and might or might not come nearer.

The sky behaved in the manner of a Gustave Doré engraving. A crack opened and a shaft of vivid sunlight darted down like God's vengeance upon the offending sea.

Ricky tingled from head to foot. The room had stealthily become much too small. He was invaded by an urge to prove himself to himself. "I may have made a muck of my espionage," he thought, "but, by gum, I'm not going to stay in my bedroom with pins-and-needles because a couple of clouds are having it off up there. To hell with them."

He fished a light raincoat out of his rucksack and ran downstairs, pulling it on as he went. The elderly clerk was asleep behind his desk.

Outside there was a stifled feeling in the air, as if the town held its breath. Sounds—isolated footsteps, desultory voices, and the hiss of tires on the road— were all exaggerated. The sky was now so black that twilight seemed to have fallen on Saint Pierre-des-Roches.

Forked lightning wrote itself with a flourish across the heavens and almost simultaneously a gigantic tin tray banged overhead. A woman in the street crossed herself and broke into a shuffle. Ricky thought: "If I combed my hair it would crackle."

A few big drops fell like bullets in the dust and then, tremendously, the rain came down.

It really was a ferocious storm. The streets were running streams; lightning whiplashed almost continuously, thunder mingled with the din made by rain on roofs, sea, and stone. Ricky's espadrilles felt as if they had dissolved on his feet.

But he went on downhill to the sea, taking a kind of

satisfaction in pandemonium. Here was the bistro where he had breakfasted, here the first group of shops. And here the deserted front, not a soul on it, pounded by the deluge and beyond it the high tide pocked all over with rain. Le Beau Rivage overlooked this scene. Ricky could see a number of people staring out from its glassed-in portico and wondered if Ferrant were among them.

The *Island Belle* rocked at her moorings. Her gangway grated on the wharf.

Ricky saw that the administrative offices were shut, but a goods shed in which three cars were parked was open. He sheltered there. It was very dark. The rain drummed remorselessly on the roof. He got an impression of somebody else being in the shed—an impression so strong that he called out "Hallo! Anyone at home?," but there was no answer. He shook the rain from his mackintosh and hood and fished out his handkerchief to wipe his face. "This has been a rum sort of a day," he thought, and wondered how best to wind it up.

Evidently the *Island Belle* would not sail for some time. The cars and a number of crates were yet, he supposed, to be put aboard her. He thought he remembered that a notice of some sort was exhibited at the foot of the gangway: probably the time of sailing. The Cove and his own familiar island began to seem very attractive. He would find out when the *Island Belle* sailed, return to the hotel for his rucksack, pay his bill, and rejoin her.

He pulled his hood well over his face and squelched out of the shed into the storm.

It was only a short distance to the ship's moorings. Her bows rose and fell and above the storm he could hear her rubbing-strake grind against the jetty. He walked forward into the rain and was half blinded. When he came alongside the ship he stopped at the edge of the jetty and peered up, wondering if there was a watchman aboard.

The blow came as if it was part of the storm, a violence that struck him below the shoulders. The jetty was gone from under his feet. The side of the ship flew upwards. He thought, "This is abominable," and was hit in the face. Green cold enclosed him and his mouth was full of water. Then he knew what had happened.

He had fallen between the turn of the bilge and the jetty, had struck against something on his way down and had sunk and risen. Saltwater stung the back of his nose and lodged in his throat. He floundered in a narrow channel between the legs of the jetty and the sloping side of the bilge.

"Did he fall or was he pushed?" thought Ricky, struggling in his prison, and knew quite definitely that he had been pushed.

III

He had no idea how much leeway the ship's moorings allowed her or whether she might roll to such a degree that he could be crushed against the legs of the jetty, the only motionless things in a heaving universe.

His head cleared. Instinctive physical reactions had kept him afloat for the first moments. He now got himself under control. "I ought to yell," he thought and a distant thunderclap answered him. He turned on his back; the ship rolled and disclosed a faint daylight moon careering across a gap in the clouds. With great difficulty he began to swim, sometimes touching the piles and grazing his hands and feet on barnacles. The turn of the bilge passed slowly above him and at last was gone. He had cleared the bows of the *Island Belle*. There was Saint Pierre-des-Roches with the Hotel Beau Rivage and the hill and the church spire above it.

Now, should he yell for help? But there was still Somebody up there perhaps who wanted him drowned, crushed, whatever way—dead. He trod water, bobbing and ducking, and looked about him.

Not three feet away was a steel ladder.

When he reached and clung to it he still thought of the assailant who might be up there, waiting. He was now so cold that it would be better to risk anything rather than stay where he was. So he climbed, slowly. He had lost his espadrilles and the rungs bit into his feet. There was a sound like a voice, very far away: In his head, he thought, not real. Halfway up he paused. Everything had become quiet. It no longer rained.

"Hey! Hey there! Are you all right?"

For a moment he didn't know where to look. The voice seemed to have come out of the sky. Then he saw, in the bows of the ship, leaning over the taffrail, a man in oilskins and sou'wester. He waved at Ricky.

"Are you OK, mate?" shouted the man.

Ricky tried to answer but could only produce a croak.

"Hang on, I'll be with you. Hang on."

Ricky hauled himself up another three rungs. His reeling head was just below the level of the jetty. He pushed his left arm through the rungs of the ladder and hung there, clinging with his right hand. He heard boots clump down the gangway and along the jetty towards him.

"You'll be all right," said the voice, close above him. He let his head flop back. The face under the sou'wester was red and concerned and looked very big against the sky. An arm and a purplish hand reached down. "Come on, then," said the voice, "only a couple more."

"I'm sort of—gone—" Ricky whispered.

"Not you. You're fine. Make the effort, Jack."

He made the effort and was caught by the arms and saved.

He lay on the jetty saying, "I'm sorry, I'm so sorry," and being sick.

The man was very kind. He took off his oilskin and spread it over Ricky, whose teeth now chattered like castanets. He lay on his back and saw the clouds part and disperse. He felt the sun on his face.

"You're doing good, mate," said the man. "How's about we go on board and take a drop of something for the cold? You was aboard us this morning? That right?"

"Yes. This morning."

"Up she rises. Take it easy. Lovely."

He was on his feet. They began to move along the jetty.

"Is there anybody else?" Ricky said.

"How'd you mean, anybody else?"

"Watching."

"You're not yourself. You'll be all right. Here we go, then."

Ricky made heavy work of the gangway. Once on board he did what he was told. The man took him into the little saloon. He helped him strip and brought him a vest and heavy underpants. He lay on a bench and was covered with a blanket and overcoats and given half a tumbler of raw whiskey. It made him gasp and shudder but it ran through him like fire. "Super," he said. "That's super."

"What happened, then? Did you slip on the jetty or what?"

"I was pushed. No, I'm not wandering and I'm not tight—yet. I was given a bloody great shove in the back. I swear I was. Listen."

The man listened. He scraped his jaw and eyed Ricky and every now and then wagged his head.

"I was looking up at the deck, trying to see if anyone was about. I wanted to know when she sails. I was on the edge almost. I can feel it now—two hands hard in the small of my back. I took a bloody great stride into damnall and dropped. I hit something. Under my eye, it was."

The man leaned forward and peered at his face. "It's coming up lovely," he admitted. "I'll say that for you."

"Didn't you see anybody?"

"Me! I was taking a bit of kip, mate, wasn't I? Below. Something woke me, see. Thunder or what-have-you and I come up on deck and there you was, swimming and ducking and grabbing the ladder. I hailed you but you didn't seem to take no notice. Not at first you didn't."

"He must have been hiding in the goods shed. He must have followed me down and sneaked into the shed."

"Reckon you think you know who done it, do you? Somebody got it in for you, like?" He stared at Ricky. "You don't look the type," he said. "Nor yet you don't sound like it, neither."

"It's hard to explain," Ricky sighed. He was beginning to feel sleepy.

"Look," said the man, "we sail at six. Was you thinking of sailing with us, then? Just to know, like. No hurry."

"Oh yes," Ricky said. "Yes, please."

"Where's your dunnage?"

Ricky pulled himself together and told him. The man said his mate, the second deckhand, was relieving him as watchman at four-thirty. He offered to collect Ricky's belongings from the hotel and pay his bill. Ricky fished his waterproof wallet out of an inside pocket of his raincoat and found that the notes were not too wet to be presentable.

"I can't thank you enough," he said. "Look. Take a taxi. Buy yourself a bottle of Scotch from me. You will, won't you?"

He said he would. He also said his name was Jim Le Compte and they'd have to get Ricky dressed proper and sitting up before the Old Man came aboard them.

And by six o'clock Ricky was sitting in the saloon fully dressed with a rug over his knees. It was a smoother crossing than he had expected, and rather to his surprise he was not seasick, but slept through most of it. At Montjoy he said goodbye to his friend. "Look," he said, "Jim, I owe you a lot already. Will you do something more for me?"

"What would that be?"

"Forget about there being anyone else in it. I just skidded and fell. Please don't think," Ricky added, "that I'm in any sort of trouble. Believe me, I'm not. Word of honor. But—will you be a good chap and leave it that way?"

Le Compte looked at him for some moments with his head on one side. "Fair enough, squire," he said at last. "If that's the way you want it. You skidded and fell."

"You *are* a good chap," said Ricky. He went ashore carrying a rucksack full of wet clothes and took a taxi to the Cove.

He let himself in and went straight upstairs, passing Mrs. Ferrant who was speaking on the telephone.

When he entered his room a very tall man rose from the armchair.

It was his father.

IV

"So you see I'm on duty," said Alleyn. "Fox and I have got a couple of tarted-up apartments at the Neo-Ritz or whatever it calls itself in Montjoy, the use of a police car, and a tidy program of routine work ahead. I wouldn't have any business talking to you, Rick, except that by an exasperating twist you may turn out to be a source of information."

"Hi!" said Ricky excitedly. "Is it about Miss Harkness?"

"Why?" Alleyn asked sharply.

"I only wondered."

"I wouldn't dream of telling you what it's about

normally, but if we're to get any further I think I'll have to. And Rick—I want an absolute assurance that you'll discuss this business with nobody. But nobody. In the smallest degree. It must be as if it'd never been. Right?"

"Right," said Ricky and his father thought he heard a tinge of regret.

"Nobody," Alleyn repeated. "And certainly not Julia Pharamond."

Ricky blushed.

"As far as you're concerned, Fox and I have come over to discuss a proposed adjustment to reciprocal procedure between the island constabulary and the mainland police. We shall be sweating it out at interminable and deadly boring meetings. That's the story. Got it?"

"Yes, Cid." ("Cid," deriving from C.I.D., was the name Ricky and his friends gave his father.)

"Yes. And nobody's going to believe it when we start nosing round at the riding stables. But never mind. Let's say that as we were here, the local chaps thought they'd like a second opinion. By the way, talking about local chaps, the Super at Montjoy who called us in hasn't helped matters by bursting his appendix and having an urgent operation. The local sergeant at the Cove, Plank—but of course you know Plank—is detailed to the job."

"He's nobody's fool."

"Good. Now, coming back to you. The really important bit to remember is that we must be held to take no interest whatever in Monsieur Ferrant's holidays and we've never even heard of Sydney Jones."

"But," Ricky ventured, "I've told the Pharamonds about his visit to you and Mum."

"Damn. All right, then. It passed off quietly and nothing has ever come of it."

"If you say so."

"I do say so. Loud and clear."

"Yes, Cid."

"Good. All right. Are you hungry, by the way?"

"Now you mention it."

"Could that formidable lady downstairs be persuaded to give us both something to eat?"

"I'm sure. I'll ask her."

"You'd better tell her you slid on the wet wharf and
banged your cheek on a stanchion."

"She'll think I was drunk."

"Good. You smell like a Scotch hangover anyway.
Are you sure you're all right, old boy? Sure?"

"Fine. Now. I'll have a word with Mrs. F."

When he'd gone, Alleyn looked out the window at
the darkening Cove and turned over Ricky's account of
his visit to Saint Pierre-des-Roches and the events that
preceded it. People, he reflected, liked to talk about
police cases in terms of a jigsaw puzzle, and that was
fair enough as far as it went. But in this instance he
couldn't be sure that the bits all belonged to the puzzle.
"Only connect" Forster owlishly laid down as the
novelist's law. He could equally have been setting out a
guide for investigating officers.

There had never been any question of Ricky
following in his father's footsteps. From the time when
his son went to his first school, Alleyn had been at
pains to keep his job at a remove as far as the boy was
concerned. Ricky's academic career had been more
than satisfactory and about as far removed from the
squalor, boredom, horror, and cynicism of a policeman's lot as it would be possible to imagine.

And now? Here they were, both of them, converging
on a case that might well turn out to be all compact of
such elements. And over and above everything else,
here was Ricky escaped from what, almost certainly,
had been a murderous attack, the thought of which
sent an icy spasm through his father's stomach. Get
him out of it, smartly, now, before there was any
further involvement, he thought—and then had to
recognize that already Ricky's involvement was too far

advanced for this to be possible. He must be treated as
someone who might, himself in the clear, provide the
police with "helpful information."

And at the back of his extreme distaste for this
development why was there an indefinable warmth, a
latent pleasure? He wondered if perhaps an old
loneliness had been, or looked to become, a little
assuaged.

Ricky came back with the assurance that Mrs.
Ferrant was concocting a dish the mere smell of which
would cause the salivary glands of a hermit to spout
like fountains.

"She's devoured by curiosity," he said. "About you.
Why you're here. What you do. Whether you're cross
with me. The lot. She'd winkle information out of a
Trappist monk, that one would. I can't wait."

"For what?"

"For her to start on you."

"Rick," Alleyn said. "She's Mrs. Ferrant, and
Ferrant, you tell me, is mysteriously affluent, goes in
for solitary night fishing, pays dressy visits to Saint
Pierre-des-Roches, and seems to be thick with Jones.
With Jones who also visits there and goes to London
carrying paint and who, since he's found out your
father is a cop, has taken a scunner to you. You think
Jones dopes. So do I. Ferrant seems to have a bully's
ascendancy over Jones. One of them, you think, tried
to murder you. It follows that you watch your step with
Mrs. Ferrant, don't you agree?"

"Yes, of course. And I always have. Not because of
any of that but because she's so bloody insatiable.
About the Pharamonds in particular. Especially about
Louis."

"Yes?"

"Yes. And I'll tell you what. I think when she was
cooking or whatever she did up at L'Esperance, she
had a romp on the side with Louis."

"Why?"

"Because of the way he talks about her. The bedside manner. And—well, because of that kid."

"The Ferrant kid?"

"That's right. There's a look. Unmistakable, I'd have thought. Dark and cheeky and a bit slyboots."

"Called?"

"Wait for it."

"Louis?"

Ricky nodded.

"It's as common a French name as can be," said Alleyn.

"Yes, of course," Ricky agreed, "and it'd be going altogether too far, one would think, wouldn't one? To christen him that if Louis was—" He made a dismissive gesture. "It's probably just my dirty mind after all. And—well—"

"You don't like Louis Pharamond?"

"Not much. Does it show?"

"A bit."

"He was on that voyage when you met them, wasn't he?" Ricky asked. Alleyn nodded. "Did you like him?"

"Not much."

"Good."

"Which signifies," Alleyn said, "damnall."

"He had something going with Miss Harkness."

"For pity's sake!" Alleyn exclaimed, "how many more and why do you think so?"

Ricky described the incident on the cliffs. "It had been a rendezvous," he said rather importantly. "You could tell."

"I don't quite see how when you say you were lying flat on your face behind a rock, but let that pass."

Ricky tried not to grin. "Anyway," he said, "I bet I'm right. He's a prowler."

"Rick," Alleyn said after a pause, "I'm here on a sort of double job which is my Assistant Commissioner's Machiavellian idea of economy. I'm here because the local police are worried about the death of Dulcie

Harkness and have asked us to nod in and I'm also supposed in an offhand, carefree manner to look into the possibility of this island being a penultimate station in one of the heroin routes into Great Britain."

"Laws!"

"Yes. Of course you've read about the ways the trade is run. Every kind of outlandish means of transit is employed—electric light-fittings, component parts for hearing aids, artificial limbs, fat men's navels, anything hollow—you name it. If the thing's going on here there's got to be some way of getting the stuff out of Marseilles, where the conversion into heroin is effected, across to Saint Pierre, from there to the island and thence to the mainland. Anything suggest itself?"

"Such as why did Jones cut up so rough when I trod on his paint?"

"Go on."

"He does seem to make frequent trips—Hi!" Ricky said, interrupting himself. "Would this mean Jerome et Cie were in it or that Jones was on his own?"

"Probably the former but it's anyone's guess."

"And Ferrant? The way he behaved with Syd at Saint Pierre. Could they be in cahoots? Is there anything on Ferrant?"

"The narcotics boys say he's being watched. Apparently he makes these pleasure trips rather often and has been known to fly down to Marseilles and the Côte d'Azur where he's been seen hobnobbing with recognized traders."

"But what's he supposed to *do?*"

"They've nothing definite. He may have the odd rendezvous on calm nights when he goes fishing. Suppose—and this is the wildest guesswork—but suppose a gentleman with similar propensities puts out from Saint Pierre with a consignment of artists' paints. They've been opened at the bottom and capsules of heroin pushed up and filled in nice and tidy with paint. Then a certain amount is squeezed out at the top and the tubes messed about to look used. And in due course they go into Syd Jones's paint box among his rightful materials and he takes one of his trips over to London. The stuff he totes round to shops and artists' studios is of course pure as pure. The customs people have got used to him and his paint box. They probably did their stuff at some early stages before he began to operate. Even now, if they got curious, the odds are they'd hit on the wrong tube. One would suppose he doesn't distribute more than a minimum of the doctored jobs among his legitimate material. Of which the vermillion you put your great hoof on was one."

Alleyn stopped. He looked at his son and saw a familiar glaze of incredulity and interest on his open countenance.

"Don't get it wrong," he said. "That may be all my eye. Mr. Jones may be as pure as the driven snow. But if you can find another reason for him taking such a scunner on you, let's have it. Rick, consider. You visit his 'Pad' and show an interest in his Jerome et Cie paint. A few days later you tread on his vermillion and try to pick up the tube. You send him to us and when he gets there he's asked if he's messing about with drugs. On top of that he learns that your pop's a cop. He sets out on a business trip to headquarters and who does he find dodging about among the cargo? You, Chummy. He's rattled and lets fly, accusing you of the first offense he can think of that doesn't bear any relation to his actual goings-on. And to put the lid on it you dog his footsteps almost to the very threshold of Messrs. Jerome et Cie. And don't forget, all this may be a farrago of utter nonsense."

"It adds up, I suppose. Or does it?"

"If you know a better 'ole'—"

"What about Ferrant, then? Are they in cahoots over the drug racket?"

"It could be. It looks a bit like it. And Ferrant it is who finds you—what exactly *were* you doing? Show me."

"Have a heart."

"Come on." Alleyn picked up a copy of yesterday's *Times*. "Show me." Ricky opened it and tore a hole in the center fold. He then advanced his eye to the hole, screwed up his face, and peered through.

Alleyn looked over the top of the *Times*. "Boh!" he said.

Mrs. Ferrant came in.

"Your bit of supper's ready," she said, regarding them with surprise. "In the parlor."

Self-conscious, they followed her downstairs.

The aroma—delicate, pervasive, and yet discreet— welcomed them into the parlor. The dish, elegantly presented, was on the table. The final assembly had been completed, the garniture was in place. Mrs. Ferrant, saucepan in hand, spooned the shellfish sauce over hot fillets of sole.

"My God!" Alleyn exclaimed. "Sole *à la Dieppoise!*"

His success with the cook could only be compared to that of her masterpiece with him. Ricky observed, with mounting wonderment and small understanding, since the conversation was in French, the rapprochement his father instantly established with Mrs. Ferrant. He questioned her about the sole, the shrimps, the mussels. In a matter of minutes he had elicited the information that Madame (as he was careful to call her) had a *maman* who actually came from Dieppe and from whom she inherited her art. He was about to send Ricky out at the gallop to purchase a bottle of white Burgundy when Mrs. Ferrant, a gratified smirk twitching at her lips, produced one. He kissed her hand and begged her to join them. She consented. Ricky's eyes opened wider and wider.

As the strange little feast progressed he became at least partially tuned in. He gathered that his father had steered the conversation around to the Pharamonds and the days of her service up at L'Esperance. "Monsieur Louis" came up once or twice. He was

sophisticated. A very mondain type, was he not? One
might say so, said Mrs. Ferrant with a shrug. It was her
turn to ask questions. Monsieur Alleyn was well
acquainted with the family, for example? Not to say
"well." They had been fellow passengers on an ocean
voyage. Monsieur's visit was unanticipated by his son,
was it not? But entirely so. It had been pleasant to
surprise him. So droll the expression, when he walked
in. Jaw dropped, eyes bulging. Alleyn gave a lively
imitation and slapped his son jovially on the shoulder.
Ah yes, for example, his black eye, Mrs. Ferrant
inquired, and switching to English asked Ricky what
he'd been doing with himself, then, in Saint Pierre.
Had he got into bad company? Ricky offered the fable
of the iron stanchion. Her stewed-prune eyes glittered
and she said something in French that sounded like *à
d'autres:* Ricky wondered whether it was the equivalent of "tell us another."

"You got yourself in a proper mess," she pointed
out. "Dripping wet those things are in your rucksack."

"I got caught in the thunderstorm."

"Did it rain seaweed, then?" asked Mrs. Ferrant and
for the first time in their acquaintance gave out a cackle
of amusement in which, to Ricky's fury, his father
joined.

"Ah, Madame!" said Alleyn with a comradely look
at Mrs. Ferrant. *"Les jeunes hommes!"*

She nodded her head up and down. Ricky wondered
what the hell she supposed he'd been up to.

The sole *à la Dieppoise* was followed by the lightest
of sorbets, a cheese board, coffee and cognac.

"I have not eaten so well," Alleyn said, "since I was
last in Paris. You are superb, Madame."

The conversation proceeded bilingually and drifted
around to Miss Harkness and to what Alleyn, with, as
his son felt, indecent understatement, referred to as *son
contretemps équestre.*

Mrs. Ferrant put on an air of grandeur, of somber

loftiness. It had been unfortunate, she conceded. Miss Harkness's awful face and sightless glare flashed up in Ricky's remembrance.

She had perhaps been of a reckless disposition Alleyn hinted. In more ways than one, Mrs. Ferrant agreed and sniffed very slightly.

"By the way, Rick," Alleyn said. "Did I forget to say? Your Mr. Jones called on us in London?"

"Really?" said Ricky, managing to sound surprised. "What on earth for? Selling Mummy his paints?"

"Well—advertising them, shall we say. He showed your mother some of his work."

"What did she think?"

"I'm afraid, not a great deal."

It was Mrs. Ferrant's turn again. Was Mrs. Alleyn, then, an artist? An artist of great distinction, perhaps? And Alleyn himself? He was on holiday no doubt? No, no, Alleyn said. It was a business trip. He would be staying in Montjoy for a few days but had taken the opportunity to visit his son. Quite a coincidence, was it not, that Ricky should be staying at the Cove. Lucky fellow!, Alleyn cried catching him another buffet and bowing at the empty dishes.

Mrs. Ferrant didn't in so many words ask Alleyn what his job was but she came indecently close to it. Ricky wondered if his father would sidestep the barrage, but no, he said cheerfully that he was a policeman. She offered a number of exclamations. She would never have dreamed it! A policeman! In English she accused him of "having her on" and in French of not being the type. It was all very vivacious and Ricky didn't believe a word of it. His ideas on Mrs. Ferrant were undergoing a rapid transformation, due in part, he thought, to her command of French. He couldn't follow much of what she said but the sound of it lent a gloss of sophistication to her general demeanor. It put her into a new category. She had become more formidable. As for his father: it was as if some frisky stranger laughed and flattered and almost flirted. Was this The Cid? What were they talking about now? About Mr. Ferrant and his trips to Saint Pierre and how he would never eat as well abroad as he did at home. He had business connections in France perhaps? No. Merely family ones. He liked to keep up with his aunts—

Ricky had had a long, painful and distracting day of it. Impossible to believe that only this morning he and Sydney Jones had leaned nose to nose across a crate of fish on a pitching deck. And how odd those people looked, scuttling about so far below. Like woodlice. Awful to fall from the balcony among them. But he *was* falling: down, down into the disgusting sea.

"Arrrach!" he tried to shout and looked into his father's face and felt his hands on his shoulders. Mrs. Ferrant had gone.

"Come along, old son," Alleyn said, and his deep voice was very satisfactory. "Bed. Call it a day."

V

Inspector Fox was discussing a pint of mild-and-bitter when Alleyn walked into the bar at the Cod-and-Bottle. He was engaged in dignified conversation with the landlord, three of the habituals, and Sergeant Plank. Alleyn saw that he was enjoying his usual success. They hung upon his words. His massive back was turned to the door and Alleyn approached him unobserved.

"That's where you hit the nail smack on the head, sergeant," he was saying. "Calm, cool, and collected. You've had the experience of working with him?"

"Well," said Sergeant Plank clearing his throat, "in a very subsidiary position, Mr. Fox. But I remarked upon it."

"You remarked upon it. Exactly, So've I. For longer than you might think, Mr. Maistre," said Fox, drawing the landlord into closer communion. "And a gratifying experience it's been. However," said Mr. Fox who had suddenly become aware of Alleyn's approach, *"quoi qu'il en soit."*

The islanders were bilingual, and Mr. Fox never let slip an opportunity to practice his French or to brag, in a calm and stately manner, of the excellencies of his superior officer. It was seldom that Alleyn caught him at this exercise and when he did, gave him fits. But that made little difference to Fox, who merely pointed out that the technique had proved a useful approach to establishing comfortable relations with persons from whom Alleyn hoped to obtain information.

"By and large," Mr. Fox had said, "people like to know about personalities in the Force so long as they're in the clear themselves. They get quite curious to meet you, Mr. Alleyn, when they hear about your little idiosyncrasies: it takes the stiffness out of the first inquiries, if you see what I mean. In theatrical parlance," Fox had added, "they call it building up an entrance."

"In common or garden parlance," Alleyn said warmly, "it makes a bloody great fool out of me." Fox had smiled slightly.

On this occasion it was clear that the Foxian method had been engaged and, it was pretty obvious, abetted by Sergeant Plank. Alleyn found himself the object of fixed and silent attention in the bar of the Cod-and-Bottle and the evident subject of intense speculation.

Mr. Fox, who was infallible at remembering names at first hearing, performed introductions, and Alleyn shook hands all round. Throats were cleared and boots were shuffled. Bob Maistre deployed his own technique as host and asked Alleyn how he'd found the young chap, then, and what was all this they'd heard

about him getting himself into trouble over to Saint
Pierre? Alleyn gave a lively account of his son losing his
footing on the wet jetty, hitting his jaw on an iron
stanchion, and falling between the jetty and the *Island
Belle*.

"Could have been a serious business," he said, "as
far as I can make out. No knowing what might have
happened if it hadn't been for this chap aboard the
ship—Jim Le Compte, isn't it?"

It emerged that Jim Le Compte was a Cove man and
this led easily to the introduction of local gossip and,
easing around under Plank's pilotage, to Mr. Ferrant
and to wags of the head and knowing grins suggesting
that Gil Ferrant was a character, a one, a bit of a lad.

"He's lucky," Alleyn said lightly, "to be able to
afford jaunts in France. I wish I could."

This drew forth confused speculations as to Gil
Ferrant's resources: his rich aunties in Brittany, his
phenomenal luck on the French lotteries, his being, in
general, a pretty warm customer.

This turn of conversation was, to Alleyn's hidden
fury, interrupted by Sergeant Plank, who offered the
suggestion that no doubt the Chief Super's professional duties sometimes took him across the Channel.
Seeing it was expected of him, Alleyn responded with
an anecdote or two about a sensational case involving
the pursuit and arrest in Marseilles, with the assistance
of the French force, of a notable child-killer. This, as
Fox said afterwards, went down like a nice long drink
but, as he pointed out to Sergeant Plank, had the
undesirable effect of cutting off any further local
gossip. "It was well meant on your part, Sarge," Mr.
Fox conceded, "but it broke the thread. It stopped the
flow of info."

"I'm a source of local info myself, Mr. Fox,"
Sergeant Plank ventured. "In my own person, I am."

"True enough as far as it goes, Sarge, but you're
overlooking a salient factor. As the Chief Super has

frequently remarked, ours is a solitary class of employment. We can and in your own type of patch, the village community, we often do, establish friendly relations. Trespassing, local vandalism, creating nuisances, trouble with neighbors and they're all over you, but let something big turn up and you'll find yourself out on your own. They'll herd together like sheep and you won't be included in the flock. It can be uncomfortable until you get used to it."

Fox left a moment or two for this to sink in. He then cleared his throat and continued. "The effect of the diversion," he said, "was this. The thread of local gossip being broken what did they do? They got all curious about the Chief. What's he here for? Is it the Harkness fatality and if not what is it? And if it is why is it? Enough to create the wrong atmosphere at the site of investigation."

Whether or not these pronouncements were correct, the atmosphere at Leathers the next morning, as disseminated by Mr. Harkness, the sole occupant, was far from comfortable. Alleyn, Fox, and Plank arrived at eight-thirty to find shuttered windows and a notice pinned to the front door: "Stables Closed till Further Notice." They knocked and rang to no effect.

"He'll be round at the back," Plank said and led the way to the stables.

At first they seemed to be deserted. A smell of straw and horse droppings hung on the air, flies buzzed, and in the old open coach house a couple of pigeons waddled about the floor, pecked here and there, and flew up to the rafters where they defecated offhandedly on the roof of the battered car. In the end loose-box the sorrel mare reversed herself, looked out, rolled her eyes, pricked her ears at them, and trembled her nostrils in an all but inaudible whinny.

"Will I see if I can knock Cuth Harkness up, sir?" offered Plank.

"Wait a bit, Plank. Don't rush it."

Alleyn strolled over to the loose-box. "Hullo, old girl," he said, "how goes it?" He leaned on the half-door and looked her over. The near foreleg was still bandaged. She nibbled his ear with velvet lips. "Feeling bored, are you?" he said and moved down the row of empty loose-boxes to the coach house.

There was the coil of old wire where Ricky had seen it, hanging from a peg above a pile of empty sacks. It was rather heavier than picture-hanging wire and looked as if it had been there for a long time. But as Ricky had noticed, there was a freshly cut end. Alleyn called Fox and the sergeant over. Plank's boots, being of the regulation sort, loudly announced his passage across the yard. He changed to tiptoe and an unnerving squeak.

"Take a look," Alleyn murmured.

"I reckon," Plank said after a heavy-breathed examination. "That could be it, Mr. Alleyn. I reckon that would fit."

"Do you, by George," Alleyn said.

There was an open box in the corner filled with a jumble of odds and ends and a number of tools, among them a pair of wire cutters. With uncanny speed Alleyn used them to nip off three inches of wire from the reverse end.

"That, Sergeant Plank," he said as he replaced the cutters, "is something we must never, never do."

"I'll try to remember, sir," said Sergeant Plank, demurely.

"Mr. Harkness," Fox said, "seems to be coming, Mr. Alleyn."

And indeed he could be heard coughing hideously inside the house. Alleyn reached the door in a breath and the other two stood behind him. He knocked briskly.

Footsteps sounded in the passage and an indistinguishable grumbling. A lock was turned and the door dragged open a few inches. Mr. Harkness, blinking and unshaven, peered out at them through a little gale of Scotch whiskey.

"The stables are closed," he said thickly and made as if to shut the door. Alleyn's foot was across the threshold.

"Mr. Harkness?" he said. "I'm sorry to bother you. We're police officers. Could you give us a moment?"

For a second or two he neither spoke nor moved. Then he pulled the door wide open.

"Police, are you?" Mr. Harkness said. "What for? Is it about my poor sinful niece again, God forgive her, but that's asking too much of Him. Come in."

He showed them into his office and gave them chairs and seemed to become aware, for the first time, of Sergeant Plank.

"Joey Plank," he said. "You again. Can't you let it alone? What's the good? It won't bring her back. Vengeance is mine saith the Lord and she's finding that out for herself where she's gone. Who are these gentlemen?"

Plank introduced them. "The Chief Superintendent is on an administrative visit to the island, Mr. Harkness," he said, "and has kindly offered to take a wee look-see at our little trouble."

"Why do you talk in that silly way about it?" Mr. Harkness asked fretfully. "It's not a little trouble, it's hell and damnation and she's brought it on herself and I'm the cause of it. I'm sorry," he said and turned to Alleyn with a startling change to normality. "You'll think me awfully rude but I daresay you'll understand what a shock this has been."

"Of course we do," Alleyn said. "We're sorry to break in on you like this but Superintendent Curie in Montjoy suggested it."

"I suppose he thinks he knows what he's talking about," Mr. Harkness grumbled. His manner now suggested a mixture of hopelessness and irritation. His eyes were bloodshot, his hands unsteady, and his breath was dreadful. "What's this about the possibility of foul play? What do they think I am, then? If there was any chance of foul play wouldn't I be zealous in the pursuit of unrighteousness? Wouldn't I be sleepless night and day as the hound of Heaven until the awful truth was hunted down?" He glared moistly at Alleyn. "Well," he shouted. "Come on! *Wouldn't I?*"

"I'm sure you would," Alleyn hurriedly agreed.

"Very natural and proper," said Fox.

"You shut up," said Mr. Harkness but absently and without rancor.

"Mr. Harkness," Alleyn began and checked himself. "I'm sorry—should I be giving you your rank? I don't know—"

The shaky hand drifted to the toothbrush moustache. "I don't insist on it," the thick voice mumbled. "Might of course. But let it pass. 'Mr.' is good enough." The wraith of the riding master faded and the distracted zealot returned. "Pride," said Mr. Harkness, "is the deadliest of all the sins. You were saying?"

He leaned toward Alleyn with a parody of anxious attentiveness.

Alleyn was very careful. He explained that in cases of fatality the police had a duty to eliminate the possibility of any verdict but that of accident. Sometimes, he said, there were features that at first sight seemed to preclude this. "More often than not," he said, "these features turn out to be of no importance, but we do have to make sure of it."

With an owlish and insecure parody of the conscientious officer, Mr. Harkness said: "Cer'nly. Good show."

Alleyn, with difficulty, took him through the period between the departure and return of the riding party. It emerged that Mr. Harkness had spent most of the day in the office concocting material for religious hand-outs. He gave a disjointed account of locking his niece in her room and of her presumed escape and said distractedly that some time during the afternoon, he could not recall when, he had gone into the barn to pray but had noticed nothing untoward and had met nobody. He began to wilt.

"Where did you have your lunch?" Alleyn asked.

"Excuse me," said Mr. Harkness and left the room.

"Now what!" Mr. Fox exclaimed.

"Call of nature?" Sergeant Plank suggested.

"Or the bottle," Alleyn said. "Damn."

He looked about the office: at faded photographs of equestrian occasions, of a barely recognizable and slim Mr. Harkness in the uniform of a mounted-infantry regiment. A more recent photograph displayed a truculent young woman in jodhpurs displaying a sorrel mare.

"That's Dulce," said Sergeant Plank. "That was," he added.

The desk was strewn with bills, receipts, and a litter of brochures and pamphlets, some of a horsey description, others proclaiming in dated, execrable type the near approach of judgment and eternal damnation. In the center was a letter pad covered in handwriting that began tidily and deteriorated into an illegible scrawl. This seemed to be a draft for a piece on the lusts of the flesh. Above and to the left of the desk was the corner cupboard spotted by Ricky and Jasper Pharamond. The door was not quite closed and Alleyn flipped it open. Inside was the whiskey bottle and behind this, as if thrust out of sight, but still distinguishable, the card with a red-ink skull and crossbones and the legend—"BEWARE!!! THIS WAY LIES DAMNATION!!!" The bottle was empty.

Alleyn reached out a long finger and lifted a corner of the card, exposing a small carton half filled with capsules.

"Look at this, Br'er Fox," he said.

Fox put on his spectacles and peered.

"Well, well," he said and after a closer look: "*Simon*

Frères. Isn't there something, now, about Simon Frères?"

"Amphetamines. Dexies. Prohibited in Britain," Alleyn said. He opened the carton and shook one capsule into his palm. He had replaced the carton and pocketed the capsule when Fox said, "Coming."

Alleyn shut the cupboard door and was back in his chair as an uneven footstep announced the return of Mr. Harkness. He came in on a renewed fog of Scotch.

"Apologize," he said. "Bowels, all to blazes. Result of shock. You were saying?"

"I'd said all of it, I think," Alleyn replied. "I was going to ask, though, if you'd mind our looking over the ground outside. Where it happened and so on."

"Go where you like," he said, "but don't, please, please, don't ask me to come."

"Of course, if you'd rather not."

"I dream about that gap," he whispered. There was a long and difficult silence. "They made me see her," he said at last. "Identification. She looked awful."

"I know."

"Well," he said with one of his most disconcerting changes of manner. "I'll leave you to it. Good hunting." Incredibly he let out a bark of what seemed to be laughter and rose with difficulty to his feet. He had begun to weep.

They had reached the outside door when he erupted into the passage and ricocheting from one wall to the other, advanced toward Alleyn upon whom he thrust a pink brochure.

Alleyn took it and glanced at flaring headlines.

"WINE IS A MOCKER" he saw.

"STRONG DRINK IS RAGING."

"Read," Mr. Harkness said with difficulty, "mark, learn and inwardly indigestion. See you on Sunday."

He executed an abrupt turn and once more retired, waving airily as he did so. His uneven footsteps faded down the passage.

Fox said thoughtfully: "He won't last long at that rate."

"He's not himself, Mr. Fox," Plank said, rather as if he felt bound to raise excuses for a local product. "He's very far from being himself. It's the liquor."

"You don't tell me."

"He's not used to it, like."

"He's learning, though," Fox said.

Alleyn said: "Didn't he drink? Normally?"

"T.T. Rabid. Hellfire according to him. Since he was Saved," Plank added.

"Saved from what?" Fox asked. "Oh, I see what you mean. Eternal damnation and all that carry-on. What was that about 'See you Sunday'? Has anything been said about seeing him on Sunday?"

"Not by me," Alleyn said. "Wait a bit."

He consulted the pink brochure. Following some terrifying information about the evils of intemperance it went on to urge a full attendance at the Usual Sunday Gathering in the Old Barn at Leathers with Service and Supper, Gents 50p, Ladies a Basket. Across these printed instructions a wildly irregular hand had scrawled: "Special! Day of Wrath!! May 13th!!! Remember!!!!"

"What's funny about May thirteenth?" asked Plank and then: "Oh. Of course. Dulcie."

"Will it be a kind of memorial service?" Fox speculated.

"Whatever it is, we shall attend it," said Alleyn. "Come on." And he led the way outside.

The morning was sunny and windless. In the horse paddock two of the Leathers string obligingly nibbled each other's flanks. On the hillside beyond the blackthorn hedge three more grazed together, swishing their tails and occasionally tossing up their heads.

"Peaceful scene, sir?" Sergeant Plank suggested.

"Isn't it?" Alleyn agreed. "Would that be the Old Barn?" He pointed to a building at some distance from the stables.

"That's it, sir. That's where they hold their meetings. It's taken on surprising in the district. By all accounts he's got quite a following."

"Ever been to one, Plank?"

"Me, Mr. Alleyn? Not in my line. We're C of E, me and my Missus. They tell me this show's very much in the blood-and-thunder line."

"We'll take a look at the barn later."

They walked down to the gap in the hedge.

An improvised but sturdy fence had been built, enclosing the area where the sorrel mare had taken off for her two jumps. Pieces of raised and weathered board covered the hoofprints.

"Who ordered all this?" Alleyn asked. "The Super?"

After a moment Plank said: "Well, no sir."

"You did it on your own?"

"Sir."

"Good for you, Plank. Very well done."

"Sir," said Plank, crimson with gratification.

He lifted and replaced the boards for Alleyn. "There wasn't anything much in the way of human prints," he said.

"There's been heavy rain. And, of course, horses' hoofprints all over the shop."

"You've saved these."

"I took casts," Plank murmured.

"You'll be getting yourself in line for a halo," said Alleyn and they moved to the gap itself. The blackthorn in the gap had been considerably knocked about. Alleyn looked over it and down and across to the far bank where a sort of plastic tent had been erected. Above and around this a shallow drain had been dug.

"That's one hell of a dirty great jump," Alleyn said.

There was a massive slide down the near bank and a scramble of hoofprints on the far one.

"As I read them," Plank ventured, "it looks as if the mare made a mess of the jump, fell all ways down this bank, and landed on top of her rider on the far side."

"And it looks to me," Alleyn rejoined, "as if you're not far wrong."

He examined the two posts on either side of the gap. They were half hidden by blackthorn, but when this was held aside, scars, noticed by Ricky, were clearly visible: on one post thin, rounded grooves, obviously of recent date; on the other, similar grooves dragged upwards from the margin. Both posts were loose in the ground.

At considerable discomfort to himself, Alleyn managed to clear a way to the base of the left-hand post and crawl up to it.

"The earth's been disturbed," he grunted. "Around the base."

He backed out, groped in his pocket, and produced his three inches of fencing wire from the coach house.

"Here comes the nitty-gritty bit," said Fox.

He and Plank wrapped handkerchiefs around their hands and held back obstructing brambles. Alleyn cupped his scratched left hand under one of the grooves and with his right finger and thumb insinuated his piece of wire into it. It fitted snugly.

"Bob's your uncle," said Fox.

"A near relation at least. Let's try elsewhere."

They did so with the same result on both posts.

"Well, Plank," Alleyn said, sucking the back of his hand, "how do you read the evidence?"

"Sir, like I did before, if you'll excuse my saying so, though I hadn't linked it up with that coil in the coach house. Should have done, of course, but I missed it."

"Well?"

"It looks like there was this wire, strained between the posts. It'd been there a long time because coming as we now know from the lot in the coach house it must have been rusty." Plank caught himself up. "Here. Wait a mo," he said. "Forget that. That was silly."

"Take your time."

"Ta. No. Wipe that. Excuse me, sir. But it had been

there a long time because the wire marks are overgrown by thorn."

Fox cleared his throat.

"What about that one, Fox?" Alleyn said.

"It doesn't follow. Not for sure. It wants closer examination," Fox said. "It could have been rigged from the far side."

"I think so. Don't you, Plank?"

"Sir," said Plank, chastened.

"Go on, though. When was it removed from the barn?"

"Recently. Recently it was, sir. Because the cut end was fresh."

"Where is it?"

"We don't know that, do we, sir?"

"Not on the peg in the coach house, at least. That lot's in one piece. What does all this seem to indicate?"

"I'd kind of thought," said Plank carefully, "it pointed to her having cut it away before she attempted the jump. It's very dangerous, sir, isn't it, in horse jumping—wire is. Hidden wire."

"Very."

"Would the young chap," Fox asked, "have noticed it if it was in place when he jumped?"

Alleyn walked back to the prints of the sorrel mare's takeoff and looked at the gap.

"Old wire. It wouldn't catch the light, would it? We'll have to ask the young chap."

Plank cleared his throat. "Excuse me, sir," he said. "I did carry out a wee routine check along the hedgerow, and there's no wire there. I'd say never has been."

"Right." Alleyn hesitated for a moment. "Plank," he said, "I can't talk to your Super till he's off the danger list so I'll be asking you about matters I'd normally discuss with him."

"Sir," said Plank, fighting down any overt signs of gratification.

"Why was it decided to keep the case open?"

"Well, sir, on account really of the wire. I reported what I could make out of the marks on the posts and the Super had a wee look-see. That was the day he took bad with the pain, like. It were that evening his appendix bust and they operated on him and his last instructions to me was: 'Apply for an adjournment and keep your trap shut. It'll have to be the Yard.'"

"I see. Has anything been said to Mr. Harkness about the wire?"

"There has but bloody-all come of it. Far's I could make out it's been there so long he'd forgotten about it. *Was* there, in fact before he bought the place. He reckons Dulcie went down and cut it away before she jumped, which is what I thought seemed to make sense if anything he says can be so classed. But Gawd knows," said Plank removing his helmet and looking inside it as if for an answer, "he was that put about there was no coming to grips with the man. Would you care to take a look at the far bank, sir? Where she lay?"

They took a look at it and the horses in the field came and took a look at them, blowing contemptuously through their nostrils. Plank removed his tent and disclosed the pegs he had driven into the ground around dead Dulcie Harkness.

"And you took photographs, did you?" Alleyn asked.

"It's a bit of a hobby with me," Plank said and drew them from a pocket in his tunic. "I carry a camera round with me," he said. "On the off-chance of a nice picture."

Fox placed his glasses, looked, and clicked his tongue. "Very nasty," he said. "Very unpleasant. Poor girl."

Plank, who contemplated his handiwork with a proprietary air, his head slightly tilted, said absently: "You wouldn't hardly recognize her if it wasn't for the shirt. I used a sharper aperture for this one," and he gave technical details.

Alleyn thought of the picture in the office of a big blowsy girl in a check shirt, exhibiting the sorrel mare. He returned the photographs to their envelope and put them in his pocket. Plank replaced the tent.

Alleyn said: "From the time the riding party left until she was found, who was here? On the premises?"

"There again!" Plank cried out in vexation. "What've we got? Sir, we've got Cuth Harkness and that's it. Now then!" He produced his notebook, wetted his thumb, and turned pages. "Harkness. Cuthbert," he said and changed to his police-court voice.

"I asked Mr. Harkness where he and Miss Harkness and Mr. Sydney Jones were situated and how employed subsequent to the departure of the riding party. Mr. Harkness replied that he instructed Jones to drive into Montjoy and collect horse fodder, which he later did. At this point Mr. Harkness broke down and spoke very confusedly about Mr. Jones—something about him not having got the mare reshod as ordered. He shed tears considerably. Mr. Jones, on being interviewed, testified that Mr. Harkness had words with the deceased who was in her room but who looked out of her window and spoke to him, he being at that time in the stable yard. I asked Mr. Harkness 'Was she locked in her room?' He said she had carried on to that extent that he went quietly upstairs and turned the key in her door, which at this point was in the outside lock. When I examined the door, the key was in the inside lock and was in the unlocked position. I noted a gap of three-quarters of an inch between door and floor. I noted a thin rug laying in the gap. I pointed this out to Mr. Harkness who told me that he had left the key in the outside lock. I examined the rug and the area where it lay and formed the opinion it had been dragged into the room. The displacement of dust on the floor caused me to form this opinion, which was supported by Mr. Harkness to the extent that the deceased had effected an escape in this manner when a schoolgirl."

Plank looked up. "I have the key, sir," he said.

"Right. So your reading is that she waited until her uncle was gone and then poked the key onto the mat. With what?"

"She carried one of those old-time pocket knives with a spike for getting stones out of hooves. It was in her breeches pocket."

"'*First Steps in Easy Detection,'*" Alleyn murmured.

"Sir?"

"Yes, all right. Could be. So you read it that at some stage after this performance she let herself out, went downstairs, cut away the wire and dumped it we don't know where. But replaced the cutters—"

Fox said: "Ah. Yes. There's that."

"—and then saddled up the mare and rode to her death. I can't," said alleyn, rubbing his nose, "get it to run smoothly. It's got a spurious feel about it. But then, of course, one hasn't known that poor creature. What was she *like,* Plank?"

After a considerable pause Plank said: "Big."

"One could see that. As a character? Come on, Plank."

"Well," said Plank, a countryman, "if she'd been a mare you'd of said she was always in season."

"That's a peculiar way of expressing yourself, Sergeant Plank," Fox observed austerely.

"My son said something to much the same effect," said Alleyn.

They returned to the yard. When they were halfway up the horse paddock Alleyn stooped and poked at the ground. He came up with a small and muddy object in the palm of his hand.

"Somebody's lost a button," he said. "Rather a nice one. Off a sleeve, I should think."

"I never noticed it," said Plank.

"It'd been trodden by a horse into the mud."

He put it in his pocket.

"What's the vet called, Plank?" he asked.

"Blacker, sir, Bob."

"Did you see the cut on the mare's leg?"

"No, sir. He'd bandaged her up when I looked at her."

"Like it or lump it, he'll have to take it off. Ring him up, Plank."

When Mr. Blacker arrived he seemed to be, if anything, rather stimulated to find police on the spot. He didn't even attempt to hide his curiosity and darted avid little glances from one to the other.

"Something funny in the wind, is there?" he said, "or what?"

Alleyn asked if he could see the injury to the mare's leg. Blacker demurred, but more as a matter of form, Alleyn thought, than with any real concern. He went to the mare's loose-box and was received with that air of complete acceptance and noninterest that animals seem to reserve for veterinary surgeons.

"How's the girl, then?" asked Mr. Blacker.

She was wearing a halter. He moved her about the loose-box and then walked her around the yard and back.

"Nothing much the matter *there,* is there?" Plank ventured.

The mare stretched out her neck toward Alleyn and quivered her nostrils at him.

"Like to take hold of her?" the vet asked.

Alleyn did. She butted him uncomfortably, drooled slightly, and paid no attention to the removal of the bandage.

"There we are," said Mr. Blacker. "Coming along nicely."

Hair was growing in where it had been shaved off around the cut, which ran horizontally across the front of the foreleg about three inches above the hoof. It had healed, as Mr. Blacker said, good and pretty and they'd have to get those two stitches out, wouldn't they? This was effected with a certain display of agitation on the part of the patient.

Alleyn said: "What caused it?"

"Bit of a puzzle, really. There were scratches from the blackthorn, which you'll have seen was knocked about, and bruises and one or two superficial grazes, but she came down in soft ground. I couldn't find anything to account for this cut. It went deep, you know. Almost to the bone. There wasn't anything of the sort in the hedge but, my God, you'd have said it was wire."

"Would you indeed?" Alleyn put his hand in his pocket and produced the few inches of wire he had cut from the coil in the coach house. He held it alongside the scar.

"Would that fit?" he asked.

"By God," said Mr. Blacker, "it certainly would."

Alleyn said, "I'm very much obliged to you, Blacker."

"Glad to be of any help. Er—yes—er," said Mr. Blacker, "I suppose, er, I mean, er—"

"You're wondering why we're here? On departmental police business, but your Super finding himself out of action suggested we might take a look at the scene of the accident."

They were in the stable yard. The Leathers string of horses had moved to the brow of the hill. "Which," Alleyn asked, "is Mungo, the wall-eyed bay?"

"That thing!" said Blacker. "We put it down a week ago. Cuth always meant to, you know, it was a wrong 'un. He'd taken a scunner on it after it kicked him. Way he talked about it, you'd have thought it was possessed of a devil. It was a real villain, I must say. Dulce fancied it, though. Thought she'd make a show jumper of it. Fantastic! Well, I'll be on my way. Morning to you."

When he had gone Alleyn said: "Shall we take a look at the barn? If open."

It was a stone building standing some way beyond

the stables and seemed to bear witness to the vanished farmstead, said by Plank to have predated Leathers. There were signs of a thatched roof having been replaced by galvanized iron. They found a key above the door, which carried the legend "Welcome to all" in amateurish capitals.

"That lets us in," said Fox, drily.

The interior was well lit from uncurtained windows. There was no ceiling to hide the iron roof and birds could be heard scruffling about outside. The hall wore that air of inert expectancy characteristic of places of assembly caught, as it were, by surprise. A group of about a hundred seats, benches of various kinds, and a harmonium faced a platform approached by steps, on which stood a table, a large chair, and six smaller ones. The table carried a book prop and an iron object that appeared to symbolize fire, flanked by a cross and a sword.

"That'll be Chris Beale, the smith's, work," said Plank, spotting it. "He's one of them."

The platform, set off by curtains, was backed by a whitewashed wall with a central door. This was unlocked and opened into a room fitted with a gas boiler, a sink, and cupboards with crockery. "'Ladies a basket' we must remember," Alleyn muttered and returned to the platform. Above the door and occupying half of the width of the wall hung an enormous placard, scarlet and lettered in white. "THE WAGES OF SIN," it alarmingly proclaimed, "ARE DEATH."

The side walls, also, were garnished with dogmatic injunctions including quotations from the twenty-seventh chapter of Deuteronomy. One of these notices attracted Mr. Fox's attention. "Watch," it said, "For ye know not at what Hour the Master Cometh."

"Do they reckon they do?" Fox asked Plank.

"Do what, Mr. Fox?"

"Know," Fox said. "When."

As if as in answer to his inquiry the front door opened to reveal Mr. Harkness. He stood there, against the light, swaying a little and making preliminary noises. Alleyn moved toward him.

"I hope," he began, "you don't mind our coming in. It does say on the door—"

A voice from within Mr. Harkness said, "Come one, come all. All are called. Few are chosen. See you Sunday." He suddenly charged down the hall and up the steps, most precariously, to the door on the platform. Here he turned and roared in his more familiar manner. "It will be an unexamplimented experience. Thank you."

He gave a military salute and plunged out of sight.

"I'll think we'll have it at that," said Alleyn.

6

Morning at the Cove

I

AT HALF-PAST NINE on that same morning, Ricky chucked his pen on his manuscript, ran his fingers through his hair, and plummeted into the nadir of doubt and depression that from time to time so punctually attends upon dealers in words. "I'm no good," he thought, "it's all a splurge of pretension and incompetence. I write about one thing and something entirely different is trying to emerge. Or is there quite simply nothing there *to* emerge? Over and out."

He stared through the window at a choppy and comfortless harbor and his thoughts floated as inconsequently as driftwood among the events of the past weeks. He wallowed again between ship and jetty at Saint Pierre-des-Roches. He thought of Julia Pharamond and that teasing face was suddenly replaced by the frightful caved-in mask of dead Dulcie. Ferrant returned to make a fool of him and he asked himself for the hundredth time if it had been Ferrant or Syd Jones who tried to drown him. And for the hundredth time he found it a preposterous notion that anybody should try to drown him. And yet knew very well that it had been so and that his father believed him when he said as much.

So now he thought of his father and of Br'er Fox, who was his godfather. He wondered how exactly they behaved when they worked together on a case and if at that moment they were up at Leathers. Detecting. And then, with a certainty that quite astonished him, Ricky tumbled to it that the reason why he couldn't write that morning was not because the events of the day before had distracted him or because he was bruised and sore and looked a sight or because the horror of Dulcie Harkness had been revived but simply because he wanted very badly indeed to be up there with his father, finding out about things.

"Oh *no*!" he thought. "I won't take that. That's not my scene. I've other things to do. Or have I?" He was very disturbed.

He hadn't seen any of the Pharamonds since the day of the postponed inquest. Jasper had rung up and asked him to dinner but Ricky had said he was in a bad patch with his work and had promised himself there would be no more junkets until he had got over it. He could hear Julia in the background shouting instructions.

"Tell him to bring his book and we'll all write it for him."

Jasper had explained that Julia was in the bath and she, in the background, screamed that umbrage would be taken if Ricky didn't come. It had emerged that the next day the Pharamonds were flying over to London to see the ballet and meant to stay on for a week or so if anything amusing offered. Ricky had stuck to his guns and not dined at L'Esperance and had wasted a good deal of the evening regretting it.

He wondered if they were still in London. Did they always hunt in a pack? Were they as rich as they seemed to be? Julia had said that Jasper had inherited a fortune from his Brazilian grandfather. And had Louis also inherited a fortune? Louis didn't seem to do work of any description. Jasper was at least writing a book about the binomial theorem but Louis—Ricky wouldn't be surprised if Louis was a bit hot: speculated rashly, perhaps, or launched slightly dubious companies. But then he didn't care for Louis and his bedroom eyes. Louis was the sort of man that women, God knew why, seemed to fall for. Even his cousin Julia when they danced together.

Julia. It would perhaps be just as well, bearing in mind his father's strictures upon talkativeness, if Julia were still in London. If she were at L'Esperance she would wish to know why his father was here; she would ask them both to dinner and say—he could see her magnolia face and her impertinent eyes—that they were slyboots, both of them. Perhaps his father would not go, but sooner or later he, Ricky, would, and once under the spell, could he trust himself not to blurt something out? No, it would be much better if the Pharamonds had decided to prolong their London visit. Much better.

And having settled that question he felt braced and took up his pen.

He heard the telephone ring and Mrs. Ferrant come out of the kitchen, releasing televisual voices from within.

He knew it was going to be for him and he knew it would be Julia.

Mrs. Ferrant shouted from the foot of the stairs and returned to the box.

As usual Ricky felt as if he had sunk much too

rapidly in a fast lift. The telephone was in the passage and before he picked up the receiver he could hear it gabbling. Julia was admonishing her daughter. "All I can say, Selina, is this. Putting mud in Nanny's reticule is the unfunniest thing you could possibly do and just *so* boring that I can't be bothered talking about it. Please go away."

"I've only just come," Ricky said.

"Ricky?"

"None other."

"You sound peculiar."

"I'm merely breathless."

"Have you been running?"

"No," said Ricky crossly. He took a plunge. "You have that effect on me," he said.

"Smashing! I must tell Jasper."

"When did you come back?"

"Just this moment. The ballet was out of this world. And there were some fantastic parties. Lots of jolly chums."

Ricky was stabbed by jealousy. "How lovely," he said.

"I've rung up to know if it can possibly be true that your superb papa is among us."

"Here we go," Ricky thought. He said. "How did you know?"

"Louis caught sight of him in the hotel last night."

"But—I thought you said you'd only just got back."

"Louis didn't come to London. He doesn't like the ballet. He stayed at the Hotel Montjoy to escape from Selina and Julietta. Has Troy come too?"

"No, she's busily painting a tree in London."

"Louis says your papa seemed to be hobnobbing with an elderly policeman."

"There's meant to be some sort of reorganization going on in the force."

"Are they going to raise Sergeant Plank to dizzy heights? I'd like that, wouldn't you?"

"Very much."

"You're huffy, aren't you?"

"No!" Ricky cried. "I'm not. Never less."

"Nevertheless what?"

"I didn't say 'nevertheless.' I said I was never less huffy."

"Well then, you're being slyboots as usual and not divulging some dynamic bit of gossip." A pause and then the voice said, "Ricky, dear. I don't know why I tease you."

"I don't mind."

"Promise? Very well, then, is it in order for us to ring up your father and ask him to dine? Or lunch?"

"Yes—well—yes, of course. He'd adore it. Only thing: he *is* very much occupied it seems."

"Does it? Well, one can but try," she said coolly. Ricky felt inclined to say, "Who's being huffy now?" but he only made vague noises and felt wretched.

"Of course you'd be invited too," she threw out.

"Thank you, Julia."

"You still sound odd."

"I fell in the sea at Saint Pierre."

"How too extraordinary! What were you doing in Saint Pierre? Or in the sea if it comes to that? Never mind. You should have said so at once and we wouldn't have been at cross-purposes like funny men on the box. Ricky?"

"Yes, Julia."

"Has the inquest been reopened?"

"No."

"I see. I feel we shall never get rid of Miss Harness."

"Harkness."

"I don't do it on purpose. To me she is Harness."

"I know."

"I hoped in my shallow way that the ballet and fun things would put her out of my head. But they haven't." She added hurriedly, furtively almost, "I dream about it. Seeing her. Isn't that awful?"

"I'm so terribly sorry. So do I, if it's any comfort."

"You do? Not fair to say I'm glad. Ricky—don't answer if you musn't—but Ricky—was she murdered?"

"I don't know. Honestly. How could I?"

"Your father."

"Julia—please don't."

"I'm sorry. How's your book going?"

"Not very fast."

"How's Mr. Jones? At least I can ask you how Mr. Jones is."

"Oh God!" Ricky said under his breath, and aloud: "He's away. Over at Saint Pierre-des-Roches."

"I see. I think I must find out what Selina is doing. It's Nanny's evening off and there's an ominous silence. Goodbye."

"I've been thinking a lot about all of you."

"Have you?"

"Goodbye."

"Goodbye."

Ricky was cast down by this exchange. It had been miserably unsatisfactory. He felt that the relationship so elegantly achieved with Julia had been lost in a matter of minutes and there he was floundering about among evasions and excuses while she got more and more remote. She hadn't spluttered. Not once.

Mrs. Ferrant opened the kitchen door, releasing the honeyed cajolements of a commercial jingle and the subtle aroma of a béarnaise sauce.

"I didn't think to ask," she said, "did you happen to see him over in Saint Pierre?"

"Yes," said Ricky. "We ran into each other."

"Any message?"

"No. Nothing particular."

She said: "That black eye of yours is a proper masterpiece, isn't it?"

Ricky returned to his room.

II

Alleyn had finished outdoors at Leathers. He went inside to ask Mr. Harkness if he might look at his niece's bedroom and found him snoring hideously in his office chair. He could not be roused to a sensible condition. Alleyn, in Fox's presence, formally put his request and took the snort that followed it as a sign of consent.

They all went upstairs to Dulcie's room.

It was exactly what might have been expected. The walls were covered in horsey photographs, the drawers and wardrobe were stuffed with equestrian gear. Riding boots stood along the floor. The bed was dragged together rather than made. On a table beside it were three battered pornographic paperbacks. A tube of contraceptive pills was in the drawer: half empty.

"Must have been careless," Fox said. They began a systematic search.

After an unproductive minute or two Plank said: "You don't suppose she thought taking that dirty great jump might do the trick, do you, sir?"

"Who can tell? On what we've got it sounds more as if the jump was the climax of a blazing row with her uncle. Did they blast off at each other as a regular practice do you know, Plank?"

"Only after he took up with this funny religion, or so they reckon in the Cove. Before that they was thought to be on very pleasant terms. He taught her to ride and was uncommon proud of the way she shaped up."

Fox threw his head back in order to contemplate from under his spectacles an item of Miss Harkness's underwear. "Free in her ways," he mused, "by all accounts. By *your* account if it comes to that, Sarge."

Sergeant Plank reddened. "According to the talk," he said, "that was the trouble between them. After he took queer with his Inner Brethren he cut up rough over Dulcie's life-style. The general opinion is, he tried to hammer it out of her but what a hope. I daresay her being in the family way put the lid on it." He entered the wardrobe and was enveloped in overcoats.

"When the Pharamonds and my son went to pick up their horses they interrupted a ding-dong go during which she roared out that she was pregnant and he called her a Whore of Babylon."

"I never knew that," said Plank's voice, stuffy with clothes. "Is that a fact."

"You wouldn't get round to wondering," Fox suggested, "if his attitude could have led to anything serious?"

Plank, still red-faced, emerged from the wardrobe, "No, Mr. Fox," he said loudly. "Not to him rigging wire in the gap. Not Cuth Harkness. Not a chap like him, given over to horses and their management. And that mare the apple of his eye! It's not in the man to do it, drunk or sober, dotty or sane." He appealed to Alleyn. "I've known the man for four years and it's not on, sir, it's not bloody on. Excuse me. Like you was saying yourself, sir, about this being an affair of character. Well, there's no part of this crime, if it is a crime, in Cuth Harkness's character and I'd stake my promotion on it."

Alleyn said: "It's a point well taken. You might just remember something else they tell us."

"What's that, sir?"

"Don't get emotionally involved."

"Ah," said Fox. "There's always that, Sarge. There's always that."

"Well, I know there is, Mr. Fox. But it does seem to me—well—Considering—"

"Considering," Alleyn said, "that Harkness locked her up in her room and on pain of hellfire and damnation forbade her to jump. Considering that, would you say, Plank?"

"Yes, sir. I would."

Mr. Fox, who was replacing Miss Harkness's

undergarments with the careful devotion of a lady's maid, said generously, "Which is what you might call a glimpse of the obvious, I'll say that for it."

"Well, ta, Mr. Fox," said Plank, mollified.

Alleyn was going through the pockets of a hacking jacket that hung from the back of a chair. They yielded a grubby handkerchief, small change, and a rumpled envelope of good paper, addressed in a civilized hand. It had been opened. Alleyn drew out a single sheet with an engraved heading—L'Esperance and the address. On it was written in the same hand, "Cliffs. Thursday. Usual time. L.P."

He showed it to the others.

"'L.P.' eh," Fox remarked.

"It doesn't stand for 'long playing,'" said Alleyn, "although I suppose, in a cockeyed sense, it just might."

"Plank," he said as they drove away from Leathers. "I want you to go over everything that Sydney Jones told you about the dialogue with Harkness after the riding party left. Not only the row with Dulcie but what he said to Jones himself. We won't need your notebook again: just tell me."

Plank, who was driving, did so. Jones had described Harkness in the yard and Dulcie at her bedroom window, hurling insults at each other. Dulcie had said she could take not only the sorrel mare, but the wall-eyed Mungo over the gap in the blackthorn hedge. Her uncle violently forbad her, under threat of a hiding, to make the attempt on any of the horses, least of all the mare. He had added the gratuitous opinion that she sat a jumping horse like a sack of potatoes. She had sworn at him and banged down the window.

"And then?"

"According to Jones, Harkness had told him to drive the car to a corn merchant on the way to Montjoy and pick up some sacks of fodder."

"Rick remembers," Alleyn said, "that after the body

was found, Mr. Harkness said Jones had been told to take the mare to the smith to be reshod and that he'd given this order to get the mare out of Dulcie's way. Harkness had added that because Jones didn't carry out this order he was as good as a murderer. Didn't Jones tell you about this?"

"Not a word, sir. No, he never."

"Sure?"

"Swear to it, sir."

Fox said: "Mr. Harkness isn't what you'd call a reliable witness. He could have invented the bit about the blacksmith."

"He wasn't drinking then, Mr. Fox. That set in later," said Plank, who seemed set upon casting little rays of favorable light upon the character of Mr. Harkness. "But he was very much upset," he added. "I will say that for him. Distracted is what he was."

"However distracted," Alleyn said, "one would hardly expect him to cook up a pointless fairy tale, would one? I'd better talk to Rick about this," he said vexedly and asked Plank to drive into the Cove. "Come and take a look at your godson, Br'er Fox," he suggested, and to Plank: "Drop us round the corner at the station. You'll be able to put in half an hour catching up on routine."

"Don't make me laugh, sir," said Plank.

They passed the Ferrants' house, turned into the side lane, and pulled up at the corner cottage that was also the local police station. A compact little woman with tight hair and rosy cheeks was hoeing vigorously in the garden. Nearby a little girl with Plank's face at the wrong end of a telescope was knocking up a mud pie in a flowerpot.

Plank, all smartness, was out of the driver's seat and opening the doors in a flash.

"Is this Mrs. Plank?" Alleyn said and advanced upon her, bareheaded. She was flustered and apologized for her mucky hand. Fox was presented. He and

Alleyn admired the garden.

"It's beginning to look better," Mrs. Plank said. "It was a terrible old mess when we first came four years ago."

"Have you had many moves?" Alleyn asked them and they said this was the third.

"And that makes things difficult," Alleyn said, knowing constant transfers to be a source of discontent.

He had them talking freely in no time: about the disastrous effect on the children's education and the problems of settling into a new patch where you never knew what the locals would be like—friendly or suspicious, helpful or resentful. Of how, on the whole, the Cove people were not bad but you had to get used to being kept at a distance.

Alleyn edged the conversation around to the neighbors. Did Mrs. Plank know the Ferrants around the corner with whom his son lodged? Not well, she said shortly. Mrs. Ferrant kept herself to herself. She, Mrs. Plank, felt sorry for her. "Really?" Alleyn asked. "Why?"

Finding herself in the delicious situation where gossip could be regarded as a duty, Mrs. Plank said that what with Ferrant away in France half the time and where they got the money for it nobody knew and never taking her with him and when he was home the way he carried on so free for all that he gave her washing machines and fridges and the name he had in the Cove for his bold behavior and yet being secretive with it: well, the general feeling was that Mrs. Ferrant was to be pitied. Although, come to that, Mrs. Ferrant herself wasn't all that—

"Now then, mother," said Plank uneasily.

"Well, I know," she said, "and so do you, Joe." Alleyn had a picture of the village policeman's wife, cut off from the cozy interchange of speculative gossip, always having to watch her tongue and always conscious of being on the outside.

"I'm sure Mrs. Plank's the soul of discretion," he said. "And we're grateful for any tips about the local situation, aren't we, Plank? About Mrs. Ferrant—you were saying?"

It emerged that Mrs. Plank had acquired one friend only with whom she was on cozy terms: her next-door neighbor in the lane, a widow who, in the past, had been a sewing maid up at L'Esperance at the time when Mrs. Ferrant was in service there. Ten years ago that would be, said Mrs. Plank and added with a quick glance at her husband that Mrs. Ferrant had left to get married. The boy was not yet eleven. Louis, they called him. "Mind you," Mrs. Plank ended, "they're French."

"So are most of the islanders, mother," said Plank. She tossed her head at him. "You know yourself, Joe," she said, "there's been trouble. With him."

"What sort of trouble?" Alleyn asked.

"Maintenance," said Plank. "Child. Up to Bon Accord."

"Ah. Don't tell me. He's no good, that one," cried Mrs. Plank in triumph.

Mr. Fox said, predictably, that they'd have to get her in the force and upon that playful note they parted.

Alleyn and Fox turned right from the lane on to the front. They crossed over to the far side and looked up at Ricky's window, which was wide open. There he was with his tousled head of hair, so like his mother's, bent over his work. Alleyn watched him for a moment or two, willing him to look up. Presently he did and a smile broke over his bruised face.

"Good morning, Cid, me dear," said Ricky. "Good morning, Br'er Fox. Coming up? Or shall I come down?"

"We'll come up."

Ricky opened the front door to them. He wore a slightly shamefaced air and had a postcard in his hand.

"Mrs. F. is out marketing," he said. "Look. On the

mat, mixed up with my mail. Just arrived." He shut the door.

The postcard displayed a hectically colored view of a market square and bore a legend: *"La place-du-marché, La Tournière."* Ricky turned it over. It had a French stamp and was addressed in an awkward hand to "M. Ferrant" but carried no message.

"It's his writing," Ricky said. "He's given me receipts. That's how he writes his name. Look at the postmark, Cid."

"I am. La Tournière. Posted yesterday. Air mail."

"But he was in Saint Pierre yesterday. Even if it wasn't Ferrant who shoved me off the jetty, it certainly was Ferrant who made me look silly in the café. Where is La Tournière?"

"North of Marseilles," said his father.

"Marseilles! But that's—what?"

"At a guess, between six and seven hundred kilometers by air from Saint Pierre. Come upstairs," said Alleyn.

He dropped the card on the mat and was on the top landing before the other two were halfway up. They all moved into Ricky's room as Mrs. Ferrant fitted her key in the front door.

"How did you know she was coming?" Ricky asked.

"What? Oh, she dumped her shopping bag against the door while she fished for her key. Didn't you hear?"

"No," said Ricky.

"We haven't all got radioactive ears," said Mr. Fox, looking benignly upon his godson.

Alleyn said abruptly: "Rick, why do you think it was Ferrant who shoved you overboard?"

"Why? I don't know why. I just felt sure it was he. I can't say more than that—I just—I dunno. I was certain. Come to think of it, it might have been Syd."

"For the sake of argument we'll suppose it was Ferrant. He may have felt he'd better remove to a distant spot, contrived to get himself flown to La

Tournière, and posted this card at the airport. What time was it when you took the plunge?"

"According to my ruined wristwatch, eight minutes past three."

Fox said: "When we came into Saint Pierre at four yesterday a plane for Marseilles was taking off. If it calls at—" Mr. Fox arranged his mouth in an elaborate pout "—La Tournière; it could be there by six-thirty, couldn't it? Just?"

"Is there anything," Ricky ventured, "against him having been staying at La Tournière, and deciding to fly up to Saint Pierre by an early plane yesterday morning?"

"What was it you used to say, Mr. Alleyn?" Mr. Fox asked demurely. "'Stop laughing. The child's quite right!'"

"My very words," said Alleyn. "All right, Rick, that may be the answer. Either way, Fox, the *peloton des narcotiques*, as you would no doubt call the French drug squad, had better be consulted. Ferrant's on their list as well as ours. He's thought to consort with someone in the upper strata of the trade."

"Where?" Ricky asked.

"In Marseilles."

"I say! Could he have been under orders to get rid of me? Because Syd had reported I'd rumbled his game with the paints?"

Fox shot a quick look at Alleyn and made a rumbling noise in his throat.

Alleyn said, "Remember, we haven't anything to show for the theory about Jones and his paints. It may be as baseless as one of those cherubim that so continually do cry. But we've got to follow it up. Next time, if there is a next time, that Master Syd sets out for London with his paint box they'll take him and his flake white to pieces at Weymouth and they won't find so much as a lone pep pill in the lot. Either he's in the clear or he'll have seen the light and shut up shop."

"Couldn't—you—couldn't it be proved one way or the other?" Ricky asked.

"Such as?" said Fox who was inclined to treat his godson as a sort of grown-up infant prodigy.

"Well—" said Ricky with diminishing assurance, "such as searching his Pad."

"Presumably he's still in France," said Alleyn.

"All the better."

"Troy and I agreed," Alleyn said to Fox, "that taking one consideration with another it was better to keep our child uninformed about the policeman's lot. Clearly, we have succeeded brilliantly."

"Come off it, Cid," said Ricky, grinning.

"However, we haven't come here to discuss police law but to ask you to recall something Harkness said about his orders to Syd Jones. Do you remember?"

"Do you mean when he said he'd ordered Syd to take the sorrel mare to the blacksmith and he was in an awful stink because Syd hadn't done it? He said Syd was as good as a murderer."

"What *did* Jones do with himself?"

"I suppose he cleared off quite early. After he'd collected some horse feed, I think."

"We don't know," Fox said heavily, "who was on the premises from the time the riding party left until they returned. Apart from the two Harknesses. Or has Plank gone into that, would you say?"

"We'll ask him. All right, Rick. I don't think we'll be hounding you any more."

"I'd rather be hounded than kept out."

Fox said: "I daresay you don't care to talk about work in progress." He looked with respect at the weighted heap of manuscript on Ricky's table.

"It's a struggle, Br'er Fox."

"Would I be on the wrong wavelength if I said it might turn out to be all the better for that?"

"You couldn't say anything nicer," said Ricky. "And I only hope you're right."

"He often is," said Alleyn.

"About people at Leathers during that afternoon," Ricky said. "There is, of course, Louis Pharamond." And he described Louis's cramp and early return.

"Nobody tells us anything," Alleyn cheerfully complained. "What time would he have got back?"

"If he pushed along, I suppose about threeish. When he left he was carrying his right boot and had his right foot out of its stirrup. He's very good on a horse."

"Has he said anything about the scene at Leathers when he got there?"

Ricky stared at his father. "Funny," he said. "I don't know."

"Didn't he give evidence at the inquest, for pity's sake?"

"No. No, he didn't. I don't think they realized he returned early."

"But surely one of you must have said something about it?"

"I daresay the others did. I haven't seen them since the inquest. I should think he probably unsaddled his horse, left it in the loose-box, and came away without seeing anybody. It was there when we got back. Of course if there'd been anything untoward, he'd have said so, wouldn't he?"

After a considerable pause during which Fox cleared his throat Alleyn said he hoped so and added that as investigating officers they could hardly be blamed if they didn't know at any given time whether they were looking into a possible homicide or a big deal in heroin. It would be tidier, he said, if some kind of link could be found.

Ricky said: "Hi."

"Hi, what?" asked his father.

"Well—I'd forgotten. You might say there *is* a link."

"'Define, define, well-educated infant,'" Alleyn quoted patiently.

"I'm sure it's of no moment, mind you, but the night

I came home late from Syd's Pad—" and he described
the meeting on the jetty between Ferrant and Louis
Pharamond.

"What time," Alleyn said after a long pause, "was
this?"

"About one-ish."

"Funny time to meet, didn't you rather think?"

"I thought Louis Pharamond might go fishing with
Ferrant. I didn't know whether they'd been together in
the boat or what. It was jolly dark," Ricky said
resentfully.

"It was your impression, though, that they had just
met?"

"Yes. Well—yes, it was."

"And all you heard was Louis Pharamond saying:
'All right?' or 'OK, careful,' or 'Watch it.' Yes?"

"Yes. I'm sorry, Cid," said Ricky. "Subsequent
events have kind of wiped it."

Fox said: "Understandable."

Alleyn said perhaps it was and added that he would
have to wait upon the Pharamonds anyway. Upon this,
Ricky, looking very uncomfortable, told him about
Julia's telephone call and her intention of asking them
to dinner. "I said I knew you'd adore to but were
horribly busy. Was that OK?"

"Half of it was, at least. Yes, old boy, you were the
soul of tact. Sure you don't fancy the diplomatic after
all? How did she know I was here?"

"Louis caught sight of you in the hotel. Last night."

"I see. I don't, on the whole, think this is an occasion
for dinner parties. Will they all be at home this
morning, do you suppose?"

"Probably."

"One other thing, Rick. I'm afraid we may have to
cut short your sojourn at the Cove."

Ricky stared at him. "Oh, *no*!" he exclaimed.
"Why?"

Alleyn walked over to the door, opened it, and had

an aerial view of Mrs. Ferrant on her knees, polishing
the stairs. She raised her head and they looked into
each other's faces.

"*Bonjour, madame!*" Alleyn called out jovially,
"*Comment ça va?*"

"*Pas si mal, monsieur,*" she said.

"*Toujours affairée, n'est-ce pas?*"

She agreed. That was how it went. He said he was
about to look for her. He had lost his ball-point pen
and wondered if she had come across it in the *petit
salon* last evening after he left. Alas, no. Definitely, it
was not in the *petit salon*. He thanked her and with
further compliments reentered the room and shut the
door.

Ricky began in a highish voice. "Now, look here,
Cid—"

Alleyn and Fox simultaneously raised their fore-
fingers. Ricky, against his better judgment, giggled.
"You look like mature Gentlemen of the Chorus," he
said, but he said it quietly. "Shall I shut the window? In
case of prowlers on the pavement?"

"Yes," said his father.

Ricky did so and changed his mind about
introducing a further note of comedy. "Sorry," he said.
"But why?"

"Principally because it would be inappropriate,
supposing Ferrant returns, for you to board in the
house of your would-be murderer—if indeed he is
that."

"I want to stay. My work's going better, I think.
And—I'm sorry but I *am* mixed up in the ongoings.
And anyway he hasn't come back. Much more than all
that, I want to see it out."

They looked so gravely at him that he felt extremely
uneasy.

From the street below there came seven syncopated
toots from a car horn.

Ricky said in an artificial voice: "That's Julia."

Alleyn opened the window and leaned out. Ricky heard the familiar and disturbing voice.

"*You?*" Julia shouted. "What fun! We've been hunting you."

"I'll come down. Hold on."

He nodded to Fox. "Meet you at Plank's," he said, and to Ricky. "See you later, old boy."

As he went downstairs he thought: "Damn. He went white. He *has* got it badly."

III

Julia was in her dashing sports car and Bruno was doubled up in the token seat behind her. She was dressed in white, as Alleyn remembered seeing her in the ship, with a crimson scarf on her head and those elegant gloves. Enormous dark glasses emphasized her pallor and her remarkable mouth. She had a trick when she laughed of lifting her lip up and curving it in. This changed her into a gamine and was extremely appealing. "Poor old Rick," Alleyn thought, "he hadn't a chance. On the whole I daresay it's been good for him."

Ricky, standing back from his closed window, was able to see his father shake hands with Julia and at her suggestion get into the passenger's seat. She looked at him as she sometimes looked at Ricky and had taken off her black glasses to smile at him. She talked—vividly, Ricky was sure—and he wondered at his father's air of polite attention. When she talked like that to Ricky he felt himself develop a fatuous expression and indeed was sometimes obliged to pull his face together and shut his mouth.

His father did not look in the least fatuous.

Now Julia stopped talking and laughing. She leaned toward Alleyn and seemed to listen closely as he, still with that air of formal courtesy, spoke to her. So might her doctor or solicitor have behaved.

What could they be saying? he wondered. Something about Louis? Or could it be about him, by any chance? The thought perturbed him.

"Ricky," Alleyn was saying, "was in a bit of a spot. I'd told him not to gossip."

"And there have I been badgering him. Wretched Ricky!" cried Julia and broke into her splutter.

"He'll recover. It must be pretty obvious to everybody in the Cove, in spite of all Sergeant Plank's diplomacy, that there's something in the wind."

"About the accident, you mean?"

"Yes."

"That it wasn't an accident?"

"That it hasn't been conclusively shown that it was. Is your cousin with you this morning?"

"Louis? Or Carlotta?"

"Louis."

"You're sitting on his coat. He's gone to buy cigarettes."

"I'm sorry." He hitched the coat from under him and straightened it, pulling down the sleeves. "What a very smart hacking jacket," he said.

"It goes too far in my opinion. He hooks it over his shoulders and looks like a mass-produced David Niven."

"He's lost a sleeve button. Have I sat it off? How awful, I'd better look."

"You needn't bother. I think my daughter wrenched it off. Why do you want to see Louis?"

"In case he noticed anything out-of-the-way when he returned to Leathers."

Julia twisted around to look at her young brother-in-law. "I don't think he did, do you, Bruno?"

Bruno said in an uncomfortable voice. "I think he just said he didn't see anybody or something like that."

"And, by the way," Alleyn said, "when you jumped

that gap—a remarkable feat if I may say so—did you go down and inspect it beforehand?"

A pause. "No," Bruno muttered at last.

"Really? So you wouldn't have noticed anything particular about it—about the actual gap?"

Bruno shook his head.

"No rail, for instance, running through the thorn?"

"There wasn't a rail."

"Just the thorn? No wire?"

For a moment Alleyn thought Bruno was going to respond to this but he didn't. He shook his head, looked at the floor of the car and said nothing.

Julia winked at Alleyn and bumped her knee against his.

Bruno said: "OK if I go to the shop?"

"Of course, darling. If you see Louis tell him who's here, will you? He's buying cigarettes, probably in the Cod-and-Bottle."

Bruno slid out of the car and walked along the front, his shoulders hunched.

"You musn't mind," Julia said. "He's got a thing about jumping the gap."

"What sort of thing?"

"He thinks he may have been an incentive to the Harness."

"Harness?"

"I've got a fixation about her name. The others think I do it to be funny but I don't, poor thing."

"I gather she was hell-bent on the jump anyway."

"So she was but Bruno fancies he may have brought her up to boiling point and it makes him miserable. Only if it's mentioned. He forgets in-between and goes cliff-climbing and bird-watching. How's Cuth?" asked Julia, and when he didn't reply at once, said: "Come on, you must know Cuth. The uncle."

"In retirement."

"Well, we all know that. The maids told Nanny he's drinking himself to death out of remorse. I can't imagine how they know. Well, one can guess. Postman. Customers wanting hacks. Ricky's chum Syd before he bolted."

"Has he bolted?"

"Cagey old Ricky just said he's gone over to Saint Pierre-des-Roches, but the village thinks he bolted. According to Nanny. She has a wide circle of friends and all of them say Syd's done a bunk."

"Why do they think he's done that?"

"Well it's really—you mustn't mind this, either," said Julia opening her eyes very wide and beginning to gabble, "but you see, to begin with, Nanny says they all thought there must be funny business afloat when the inquest was adjourned and on top of that everyone knew she was going to have a baby. Well, I mean, Cuth seems to have bellowed away about it, far and wide. And as she was a constant caller at Syd's place they put two and two together." Julia stopped short. "Have you ever thought," she said in a different voice, "how *very* appropriate that expression would be if it was 'one and one together.'"

"It hadn't occurred to me."

"I make you a present of it. Where was I?"

"I think you were going to tell me something that you hoped I wouldn't mind."

"Ah! Thank you. It was just that your arrival on the scene led everyone to believe that you were hard on Syd's trail because Syd was the—what does 'putative' mean? Not that Nanny used the expression."

"'Supposed', or 'presumed.'"

"That's what I thought. The putative papa. Somehow I don't favor the theory. The next part gets vague: Nanny hurries over it rather, but the general idea seems to be that Syd was afraid Cuth would horsewhip him into marrying Dulcie."

"And what steps is Syd supposed to have taken?"

"They don't say it in so many words."

"What do they say? It doesn't matter how many words."

"They hint."

"What do they hint?"

"That Syd egged her on. To jump. Hoping."

"I see," said Alleyn.

"And then, of course, your arriving on the scene—"

"I only arrived last night."

"Nanny was at a whist-drive last night. The W.I. Some of the husbands picked their ladies up on the way home from the Cod-and-Bottle where they had been introduced to you by Sergeant Plank."

"I see," said Alleyn again.

"That's what I hoped you wouldn't mind: the whist-drive ladies all saying it looked pretty funny. It seems nobody really believes you merely came to give Sergeant Plank and the boys in blue a new look. They're all very thrilled to have you, I may say."

"Too kind."

"So are we, of course. Here they come. I expect you'd like to have your word with Louis, wouldn't you? I'll pay Ricky a little visit."

"He's got a black eye and will be self-conscious but enchanted."

Alleyn, a quick mover, was out of the car and had the door open for her. She gave him a steady look. "How very kind," she said and left him.

The presence of Louis Pharamond on the front had the effect of turning it into some kind of resort—some little harbor only just "discovered," perhaps, but shortly to be developed and ruined. His blue silk polo-necked jersey, his sharkskin trousers, his golden wristwatch, even the medallion he wore on a thin chain were none of them excessive but one felt it was only by a stroke of good luck that he hadn't gone too far with, say, some definitely regrettable ring or even an earring.

Bruno, who trailed after Louis with his hands in his denim pockets, turned into the shop. Louis advanced alone and bridged the awkward gap between himself and Alleyn with smiles and expressions of pleasurable recognition.

"This *is* a nice surprise!" he cried with outstretched hand. "Who'd have thought we'd meet again so soon!"

There was the weatherworn bench close by, where Ricky had sat in the early hours of the morning. Village worthies sometimes gathered there as if inviting the intervention of some TV commentator. Alleyn, having negotiated Louis's effusive greetings, suggested that they might move to this bench and they did so.

"I gather," he said, "you've guessed that I'm here on a job." Louis was all attention: appropriately grave, entirely correct.

"Well, yes, we have wondered, actually. The riding-school girl, isn't it? Rotten bad show." He added with an air of diffidence that one didn't, of course, want to speak out of turn, but did this mean there was any suspicion that it wasn't an accident?

Alleyn wondered how many more times he was to say that they were obliged to make sure.

"Anything else," said Louis, "is unbelievable. It's— well, I mean what could it be but an accident?" And he rehearsed the situation as it had presented itself to the Pharamonds. "I mean," he said, "she was hell-bent on doing it. And with her weight up—she was a great hefty wench, you know. Not to put too fine a point on it. I'd say she must have ridden every ounce of eleven stone. Well, it was a foregone conclusion."

Alleyn said it looked like that, certainly.

"We're trying to find out," he said, "as closely as may be, when it happened. The medical report very tentatively puts it at between four and five hours of when she was found. But even that is uncertain. She may have survived the injuries for some considerable time or she may have died immediately."

"Yes, I see."

"When did you arrive back at Leathers? I know about the cramp."

Louis sat with his lightly clasped hands between his knees. Perhaps they tightened their grasp on each other; if so, that was his only movement.

"I?" he said. "I don't know exactly. I suppose it would have been about three o'clock. I rode back by the shortest route. The cramp cleared up quite soon and I put on my boot and took most of it at an easy canter."

"When you arrived was anybody about?"

"Not a soul. I unsaddled the hack and walked home."

"Meeting anybody?"

"Meeting nobody."

"Did you happen to look across the horse paddock to the hedge?"

Louis ran his hand down the back of his head.

"I simply don't remember," he said. "I suppose I might have. If I did there was nothing out-of-the-way to be seen."

"No obvious break in the gap, for instance?"

He shook his head.

"No sign of the sorrel mare on the hillside?"

"Certainly not. But I really don't think I looked in that direction."

"I thought you might have been interested in young Bruno's jump."

"Young Bruno behaved like a clodhopper. No, I'm sorry. I'm no good to you, I'm afraid."

"You know Miss Harkness, didn't you?"

"She came to lunch one day at L'Esperance—on Ricky's first visit, by the way. I suppose he told you."

"Yes, he did. Apart from that?"

"Not to say 'knew,'" Louis said. He seemed to examine this remark and hesitated as if about to qualify it. For a second one might have almost thought it had suggested some equivocation. "She came into the pub sometimes when I was there," he said. "Once or twice, I wouldn't remember. She wasn't," Louis said, "exactly calculated to snatch one's breath away. Poor lady."

"Did you meet her on a Thursday afternoon near the foot of a track going down the cliffs?"

The movement Louis made was like a reflex action, slight but involving his whole body and instantly repressed. It almost came as a shock to find him still sitting quietly on the bench.

"Good Lord!" he said, "I believe I did. How on earth did you know? Yes. Yes, it was an afternoon when I'd been for a walk along the bay. So I did."

"Did you meet by appointment?"

That brought him to his feet. Against a background of sparkling harbor and cheerful sky he stood like an advertisement for men's wear, leaning back easily against the seawall. An obliging handful of wind lifted his hair.

"Look here," Louis said, "I don't much like all this. Do you mind explaining?"

"Not a bit. Your note was in the pocket of her hacking jacket."

"Damn," said Louis quietly. He waited for a moment and then with a graceful, impetuous movement reseated himself by Alleyn.

"I wouldn't have had this happen for the world," he said.

"No?"

"On several counts. There's Carlotta, first of all, and most of all. I mean, I know I'm a naughty boy sometimes and so does she but this is different. In the light of what's happened. It'd be horrid for Carlotta."

He waited for Alleyn to say something but Alleyn was silent.

"You do understand, I'm sure. I mean it was nothing. No question of any—attachment. You might say she simply happened to be damn good at one thing and made no bones about it. As was obvious to all. But—well, you'll understand—I'd hate Carlotta to know. For it to come out. Under the circs."

"It won't unless it's relevant."

"Thank God for that. I don't see how it possibly could be."

"Was this meeting at the cliffs the first time?"

"I'm not sure—yes, I think it might have been."

"Not according to the note. The note said 'Usual time.'"

"All right, then. It wasn't. I said I wasn't sure."

"One would have thought," Alleyn said mildly, "you'd remember."

"Basically the whole thing meant so little. I've tried to explain. It was nothing. Absolutely casual. It would have petered out, as you might say, without leaving a trace."

"You're sure of that?"

"What the hell do you mean?"

"She was pregnant."

"If you're trying to suggest—" Louis broke off. He had spoken loudly but now, after a quick look up at Ricky's window stopped short. In the silence that followed Julia's voice could be heard. Alleyn looked around and was in time to see her appear briefly at the closed window. She waved to them and then turned away. Ricky could be dimly seen in the background.

"There is absolutely no question of that," Louis said. "You can dismiss any such notion."

"Have you any theory on the parentage?"

For a moment or two he hesitated and then said that, "not to put too fine a point on it, it might be anybody." By one of those quirks of foresight Alleyn knew what his next remark would be and out it came. "She was quite a girl," Louis said.

"So I've been told," said Alleyn.

Louis waited. "Is that all you wanted to see me about?" he asked at last.

"Pretty well, I think. We'd just like to be sure about any possible callers at Leathers during the day. A tidying-up process. Routine."

"Yes, I see. I'm sorry if I didn't take kindly to being grilled."

"It was hardly that, I hope."

"Well—you did trick me over that unlucky note, didn't you?"

"You should see us when we get really nasty," Alleyn said.

"It's just because of Carlotta. You do understand?"

"I think so."

"I suppose I'm pretty hopeless," said Louis. "But still..." He stretched elaborately as if freeing himself from the situation. "Ricky seems to be enjoying the giddy pleasures of life in Deep Cove and la maison Ferrant," he said. "I can't imagine what he finds to do with himself when he's not writing."

"There's been some talk of night fishing and assignations with his landlord in the early hours of the morning, but I don't think anything's come of it. Do you ever go in for that?"

Louis didn't answer. It was as if for a split second he had become the victim of suspended animation, a "still" introduced into a motion picture with the smile unerased on his face. This hitch in time was momentary, so brief that it might have been an illusion. The smile broadened and he said: "Me? Not my scene, I'm afraid. Too keen on my creature comforts."

He took out his cigarette case and filled it with a steady hand from a new packet. "Is there anything else?" he asked.

"Not that I can think of," Alleyn said cheerfully. "I'm sorry I had to raise uncomfortable ghosts."

"Oh," Louis said, "I'll survive. I wish I could have been more help." He looked up at Ricky's window. "What's all this we hear about him taking a plunge?"

Alleyn said it appeared that Ricky had slipped on the wet wharf, knocked his face against a gangway stanchion, and fallen in.

"He's a pretty picture," he said, "and loath to display himself."

Louis said they'd soon see about that and with a sudden and uncomfortable display of high spirits, threw a handful of fine gravel at the window. Some of it miscarried and spattered on the front door. Ricky loomed up, empurpled and unwilling, behind the glass. Louis gestured for him to open the window and when he had done so shouted, "'*But soft, what light from yonder window breaks,*'" in a stagey voice. Julia appeared beside Ricky and took his arm.

"Do pipe down, Louis," she said. "You're inflaming the populace."

And indeed the populace in the shape of one doubled-up ancient-of-days on his way to the Cod-and-Bottle and three preschool-aged children had paused to gape at Louis. Two windows were opened. Mr. Mercer came out of his shop and went in again.

More dramatically, the front door of the Ferrants' house was thrown wide and out stormed Mrs. Ferrant, screaming as she came: "*Louis! Assez de bruit!* What are you doing, *Petit méchant!*"

She came face to face with Louis Pharamond, stopped dead, and shut her mouth like a trap.

"Good morning, Marie," he said. "Were you looking for me?"

Her eyes narrowed and her hands clenched. For a moment Alleyn thought she was going to have at Louis but she turned instead to him. "Pardon, Monsieur Alleyn," she said. "A stupid mistake. My son occasionally has the bad manners to throw stones." And with a certain magnificence she returned indoors.

"Let's face it," said Louis, "I am *not*, in that department, a popular boy." He looked up at Julia in the window. "We'll be late for luncheon," he called. "Coming?"

"Go and find Bruno, then," she said. "I'll be down in a moment."

Alleyn looked at his watch. "I'm running shamefully late," he said. "Will you forgive me?"

"For almost anything," Julia called, "except not coming to see us. *Au revoir.*"

IV

Ricky would not have chosen for Julia to see him with his black eye, which was half-closed and made him look as if he lewdly winked at people. He had felt sheepish and uncomfortable when she walked into his room but, although she did laugh, it was sympathetically, and at first she didn't ask him to elaborate on his accident. This surprised him, because after all it would have been a natural thing to do. Perversely, although relieved, he felt slightly hurt at the avoidance.

Nor did she tease him with questions about his father's activities, but related the Pharamonds' London adventures, asked him about his writing, and repeated her nonsense offer to help him with it. She dodged about from one topic to another. The children, she said, had become too awful. "They writhe and ogle and have suddenly turned just *so* common that I begin to think they must be changelings and not Jasper's and mine at all."

"Oh, come," said Ricky.

"I promise! Of course, I love them to distraction and put it all down to everybody but me spoiling them. We've decided that they shall have a tutor."

"Aren't they rather small for that?" Ricky ventured.

"Not at all. He needn't teach them anything, just rule them with a rod of iron and think of strenuous and exhausting games. I had rather wondered if Mr. Jones might do."

"You can't by any chance mean that?"

"Not really. It did just cross my mind that perhaps

he could teach them painting. Selina's style is rather like his own. With guidance she might develop into a sort of Granddaughter Moses. Still, as you tell me he's junketing in Saint Pierre-des-Roches these ideas are only wishful thinking on my part. I merely throw them out."

"I don't know where he is."

"Didn't you go jaunting together to Saint Pierre?"

"No, no," he said in a hurry. "Not together. Only, as it happened, at the same time. I was just a day-tripper."

"Well," said Julia gazing at his face, "you certainly do seem to have tripped in a big way."

Ricky joined painfully in her amusement. It was at this point that Julia had walked over to the window and waved to Alleyn and Louis.

"They look portentous," she said and then, with an air of understatement that was not quite successful, she said: "It's not fair."

"I don't understand? What isn't?"

"The two of them, down there. The 'confrontation.' Isn't that one of the *in* words? Oh, come off it, Ricky. You know what I mean. Diamond cut paste. One guess which is which."

This was so utterly unlike anything Julia had ever said to him in their brief acquaintance and, in its content, so acutely embarrassing, that he could find no reply. She had come close to him and looked into his face searchingly as if hesitating on the edge of some further extravagance or indiscretion.

Ricky's hands began to tingle and his heart to thump.

"Poorest Ricky," she said and gently laid her palm against his unbruised cheek, "I've muddled you. Never mind."

Ricky's thoughts were six-deep and simultaneous. He thought: "That's torn it," and at the same time, "this is it: this is Julia in my arms and these are her ribs," and "if I kiss her I'll probably hurt my face," and even, *bouleversé* though he was, "what *does* she mean about Louis?" And then he was kissing her.

"No, no," Julia was saying. "My dear boy, no. What *are* you up to! Ricky, please."

Now they stood apart. She said: "Bless my soul, you *did* take me by surprise," and made a shocked face at him. "'Out upon you, fie upon you Bold Faced Jig,'" she quoted.

"She's not even disconcerted," he thought. "I might be Selina for all she feels about it."

He said: "I'm sorry, but you do sort of trigger one off, you know."

"Do I? How lovely! It's very gratifying to know one hasn't lost the knack. I must tell Jasper, it'll be good for him."

"How can you?" Ricky said quietly.

"My dear, I'm sorry. That was beastly of me. I won't tell Jasper. I wouldn't dream of it."

She waited for a moment and then began to make conversation as if he were an awkward visitor who had, somehow or another, to be put at his ease. He did his best to respond and in some degree succeeded, but he was humiliated and confusedly resentful.

"Have you," she said at last, "had your invitation to Cuth's party?"

"His party? No."

"Not exactly a party perhaps although it's 'ladies a basket,' we must remember. *You* must remember. It's one of his services. In the barn at Leathers on Sunday. You're sure to be asked. Do come and bring your papa. Actually it seems anyone is welcome. Gents fifty pence. We've all been invited and I think we're all going although Louis may be away. It has 'The Truth!' written by hand all over it with rows of exciting marks and 'Revelation!' in enormous capitals on the last page. You must come back to L'Esperance afterwards for supper in case the baskets are not very filling."

It had been at this point that Louis threw gravel at

the window. When Ricky looked down and saw him there with Alleyn standing behind him it was if they were suddenly exhibited as an illustration to Julia's extraordinary observations. He was given, as he afterwards thought, a new look at his father—at his quietude and his air of authority. And there was handsome Louis in the foreground, all eyes and teeth, acting his boots off. Ricky understood what Julia had meant when she said it wasn't fair.

In response to Louis's gesture he opened the window and was witness to the idiotic quotation from Romeo, Julia's quelling of Louis, and Mrs. Ferrant's eruption into the scene and departure from it.

When Julia had dealt crisply with the remaining situation she shut the window and returned to Ricky.

"High time the Pharamonds removed themselves," she said. She looked directly into his eyes, broke into her laugh, kissed him rapidly on his unbruised side, and was gone.

She gave a cheerful greeting to Mrs. Ferrant as she saw herself off.

Ricky stood stock-still in his room. He heard the car start up and climb the hill to the main road. When he looked out his father had gone and the little street was deserted.

"And after all that," he thought, "I suppose I'm meant to get on with my book."

V

Around the corner in Sergeant Plank's office, Alleyn talked to his contact in Marseilles, M. l'Inspecteur Dupont. They spoke in French and were listened to with painful concentration by Mr. Fox. Dupont had one of those Provençal voices that can be raised to a sort of metallic clatter guaranteed to extinguish any opposition. It penetrated every corner of the little room and caused Mr. Fox extreme consternation.

At last, when Alleyn, after an exchange of compliments, hung up the receiver, Fox leaned back in his chair, unknitted his brow, and sighed deeply.

"It's the pace," he said heavily. "That's what gets you—that and the noise. I suppose," he added wistfully, turning to Sergeant Plank, "you had no difficulty?"

"Me, Mr. Fox? I don't speak French. We only came here four years ago. We've tried to learn it, the Missus and me, but we don't seem to make much headway and in any case the lingo they use over here's a patois. The chaps always seem to drop into it when I look in at the Cod-and-Bottle," said Plank in his simple way. Another symptom, Alleyn thought, of the country policeman's loneliness.

"Well," he said, "for what it's worth, Ferrant has been spotted in La Tournière and in Marseilles."

"I got that all right," said Fox, cheering up a little.

"And he's made a trip to a place outside Marseilles where one of the big boys hangs out in splendor and is strongly suspected. They haven't been able to pin anything on him. The old, old story."

"What are they doing about it?"

"A lot. Well—quite a lot. No flies, by and large, on the narcotics squad in Marseilles; they get the practice if they look for it and could be very active. But it's the old story. The French are never madly enthusiastic about something they haven't set up themselves. Nor, between you and me and the junkie, are they as vigilant at the ports as they might be. Still, Dupont's one of their good numbers. He's all right as long as you don't step on his amour propre. He says they've got a dossier as fat as a bible on this character—a Corsican, he is, like most of them: a qualified chemist and a near millionaire with a château halfway between Marseilles and La Tournière and within easy distance of a highly sophisticated laboratory disguised as an innocent research setup where this expert turns morphine into heroin."

"Well!" said Fox. "If they've got all this why don't they pull chummy in?"

"French law is very fussy about the necessity for detailed, conclusive, and precise evidence before going in for a knockoff. And they haven't got enough of that. What they *have* got is a definite line on Ferrant. He's been staying off and on in an expensive hotel in La Tournière known to be a rendezvous for heroin merchants. He left there unexpectedly yesterday morning. Yes, I know. Rick's idea. They've been keeping obbo on him for weeks. Apparently the tip-off came from an ex-mistress in the hell-knows-no-fury department."

"Did I catch the name Jones?" asked Fox.

"You did. Following up their line on Ferrant, they began to look out for anybody else from the island who made regular trips to Saint Pierre and they came up with Syd. So far they haven't got much joy out of that but, as you may have noticed, when I told Inspector Dupont that Jones is matey with Ferrant, the decibel count in his conversation rose dramatically. There's one other factor, a characteristic of so many cases in the heroin scene: they keep getting shadowy hints of another untraced person somewhere on a higher rung in the hierarchy, who controls the island side of operations. One has to remember the rackets are highly sophisticated and organized down to the last detail. In a way they work rather like labor gangs in totalitarian countries: somebody watching and reporting and himself being watched and reported upon all the way up to the top. One would expect an intermediary between, say, an operative like Ferrant and a top figure like the millionaire in a château outside Marseilles. Dupont feels sure there is such a character."

"What do we get out of all this?" Fox asked.

Alleyn got up and moved restlessly about the little office. A bluebottle banged at the windowpane. In the kitchen, Mrs. Plank could be heard talking to her daughter.

"What I get," Alleyn said at last, "is no doubt a great slab of fantasy. It's based on conjecture and, as such, should be dismissed."

"We might as well hear it," said Fox.

"All right. If only to get it out of my system. It goes like this. Ferrant is in La Tournière and Syd Jones is in Saint Pierre, having arrived at the crack of dawn yesterday morning. Syd is now persuaded that Ricky is spying on him and has followed him to Saint Pierre for that purpose. He has grown more and more worried and on landing rings up Ferrant. The conversation is guarded but they have an alarm code that means 'I've got to talk to you.' Ferrant comes to Saint Pierre by the early morning plane—Dupont says there's one that leaves at seven. They are to meet in the café opposite the premises of Jerome et Cie. Ricky sits in the café being a sleuth and squinting through a hole in *Le Monde* at Syd. At which ludicrous employment he is caught by Ferrant. Ricky leaves the café. Syd, who seems to have gone to pieces and given himself a jolt of something, heroin one supposes, now tells Ferrant his story and Ferrant, having seen for himself my poor child's antics with the paper and bearing in mind that I'm a copper, decides that Ricky is highly expendable. One of the two keeps tabs on Ricky, is rewarded by a thunderstorm, and takes the opportunity to shove him overboard between the jetty and the ship." Alleyn's eyes closed for half a second. "The ship," he repeated, "was rolling. Within a couple of feet of the legs of the jetty."

He walked over to the window and stood there with his back to the other men. "I suppose," he said, "he was saved by the turn of the bilge. If the ship had been lower in the water—" He broke off.

"Yes. Quite so," Fox said. Plank cleared his throat.

For a moment or two none of them spoke. Mrs. Plank in her kitchen sang mutedly and the little girl kept up what seemed to be a barrage of questions.

Alleyn turned back into the room.

"He thought it was Ferrant," he said. "I don't know quite why, apart from the conjectural motive."

"How doped up was this other type, Jones?"

"Exactly, Br'er Fox. We don't know."

"If he's on the main-line racket—and it seems he is—"

"Yes."

"And under this Ferrant's influence—"

"It's a thought, isn't it? Well, there you are," Alleyn said. "A slice of confectionery from a plain cook and you don't have to swallow it."

There was a long pause which Fox broke by saying, "It fits."

Plank made a confirmatory noise in his throat.

"So what happens next?" asked Fox. "Supposing this is the case?"

Alleyn said: "All right. For the hell of it— supposing. What *does* Ferrant do? Hang about Saint Pierre waiting—" Alleyn said rapidly—"for news of a body found floating under the jetty? Does he go back to La Tournière and report? If so, to whom? And what is Syd Jones up to? Supposing that he's got his next quota of injected paint tubes, if in fact they are injected, does he hang about Saint Pierre? Or does he lose his nerve and make a break for Lord knows where?"

"If he's hooked on dope," Fox said, "he's had it."

Plank said: "Excuse me, Mr. Fox. Meaning?"

"Meaning as far as his employers are concerned."

Alleyn said: "Drug merchants don't use drug consumers inside the organization, Plank. They're completely unpredictable and much too dangerous. If Jones is in process of becoming a junkie he's out, automatically, and if his bosses think he's a risk he might very easily be out altogether."

"Would he go to earth somewhere over there? In France?" Fox wondered. And then: "Never mind that for the moment, Mr. Alleyn. True or not, and I'd take long odds on your theory being the case, I don't at all fancy the position our young man has got himself into. And I don't suppose you do either."

"Of course I don't," Alleyn said with a violence that made Sergeant Plank blink. "I'm in two minds whether to pack him off home or what the devil to do about him. He's hell-bent on sticking round here and I'm not sure I don't sympathize with him."

Fox said: "And yet, wouldn't you say that when they do find out he escaped and came back here, they'll realize that anything he knows he'll have already handed on to you? So there won't be the same reason for getting rid of him. The beans, as you might say, are spilled."

"I'd thought of that too, Br'er Fox. These people are far too sophisticated to go about indulging in unnecessary liquidations. All the same—"

He broke off and glanced at Sergeant Plank whose air of deference was heavily laced with devouring curiosity. "The fact of the matter is," Alleyn said quickly, "I find it difficult to look objectively at the position, which is a terrible confession from a senior cop. I don't know what the drill ought to be. Should I ask to be relieved from the case because of personal involvement?"

"Joey," Mrs. Plank called from the kitchen and her husband excused himself.

"Fox," Alleyn said, "what the hell should a self-respecting copper do when his boy gets himself bogged down, and dangerously so, in a case like this? Send him abroad somewhere? If they are laying for him that'd be no solution. This lot is one of the big ones with fingers everywhere. And I can't treat Rick like a kid. He's a man and what's more I don't think he'd take it if I did and, by God, I wouldn't want him to take it."

Fox, after some consideration, said it was an unusual situation. "I can't say," he admitted, "that I can recollect anything of the sort occurring in my experience. Or yours either, Mr. Alleyn, I daresay. Very unusual. You could think, if you weren't personally concerned, that there's a piquant element."

"For the love of Mike, Fox!"

"It was only a passing fancy. You were wondering what would be the correct line to take?"

"I was."

"With respect, then, I reckon he should do as I think he wants to do. Stay put and act under your orders."

"Here?"

"Here."

"If Ferrant comes back? Or Jones?"

"It would be interesting to see the reaction when they met."

"Always supposing Ferrant's the man. Or Jones."

"That's right. It's possible that Ferrant may still be waiting for the body, you'll excuse me won't you, Mr. Alleyn, to rise. He may think it's caught up under the pier. Unless, of course, the chap in the ship has talked."

"The ship doesn't return to Saint Pierre for some days. And Ricky got the man to promise he *wouldn't* talk. He thinks he'll stick to his word."

"Yerse," said Fox. "But we all know what a few drinks will do."

"Anyway, Ferrant has probably telephoned his wife and heard that Rick's home and dry. I wonder," Alleyn said, "if he's in the habit of sending her postcards with no message."

"Just to let her know where he is?"

"And I wonder—I do very much wonder—how far, if any distance at all, that excellent cook is wise to her husband's proceedings."

Sergeant Plank returned with a plateload of

enormous cheese and pickle sandwiches and a jug of beer.

"It's getting on for three o'clock," he said, "and the Missus reckons you must be fair clemmed for a snack, Mr. Alleyn."

"Your Missus, Sergeant Plank," said Alleyn, "is a pearl among ladies and you may tell her so with our grateful compliments."

7

Syd's Pad Again

I

WHEN RICKY HAD eaten his solitary lunch he was unable to settle to anything. He had had a most disturbing morning and himself could hardly believe in it. The memory of Julia's blouse creasing under the pressure of his fingers and of herself warm beneath it, her scent, and the smooth resilience of her cheek were at once extraordinarily vivid yet scarcely to be believed. Much more credible was the ease with which she had dealt with him.

"She stopped *my* nonsense," he thought, "with one arm tied behind her back. I suppose she's a dab hand at disposing of excitable young males." For the first time he was acutely aware of the difference in their ages and began to wonder uncomfortably how old Julia, in fact, might be.

Mixed up with all this and in a different though equally disturbing key was his father's suggestion that he, Ricky, should take himself off. This he found completely unacceptable and wondered unhappily if they were about to have a family row about it. He was much attached to his father.

And then there was the case itself, muddling to a degree with its shifting focus, its inconsistencies and lack of perceptible design. He thought he would write a kind of résumé and did so and was, he felt, none the wiser for it. Turn to his work he could not.

The harbor glittered under an early afternoon sun and beyond the heads there was a lovely blue and white channel. He decided to take a walk, first looking in his glass to discover, he thought, a slightly less grotesque face. His eye, at least, no longer leered, although the area beneath it still resembled an overripe plum.

Since his return he had felt that Mrs. Ferrant not perhaps spied upon him, but kept an eye on him. He had an impression of doors being shut a fraction of a second after he left or returned to his room. As he stepped down into the street he was almost sure one of the parlor curtains moved slightly. This was disagreeable.

He went into Mr. Mercer's shop to replace his lost espadrilles with a pair from a hanging cluster inside the door. Mr. Mercer, in his dual role of postmaster, was in the tiny office reserved for Her Majesty's Mail. On seeing Ricky he hurried out carrying an airletter and a postcard.

"*Good* afternoon, sir," said Mr. Mercer winningly after a startled look at the eye. "*Can* I have the pleasure of helping you? And *may* I impose upon your kindness? Today's post was a little delayed and the boy had started on his rounds. *If* you would—You *would!* Much obliged I'm sure."

The letter was from Ricky's mother and the postcard he saw at a glance was from Saint Pierre-des-Roches with a view of that fateful jetty. For Mrs. Ferrant.

When he was out in the street he examined the card. Ferrant's writing again, and again no message. He turned back to the house and pushed the card and the espadrilles through the letter flap. He put his mother's letter in his pocket, and walked briskly down the front toward the Cod-and-Bottle and past it.

Here was the lane, surely, that he had taken that dark night when he visited Syd's Pad—a long time ago as it now seemed. The name, roughly painted on a decrepit board, hung lopsided from its signpost. "Fisherman's Steps."

"Blow me down flat," thought Ricky, "if I don't case the joint."

In the dark he had scarcely been aware of the steps, so worn, flattened, and uneven had they become, but had stumbled after Syd like a blind man only dimly conscious of the two or three cottages on either side. He saw, now, that they were unoccupied and falling into ruin. Clear of them the steps turned into a steep and sleazy path that separated areas of rank weeds littered with rusting tins. The path was heavily indented with hoofprints. "How strange," he thought. "Those were left I suppose by Dulcie's horse Mungo: 'put down' now, dead and buried, like its rider."

And here was Syd's Pad.

It must originally have been a conventional T-plan cottage with rooms on either side of a central passage. At some stage of its decline the two front rooms had been knocked into one, making the long disjointed apartment he had visited that night. The house was in a state of dismal neglect. At the back an isolated privy faced a desolation of weeds.

The hoofprints turned off to the right and ended in a morass overhung by a high bramble to which, Ricky thought, the horse must have been tethered.

It was through the marginal twigs of this bush that he surveyed the Pad and from here, with the strangest feeling of involvement in some repetitive expression of antagonism, thought he caught the slightest possible movement in one of the grimy curtains that covered the windows.

Ricky may be said to have kept his head. He realized that if there were anybody looking out they could certainly see him. The curtains, he remembered, were of a flimsy character, an effective blind from outside but probably semitransparent from within. Supposing Syd Jones to have returned and to be there at the window, Ricky himself would seem to be the spy, lurking but perfectly visible behind the brambles.

He took out his pipe, which was already filled, and lit it, making a show of sheltering from the wind. When it was going he emerged and looked about him as if making up his mind where he would go and then with what he hoped was an air of purposeful refreshment and enjoyment of the exercise, struck up the path, passing close by the Pad. The going became steeper and very rough, and before he had covered fifty feet the footpath had petered out.

He continued, climbing the hill until he reached the edge of a grove of stunted pines that smelled warm in the afternoon sun. Three cows stared him out of countenance and then tossed their heads contemptuously and returned to their grazing. The prospect was mildly attractive; he looked down on cottage roofs and waterfront and away over the harbor and out to sea where the coast of Normandy showed up clearly. He sat down and thought, keeping an eye on Syd's Pad and asking himself if he had only imagined he was watched from behind the curtain, if what he thought he had seen was merely some trick of light on the dirty glass.

Suppose Syd had returned, when and how had he come?

How far down the darkening path to subservience had Syd gone? Ricky called up the view of him through that shaming hole in *Le Monde*: the grope in the pockets, the bent head, hunched shoulders, furtively busy movements, slight jerk.

Had Syd picked up a load of doctored paint tubes from Jerome et Cie? Did Syd himself, perhaps, do the doctoring in his Pad? Was he at it now, behind his dirty curtains? If he were there, how had he come back? By air, last evening? Or early this morning? Or could there have been goings-on in the small hours—a boat from Saint Pierre? Looking like Ferrant at his night fishing?

What had happened between Ferrant and Syd, after Ricky left the café? Further bullying? Had they left together and gone somewhere for Syd to sleep it off? Or have a trip? Or what?

Ricky fetched up short. Was it remotely possible that Ferrant could by some means have injected Syd with the idea of getting rid of him, Ricky? He knew nothing of the effects of heroin, if in fact Syd had taken heroin, or whether it would be possible to lay a subject on to commit an act of violence.

And finally: had it after all been Syd who, under the influence of Ferrant or heroin or both, hid on the jetty and knocked him overboard?

The more he thought of this explanation, the more likely he felt it to be.

Almost, had he known it, he was following his father's line of reasoning as he expounded it, not half a mile away, over in Sergeant Plank's office. Almost, but not quite, because, at that point or thereabouts, Alleyn finished the last of Mrs. Plank's sandwiches and said: "There is another possibility, you know. Sydney Jones may have cut loose from Ferrant and, inspired by dope, acted on his own. Ricky says he got the impression that there was someone else in the goods shed when he sheltered there."

"Might have sneaked in for another jolt of the

stuff," Fox speculated, "and acted on the 'rush.' It takes different people different ways."

"Incidentally, Br'er Fox, his addiction might have been the reason why he didn't take the sorrel mare to the smith."

"Nipped off somewhere for a quickie?"

"And now we *are* riding high on the wings of fancy."

"I do wonder, though, if Jones supplies Mr. Harkness with those pills. 'Dexies,' you say they are. And sold in France."

"Sold in Saint Pierre quite openly, Dupont tells me."

"Excuse me," Plank asked, "but what's a dexie?"

"Street name for amphetamines," Alleyn replied. "Pep pills to you. Comparatively harmless taken moderately but far from so when used to excess. Some pop artists take them to induce, I suppose, their particular brand of professional hysteria. Celebrated orators have been said to take them—" He stopped short. "We shall see how Mr. Harkness performs in that field on Sunday," he said.

"If he can keep on his feet," Fox grunted.

"He'll contrive to do that, I fancy. He's a zealot, he's hagridden, he's got something he wants to loose off if it's only a dose of hellfire, and he's determined we shall get an earful. I back him to perform, pep pills and Scotch or no pep pills and Scotch."

"Might that," Plank ventured, "be why Syd Jones got these pills for him in the first place? To kind of work him up to it?"

"Might. Might. Might," Alleyn grunted. "Yes, of course, Plank. It might indeed, if Jones *is* the supplier."

"It'd be nice to know," Fox sighed, "where Jones and Ferrant are. Now."

And Ricky, up on his hillside, thought so too. He was becoming very bored with the prospect of the rusted roof and outside privy at Syd's pad.

He could not, however, rid himself of the notion

that Syd might be on the watch down there, just as he'd got it into his head that Mrs. Ferrant was keeping observation on him in her cottage. Had Syd crept out of his Pad and did he lie in wait behind the bramble bush, for instance, with a blunt instrument?

To shake off this unattractive fancy, he took out his mother's letter and began to read it.

Troy wrote as she talked and Ricky enjoyed her letters very much. She made exactly the right remarks, and not too many of them, about his work and told him sparsely about her own. He became absorbed and no longer aware of the countrified sounds around him: seagulls down in the Cove; intermittent chirping from the pine grove and an occasional stirring of its branches; even the distant and inconsequent pop of a shotgun where somebody might be shooting rabbits. And if subconsciously he heard, quite close at hand, footfalls on the turf, he attributed them to the three cows.

Until a shadow fell across Troy's letter and he looked up to find Ferrant standing over him with a grin on his face and a gun in his hand.

II

At about this same time—half-past three in the afternoon—Sergeant Plank was despatched to Montjoy under orders to obtain a search warrant and, if he were forced to do so, to execute it at Leathers, collecting, to that end, two local constables from the central police station.

"We'll get very little joy up there," Alleyn said, "unless we find that missing length of wire. Remember the circumstances. Sometime between about ten-thirty in the morning and six-ish in the evening and before Dulcie Harkness jumped the gap somebody rigged the wire. And the same person, after Dulcie had crashed, removed and disposed of it. Harkness, when he wasn't haranguing his niece and ineffectually locking her up, was in his office cooking up hellfire pamphlets. Jones took a short trip to the corn chandlers and back and didn't obey orders to take the mare to the smith's. We don't know where he went or what he may have done. Louis Pharamond came and went, he says, round about three. He says he saw nobody and nothing untoward. As a matter of interest somebody had dropped an expensive type of leather button in the horse paddock which he says he didn't visit. He's lost its double from his coat sleeve.

"I think you'll do well, Plank, to work out from the fence, taking in the stables and the barn. Unless you're lucky you won't finish today. And on a final note of jolly optimism, there's always the possibility that somebody from outside came in, rigged the trap, hung about until Dulcie was killed in it, and then dismantled the wire and did a bunk, taking it with him."

"Oh dear," said Plank primly.

"On which consideration you'd better get cracking. All right?"

"Sir."

"Good. I don't need to talk about being active, thorough, and diligent, do I?"

"I hope not," said Plank. And then: "I *would* like to ask, Mr. Alleyn: *is* there any connection between the two investigations—Dulcie's death and the dope scene?"

Alleyn said slowly: "That's the hundred-guinea one. There do seem to be very tenuous links, so tenuous that they may break down altogether, but for what they're worth I'll give them to you."

Plank listened with carefully restrained avidity.

When Alleyn had finished they made their final arrangements. They telephoned the island airport for details of disembarking passengers. There had been none bearing a remote resemblance to Ferrant or Jones. Plank was to telephone his own station at five-thirty to report progress. If neither Alleyn nor Fox were there, Mrs. Plank would take the message. "If by any delicious chance," Alleyn said, "you find it before then, you'd better pack up and bring your booty here and be wary about dabs."

"And I take the car, sir?"

"You do. You'd better lay on some form of transport to be sent here for us in case of an emergency. Can you do this?"

"The Super said you were to have the use of his own car, sir, if required."

"Very civil of him."

"I'll arrange for it to be brought here."

"Good for you. Off you go."

"Sir."

"With our blessing, Sergeant Plank."

"Much obliged I'm sure, sir," said Plank and left after an inaudible exchange with his wife in the kitchen.

"And what for us?" Fox asked when he had gone.

"'And what for me, my love, and what for me?'" Alleyn muttered. "I think it's about time we had a look at Mr. Ferrant's seagoing craft."

"Do we know where he keeps it? Exactly?"

"No, and I don't want to ask Madame. We'll take a little prowl. Come and say goodbye to Mrs. P."

He took the tray into the kitchen. Mrs. Plank was ironing. "That *was* kind," he said and unloaded crockery into the sink. "Is this the drill?" he asked and turned on the tap.

"Don't you touch them things!" she shouted. "Beg pardon, sir, I'm sure. It's very kind but Joe'd never forgive me."

"Why on earth not?"

"It wouldn't be fitting," she said in a flurry. "Not the thing at all."

"I don't see why. Here!" he said to the little girl who was ogling him around the leg of the table. "Can you dry?"

She swung her barrel of a body from side to side and shook her head.

"No, she can't," said her mother.

"Well, Fox can," Alleyn announced as his colleague loomed up in the doorway. "Can't you?"

"Pleasure," he said and they washed up together.

"By the way, Mrs. Plank," Alleyn asked. "Do you happen to know where Gil Ferrant berths his boat?"

She said she fancied it was anchored out in the harbor. He made great use of it, said Mrs. Plank.

"When he goes night fishing?"

"If that's what it is."

This was a surprising reaction but it turned out that Mrs. Plank referred to the possibility of philandering escapades after dark in "Fifi," which was the name of Ferrant's craft. "How *she* puts up with it I'm sure I don't know," said Mrs. Plank. "No choice in the matter I daresay."

Fox clicked his tongue against his palate and severely contemplated the glass he polished. "Fancy that," he said.

Unhampered by the austere presence of her husband, Mrs. Plank elaborated. She said that mind you, Mr. Fox, she wouldn't go so far as to say for certain but her friend next door knew for a fact that the poor girl had been seen embarking in "Fifi" after dark with Ferrant in attendance and as for her and that Jones . . . She laughed shortly and told her daughter to go into the garden and make another mud pie. The little girl did so by inches, retiring backwards with her eyes on Alleyn as if he were royalty. Predictably she tripped on the doorstep and fell, still backwards, on the wire mat. She was still roaring when they left.

"Didn't amount to much joy," Fox said disparagingly as they walked down to the front. "All this about the girl. We knew she was—what's that the prince called the tom in the play?"

"'Some road'?"

"That's right. The young chap took me to see it," said Fox, who usually referred in this fashion to his godson. "Very enjoyable piece. Well, as I was saying, we knew already what this unfortunate girl was."

"We didn't know she'd had to do with Ferrant, though. If it's true. Or that she went boating with him after dark."

"If it's true," they said together.

"Might be the longed-for link, if it *is* true," Fox said. "In any case I suppose we add him to the list."

"Oh yes. Yes. We prick him down. And if Rick's got the right idea about the attack on him, I suppose we add a gloss to the name. 'Prone to violence.'"

"There is that, too," said Fox.

They were opposite the Ferrants' cottage. Alleyn looked up at Ricky's window. It was shut and there was no sign of him at his worktable.

"I think I'll just have a word with him," he said. "If he's at home. I won't be a moment."

But Ricky was not at home. Mrs. Ferrant said he'd gone out about half an hour ago; she couldn't say in what direction. He had not left a message. His bicycle was in the shed. She supposed the parcel in the hall must be his.

"Freshening himself up with a bit of exercise, no doubt," said Fox gravely. "Heavy work, it must be, you know, this writing. When you come to think of it."

"Yes, Foxkin, I expect it must," Ricky's father said with a friendly glance at his old colleague. "Meanwhile one must pursue the elusive 'Fifi.' From Rick's story of the dead-of-night encounter between Ferrant and Louis Pharamond, it looks as if she sometimes ties up at the end of the pier. But if she anchors out in the harbor, he'll need a dinghy. There are only four boats out there. Can you pick up the names?"

Fox, who was long-sighted, said: "'Tinker.' 'Marleen.' 'Bonny Belle.' Wait a bit. She's coming round. Hold on. Yes. That's her. Second from the right, covered with a tarpaulin. 'Fifi.'"

"Damn."

"Could we get a dinghy and row out?"

"With Madame Ferrant's beady eye at the front parlor window?"

"Do you reckon?"

"I'd take a bet on it. Let's trip blithely down the pier."

They walked down the pier and stood with their hands in their pockets, ostensibly gazing out to sea. Alleyn pointed to the distant coast of France.

"To coin a phrase, don't look now, but Fifi's dinghy's below, moored to the jetty with enough line to accommodate to the tide."

"Is she though? Oh, yes." said Fox, slewing his eyes down and round. "I see. 'Fifi' on the stern. Would she normally be left like that, though? Wouldn't she knock herself out against the pier?"

"There are old tires down there for fenders. But you'd think she'd be hauled up the beach with the others. Or, of course, if the owner was aboard, tied up to 'Fifi'."

"Do we get anything out of this, then?"

"Let's get back, shall we?"

They returned to the front and sat on the weatherworn bench. Alleyn got out his pipe.

"I've got news for you, Br'er Fox," he said. "Last evening that dinghy *was* hauled up on the beach. I'm sure of it. I waited up in Rick's room for an hour until he arrived and spent most of the time looking out of the window. There she was, half blue and half white and her name across her stern. She was just on the seaward side of the high-water mark with her anchor in the sand. She'd be afloat at high tide."

"Is that so? Well, well. Now, how do you read that?" asked Fox.

"Like everything else that's turned up—with modified rapture. Ferrant may let one of his mates in the cove have the use of his boat while he's away."

"In which case, wouldn't the mate return it to the beach?"

"Again, you'd think so, wouldn't you?" Alleyn said. And after a pause. "When I left last night, at ten o'clock, the tide was coming in. The sky was overcast and it was very dark. The dinghy wasn't on the beach this morning."

He lit his pipe. They were silent for some time.

Behind them the Ferrants' front door banged. Alleyn turned quickly, half expecting to see Ricky, but it was only the boy, Louis, with his black hair sleeked like wet fur to his head. He was unnaturally tidy and French-looking in his matelot jersey and very short shorts.

He stared at them, stuck his hands in his pockets, and crossed the road, whistling and strutting a little.

"Hullo," Alleyn said. "You're Louis Ferrant, aren't you?"

He nodded. He walked over to the low wall and lounged against it as Louis Pharamond had lounged that morning: self-consciously, deliberately. Alleyn experienced the curious reaction that is induced by unexpected cross-cutting in a film, as if the figure by the wall blinked by split seconds from child to man to child again.

"Where are you off to?" he asked. "Do you ever go fishing?"

The boy shook his head and then said: "Sometimes," in an indifferent voice.

"With your father, perhaps?"

"He's not here," Louis said very quickly.

"You don't go out by yourself? In the dinghy?"

He shrugged his shoulders.

"Or perhaps you can't row," Alleyn casually suggested.

"Yes. I can. I can so row. My papa won't let

anybody but me row the dinghy. Not anybody. I can row by myself even when it's *gros temps*. Round the *musoir*, I can, and out to the *cap*. Easy."

"I bet you wouldn't go out on your own at night."

"Huh! Easy! Often! I—"

He stopped short, looked uncomfortably at the house and turned sulky. "I can so row," he muttered and began to walk away.

"I'll get you to take me out one of these nights," Alleyn said.

But Louis let out a small boy's whoop and ran suddenly, down the road and around the corner.

"Let me tell you a fairy tale, Br'er Fox," said Alleyn.

"Any time," said Fox.

"It's about a little boy who stayed up late because his mother told him to. When it was very dark and very late indeed and the tide was high, she sent him down to the strand where his papa's dinghy was anchored and just afloat and he hauled up the anchor and rowed the dinghy out to his papa's motorboat which was called 'Fifi' and he tied her up to 'Fifi' and waited for his papa who was not really his papa at all. Or *perhaps*, as it was a calm night, he rowed right out to the heads—the *cap*—and waited there. And presently his papa arrived in a boat from France that went back to France. So the little boy and his papa rowed all the way back to the pier and came home. And they left the dinghy tied up to the pier."

"And what did the papa do then?" Fox asked in falsetto.

"That," Alleyn said, "is the catch. He can hardly have bedded down with his lawful wedded wife and be lying doggo in the bedroom. Or can he?"

"Possible."

"Yes. Or," Alleyn said, "he may be bedded down somewhere else."

"Like where?"

"Like Syd's Pad, for example."

"And why's he come back? Because things are getting too hot over there?" Fox hazarded.

"Or, while we're in the inventive vein, because they might be potentially even hotter over here and he wants to clean up damning evidence."

"Where? Don't tell me. At Syd's Pad. Or," Fox said, "could it be, don't laugh, to clean up Syd?"

"Because, wait for it, Syd it was who made the attempt on Rick and bungled it and has become unreliable and expendable. Your turn."

"A digression. Reverting to the deceased. While on friendly terms with Syd at his Pad, suppose she stumbled on something," said Fox.

"What did she stumble on? Oh, I'm with you. On a doctored tube of emerald-oxide-of-chromium or on the basic supply of dope."

"And fell out with Jones on account of it being his baby and he not being prepared to take responsibility and so she threatened to grass on him," said Fox, warming to his work. "Or alternatively, yes, by gum, for Syd read Ferrant. It was *his* baby and *he* did her in. Shall I go on?"

"Be my guest."

"Anyway one, or both of them, fixes up the death trap and polishes her off," said Fox. "There you are! Bob's your uncle." He chuckled.

Alleyn did not reply. He got up and looked at Ricky's window. It was still shut. The village was very quiet at this time in the afternoon.

"I wonder where he went for his walk," he said. "I suppose he could have come back while we were on the pier."

"He couldn't have failed to see us."

"Yes, but he wouldn't butt in. He's not at his table. When he's there you can see him very clearly from the street. Good God, I'm behaving like a clucky old hen."

Fox looked concerned but said nothing.

Alleyn said: "We're not exactly active at the

moment, are we? What the hell have we got in terms of visible, tangible, put-on-table evidence? Damnall."

"A button."

"True."

"It wasn't anywhere near the fence," said Fox. "Might he just have forgotten?"

"He might, but I don't think so. Fox, I'm going to get a search warrant for Syd's Pad."

"You are?"

"Yes. We can't leave it any longer. Even if we've done no better than concoct a fairy tale, Jones does stand not only as an extremely dubious character but as a kind of link between the two crackpot cases we're supposed to be handling. I've been hoping Dupont at his end might turn up something definite and in consequence haven't taken any action with the sprats that might scare off the mackerel. But there's a limit to masterly inactivity and we've reached it."

"So we search," Fox said. He fixed his gaze upon the distant coast of France. "What d'you reckon, Mr. Alleyn?" he asked. "Has he got back? Have they both got back? Jones and Ferrant?"

"Not according to the airport people."

"By boat, then, like we fancied. In the night?"

"We'll find out soon enough, won't we? Here comes a copper in the Super's car. It's ho for the nearest beak and a search warrant."

"It'll be a pity," Fox remarked, "if nobody's there after all. Bang goes the fairy tale. Back to square one." He considered this possibility for a moment. "All the same," he said, "although I don't usually place any reliance on hunches I've got a funny kind of feeling there's somebody in Syd's Pad."

III

The really extraordinary feature of Ricky's situation was his inability to believe in it. He had to keep

reminding himself that Ferrant had a real gun of sorts
and was pointing it into the small of his back. Ferrant
had shown it to him and said it was real and that he
would use it if Ricky did not do as he was told. Even
then Ricky's incredulity nearly got the better of him
and he actually had to pull himself together and stop
himself calling the bluff and suddenly bolting down the
hill.

The situation was embarrassing rather than
alarming. When Syd Jones slouched out of the Pad
and met them and fastened his arms behind his back
with a strap, Ricky thought that all three of them
looked silly and not able to carry the scene off with
style. This reaction was the more singular in that, at the
same time, he knew they meant business and that he
ought to be deeply alarmed.

And now, here he was, back in Syd's Pad and in the
broken-down chair he had occupied on his former
visit, very uncomfortable because of his pinioned arms.
The room smelled and looked as it had before and was
in the same state of squalor. He saw that blankets had
been rigged up over the windows. A solitary shaded
lamp on the worktable gave all the light there was. His
arms hurt him and broken springs dug into his bottom.

There was one new feature, apart from the blankets.
Where there had been sketches drawing-pinned to the
wall there now hung a roughly framed canvas. He
recognized Leda and the Swan.

Ferrant lounged against the table with unconvincing insolence. Syd lay on his bed and looked seldom
and furtively at Ricky. Nothing was said and,
grotesquely, this silence had the character of a social
hiatus. Ricky had some difficulty in breaking it.

"What is all this?" he asked, his voice sounding like
somebody else's. "Am I kidnapped or what?"

"That's right, Mr. Alleyn," Ferrant said. "That's
correct. You are our hostage, Mr. Alleyn."

He was smoking. He inhaled and blew smoke out
his nostrils. "What an act!" Ricky thought.

"Do you mind telling me why?" he asked.

"A pleasure, Mr. Alleyn. A great pleasure."

Ricky thought: "If this were fiction it would be terrible stuff. One would write things like 'sneered Ferrant' and 'said young Alleyn, very quietly.'"

He said: "Well, come on, then. Let's have it."

"You're going to write a little note to your papa, Mr. Alleyn."

For the first time an authentic cold trickle ran down Ricky's spine. "To say what?" he asked.

Ferrant elaborated with all the panache of a grade-B film gangster. The message Ricky was to write would be delivered to the Cove police station—never mind by whom. Ricky said tartly that he couldn't care less by whom; what was he expected to say?

"Take it easy, take it easy," Ferrant snarled out of the corner of his mouth. He moved around the table and sat down at it. He cocked up his feet in their co-respondent shoes on the table and leveled his gun between his knees at Ricky. It was not a pose that Ricky, himself in acute discomfort, thought that Ferrant would find easy or pleasant to sustain.

He noticed that among the litter on the table were the remains of a meal: an open jackknife, cups, and a half-empty bottle of cognac. A piece of drawing paper lay near the lamp with an artist's conté pencil beside it. There was a chair on that side of the table, opposite Ferrant.

"That's the idea," said Ferrant ("purred," no doubt would be the chosen verb, thought Ricky). "We'll have a little action, shall we?"

He nodded magnificently at Syd, who got off the bed and moved to Ricky. He bent over him, not looking in his face.

"Your breath stinks, Syd," said Ricky.

Syd made a very raw reply. It was the first time he had spoken. He hauled ineffectually at Ricky and they floundered about aimlessly before Ricky got his balance. It was true that Syd smelled awful.

Obviously they wanted him on the chair, facing Ferrant. He managed to shoulder Syd off and sit on it.

"Now then," he said. "What's the drill?"

"We'll take it ve-ry nice and slow," said Ferrant and Ricky thought he'd been wanting to get the phrase off his chest, appropriate or not, as the situation developed. He repeated it: "Ni-ce and slow."

"If you want me to write you'll have to untruss me, won't you?" Ricky pointed out.

"I'm giving the orders in this scene, mate, do you mind?" said Ferrant. He nodded again to Syd, who moved behind Ricky but did not release him.

Ricky had pins and needles in his forearms. It was difficult to move them. His upper arms, still pinioned, had gone numb. Ferrant raised the gun slightly.

"And we won't try any funny business, will we?" he said. "We'll listen carefully and do what we're told like a good boy. Right?"

He waited for an answer and getting none began to lay down the law.

He said Ricky was to write a message in his own words and if he tried anything on he'd have to start again. He was to say that he was being held hostage and the price of his release was absolute inactivity on the part of the police until Ferrant and Syd had gone.

"Say," Ferrant ordered, "that if they start anything you'll be fixed. For keeps."

That was to be the message.

How many strata of thought are there at any given moment in a human brain? In Ricky's there was a kind of lethargy, a profound unbelief in the situation, a sense of nonreality, as if, in an approaching moment, he would find himself elsewhere and unmolested. With this there was a rising dry terror and an awareness of the necessity to think clearly about the immediate threat. And, overall, a desolate longing for his father.

"Suppose I won't write it," he said. "What about that?"

"Something not very nice about that. Something we don't want to do."

"If you mean you'll shoot me you must be out of your mind. Where would that get you?" Ricky asked, forcing himself (and it cost him an enormous effort) to take hold of what he supposed must be reality. "Don't be silly," he said. "What do you want? To do a bolt because you're up to your eyebrows in trouble? The hostage ploy's exploded, you ought to know that. They'll call your bluff. *You're* not going to shoot me."

Syd Jones mumbled, "You ought to know we mean business. What about yesterday? What about—"

"Shut up," said Ferrant.

"All right," said Ricky. "Yesterday. What about it? A footling attempt to do me in and a dead failure at that."

To his own surprise he suddenly lost his temper with Syd. "You've been a bloody fool all along," he shouted. "You thought I was on to whatever your game is with drugs, didn't you? It wouldn't have entered my head if you hadn't made such an ass of yourself. You thought I sent you to see my parents because my father's a cop. I sent you out of bloody kindness. You thought I was spying on you and tailed you over to Saint Pierre. You were dead wrong all along the line and did yourself a lot of harm. Now, God save the mark, you're trying to play at kidnappers. You fool, Syd. If you shot me, here, it'd be the end of you. What do you think my father'd do about that one? He'd hunt you both down with the police of two nations to help him. *You* don't mean business. Ferrant's making a monkey of you and you're too bloody dumb or too bloody doped to see it. Call yourself a painter. You're a dirty little drug-runner's sidekick and a failure at that."

Syd hit him across the mouth. His upper lip banged

against his teeth. Tears ran down his face. He lashed out with his foot. Syd fell backwards and sat on the floor. Ricky saw through his tears that Syd had the jackknife in his hand.

Ferrant, in command of a stream of whispered indecencies, rose and was frightening. He came around the table and winded Ricky with a savage jab under the ribs. Ricky doubled up in his chair and through the pain felt them lash his ankles together. Ferrant took his shoulders and jerked him upright. He began to hit him methodically with hard, openhanded slaps on his bruised face. "This is the worst thing that has ever happened to me," Ricky thought.

Now Ferrant had the knife. He forced Ricky's head back by the hair and held the point to his throat.

"Now," whispered Ferrant, "who's talking about who means business? Another squeal out of you, squire, and you'll be gagged. And listen. Any more naughty stuff and you'll end up with a slit windpipe at the bottom of the earth bog behind this shack. Your father won't find you down there in a hurry and when he does he won't fancy what he sees. *Filth*," said Ferrant, using the French equivalent. He shook Ricky by the hair of his head and slapped his face again.

Ricky wondered afterward if this treatment had for a moment or two actually served to clear rather than fuddle his wits and even to extend his field of observation. Whether this was so or not, it was a fact that he now became aware beyond the circle of light cast by the single lamp, of suitcases that were vaguely familiar. Now he recognized them, ultrasmart pieces of luggage (*"Très snob—presque cad"*—who had said that?) suspended from Ferrant's gloved hands as he walked down the street to the jetty in the early hours of the morning.

He saw, blearily, the familiar paint box lying open on the table with a litter of tubes and an open carton beside it. He even saw that one tube had been opened at the bottom and was gaping.

"They're cleaning up," he thought. And then: "They're cooking up a getaway with the stuff. Tonight. They saw me watching the Pad, and they saw me up by the pine grove, and they hauled me in. Now they don't know what to do with me. They're improvising."

Ferrant thrust his face at him. "That's for a start," he said. "How about it? You'll write this message? Yes?"

Ricky tried to speak but found that his tongue was out of order and his upper lip bled on the inside and wouldn't move. He made ungainly noises. Syd said: "Christ, you've croaked him."

Ricky made an enormous effort. "Won't work," he hoped he'd said. Ferrant listened with exaggerated attention.

"What's that? Won't work? Oh, it'll work, don't worry," he said. "Know how? You're going down to the pier with us, see? And if your papa and his bloody fuzz start anything, you'll croak." He touched Ricky's throat with the point of the knife. "See? Feel that? Now, get to it. Tell him."

They released his right arm and strapped the left to the chair. Ferrant pushed the drawing paper toward him and tried to shove the pencil into his tingling hand. "Go on," he said. "Go on. Take it. Take it."

Ricky flexed his fingers and clenched and un- clenched his hand. He felt horribly sick. Ferrant's voice receded into the distance and was replaced by a thrumming sound. Something hard pressed against his forehead. It was the table. "But I haven't passed out," he thought. "Not quite."

Syd Jones was saying: "No, Gil, don't. Hell, Gil, not now. Not yet. Look, Gil, why don't we gag him and tie him up and leave him? Why don't we finish packing the stuff and stay quiet till it's time and just leave him?"

"Do I have to go over it again? Look. So he doesn't turn up. So his old man's asking for him. Marie reckons he's suspicious. They'll be watching, don't you worry. All right. So we leave him here and we walk straight into it. But if we've got him between us and look like we mean business, they won't do a bloody thing. They can't. We'll take him in the dinghy as far as the boat and tip him overboard. By the time they've fished him out, we're beyond the heads and on our way."

"I don't like it. Look at him. He's passed out."

Ricky stayed as he was. When Ferrant jerked his head back he groaned, opened his eyes, shut them again, and, when released, flopped forward on the table. "I must listen, listen, listen," he thought. It was a horrid task; so much easier to give up, to yield, voluptuously almost, to whatever punch, slap, or agonizing tweak they chose to deal out. And what to do about writing? What would be the result if he did write—write what? What Ferrant had said—write to his father.

"Go on," Ferrant was saying. "Get to it. You know what to put. Go on."

His head was jerked up again by the hair. Perhaps his scalp rather than his mouth hurt most.

His fingers closed around the conté pencil. He dragged his hand over the paper.

Kidnapped," he wrote, "*OK. They say if you're inactive till they've gone I won't be hurt. If not I will. Sorry.*" He made a big attempt at organized thinking. "*P.A.D.*," he wrote as a signature and let the pencil slide out of his grip.

Ferrant read the message. "What's this 'P.A.D.'?" he demanded.

"Initials. Patrick Andrew David," Ricky lied and thought it sounded like royalty.

"What's this 'Ricky' stuff then?"

"Nickname. Always sign P.A.D."

The paper was withdrawn. His face dropped painfully on his forearm and he closed his eyes. Their voices faded and he could no longer strain to listen. It would be delicious if in spite of the several pains that competed for his attention, he could sleep.

There was no such thing as time, only the rise and ebbing of pain to which a new element had been added, cutting into his ankles as if into the sorrel mare's near fore.

IV

It took much longer than they had anticipated to get their search warrant. The magistrates court had risen and Alleyn was obliged to hunt down a Justice of the Peace in his home. He lived some distance on the far side of Montjoy in an important house at the foot of a precipitous lane. They had trouble finding him and when found he turned out to be a fusspot and a ditherer. On the return journey the car jibbed at the steep ascent and wouldn't proceed until Fox had removed his considerable weight and applied it to the rear. Whereupon Alleyn, using a zigzagging technique, finally achieved the summit and was obliged to wait there for his laboring colleague. They then found that there was next to no petrol left in the tank and stopped at the first station to fill up. The man asked them if they knew they had a slow puncture.

By the time they got back to the Cove dusk was falling and Sergeant Plank had twice rung up from Leathers. Mrs. Plank, the victim of redundancy, reported that there was nothing to report but that he would report again at seven-thirty. She offered them high tea, which they declined. Alleyn left Fox to take the call, saying he would look in for a fleeting moment on Ricky, who would surely have returned from his walk.

So he went around the corner to the Ferrants' house. Ricky's window was still shut. The boy, Louis, admitted Alleyn.

Mrs. Ferrant came out of her kitchen to the usual accompaniment of her television.

"Good evening, monsieur," she said. "Your son has not yet returned."

The idiot insistence of a commercial jingle blared to its conclusion before Alleyn spoke.

"He's rather late, isn't he?" Alleyn said.

She lifted her shoulders. "He has perhaps walked to Bon Accord and is eating there."

"He didn't say anything about doing that?"

"No. There was no need."

"You would wish to know because of the meal, madame. It was inconsiderate of him."

"*C'est peu de chose.*"

"Has he done this before?"

"Once, perhaps. Or more than once. I forget. You will excuse me, monsieur. I have the boy's meal to attend to."

"Of course. Forgive me. Your husband has not returned?"

"No, monsieur. I do not expect him. Excuse me."

When she had shut the kitchen door after her, Alleyn lifted his clenched fist to his mouth, took in a deep breath, waited a second, and then went upstairs to Ricky's room. Perhaps there would be a written message there that he had not, for some reason, wished to leave with Mrs. Ferrant.

There was no message. Ricky's manuscript, weighted by a stone, was on his table. A photograph of his parents stared past his father at the empty room. The smell of Ricky, a tweed and shaving-soap smell mixed with his pipe, hung on the air.

"She was lying," he thought. "He hasn't gone to Bon Accord. What the hell did he say was the name of that pub, where they lunched?" "Fisherman's Rest" clicked up in his police-drilled memory. He returned to the worktable. On a notepad Ricky had written a telephone number and after it L'E.

"He'd not go there," Alleyn thought. "Or would he? If Julia rang him up? Not without letting me know. But he couldn't let me know."

There was more writing—a lot of it—on an underleaf of the notepad. Alleyn saw that it was a quite exhaustive breakdown of the circumstances surrounding Ricky's experiences before and during his visit to Saint Pierre-des-Roches.

Alleyn momentarily closed his eyes. "Madame F.," he thought, "has no doubt enjoyed a good read."

He took down the L'Esperance number and left a message under the stone. "Sorry I missed you, Cid."

"She'll read it, of course," he thought and went downstairs. The kitchen door was ajar and the television silent.

"*Bon soir, madame*" he called out cheerfully and let himself out.

Back at the police station he rang the Fisherman's Rest at Bon Accord and to a background of bar conviviality was told that Ricky was not, and had not been, there. Fox, who had yielded to Mrs. Plank's renewed hospitality, listened with well-controlled consternation.

Alleyn then rang L'Esperance. He was answered by a voice that he recognized as Bruno's.

"Hullo," he said. "Alleyn, here. I'm sorry to bother you but is Rick by any chance with you?"

"No, sir, we haven't seen him since—"

He faded out. Alleyn heard his own name and then, close and unmistakable, Julia's voice.

"It's you! What fun. Have you mislaid your son?"

"I seem to have, for the moment."

"We've not seen him since this morning. Could he be hunting you down in your smart hotel? Perhaps he's met Louis and they're up to no good in Montjoy."

"Is Louis in Montjoy?"

"I think so. *Carlotta*," cried Julia musically, "is Louis in Montjoy?" And after a pause, into the receiver: "She doesn't seem to know."

"I'm so sorry to have bothered you."

"You needn't be. Quite to the contrary. Hope you find him."

"I expect I shall," he said quite gaily. "Good-bye and thank you."

When he had hung up, he and Fox looked steadily at each other.

Fox said: "There'll be a simple explanation, of course."

"If there is," Alleyn said, "I'll knock his block off," and contrived to laugh. "You think of one, Fox," he said. "I can't."

"Such as gone for a walk and sprained an ankle?"

"All right. Yes. That."

"He wouldn't be up at Leathers? No. Plank would have said."

The telephone rang.

"That'll *be* Plank," said Fox and answered it. "Fox here. Yes. Nothing, eh? I'll ask the Chief." He looked at Alleyn who, with a most uncharacteristic gesture, passed his hand across his eyes.

"Tell him to—no, wait a moment. Tell them to knock off and report back here. And—you might just ask—"

Fox asked and got the expected reply.

"By God," said Alleyn. "I wish this hadn't happened. Damn the boy, I ought to have got him out of it to begin with."

After a longish pause, Fox said: "I'm not of that opinion, if you don't mind my saying so, Mr. Alleyn."

"I don't mind, Br'er Fox. I hope you're right."

"It'll just turn out he's taken an extra long walk."

"You didn't hear Mrs. Ferrant. I think she knows something."

"About the young chap?"

"Yes."

Fox was silent.

"We must, of course, do what we'd do if someone came into the station and reported it," Alleyn said.

"Tell them to wait," Fox said promptly. "Give him until it gets dark and then if he hadn't turned up we'd—well—"

"Set up a search."

"That's right," said Fox uncomfortably.

"In the meantime we've got the official search on hand. Did Plank say what he'd beaten up in the way of help?"

"The chaps he's got with him. A couple of coppers from the Montjoy factory," said Fox, meaning the police station.

"We'll take them with us. After all, we don't know what we'll find there, do we?" said Alleyn.

8

Night Watches

I

THE THING THEY got wrong in the gangster films, Ricky thought, was what it did to you being tied up. The film victims, once they were released, did one or two obligatory staggers and then became as nimble as fleas and started fighting again. He knew that when, if ever, he was released, his legs would not support him, his arms would be senseless, and his head so compounded of pain that it would hang down and wobble like a wilted dahlia.

He could not guess how long it was since they gagged him. Jones had made a pad out of rag and Ferrant had forced it between his teeth and bound it with another rag. It tasted of turpentine and stung his cut lip. They had done this when Syd said he'd heard something outside. Ferrant had switched off the light and they were very still until there was a scratching at the door.

"It's the kid," Ferrant said.

He opened the door a little way and after a moment shut it again very quietly. Syd switched on the light. Young Louis was there. He wore a black smock like a French schoolboy and a beret. He had a satchel on his back. His stewed-prune eyes stared greedily at Ricky out of a blackened face.

Ferrant held out his hand and Louis put a note in it. Ferrant read it—it was evidently very short—and gave it to Syd.

Louis said: "Papa, he asked me if I could row the boat."

"Who did?"

"The fuzz. He asked if I was afraid to go out in her at night."

"What'd you say?"

"I said I wasn't. I didn't say anything else, Papa. Honest."

"By God, you better not."

"Maman says he's getting worried about *him*." Louis pointed to Ricky. "You got him so he can't talk, haven't you, Papa? Have you worked him over? His face looks like you have. What are you going to do with him, Papa?"

"*Tais-toi donc*. Keep your tongue behind your teeth. *Passe-moi la boustifaille*."

Louis gave him the satchel.

"Good. Now, there is more for you to do. Take this envelope. Do not open it. You see it has his name on it. The detective's name. Listen carefully. You are to push it under the door at the police station and nobody must see you. Do not put it through the slot. Under the door. Then push the bell and away home quick and silent before the door is opened. Very quick. Very silent. And nobody to see you. Repeat it."

He did, accurately.

"That is right. Now go."

"I've blacked my face. Like a gunman. So's nobody can see me."

"Good. The light, Syd."

Syd switched it off, and on again when the door was shut.

"Is he safe?" Syd asked.

"Yes. Get on with it."

"We can't take—" Syd stopped short and looked at Ricky. "Everything," he said.

They had paid no attention to him for a long time. It was as if by trussing him up they had turned him into an unthinking as well as an inanimate object.

They had been busy. His chair had been turned away from the table and manhandled excruciatingly to bring him face to the wall. There had been some talk of a blindfold, he thought, but he kept his eyes shut and let his head flop and they left him there, still gagged, and could be heard moving purposefully about the room.

He opened his eyes. Leda and the Swan had gone from their place on the wall and now lay face down on the floor, close to his feet. He recognized the frame and wondered bemusedly by what means it had hung up there because there was no cord or wire to be seen although there were the usual ring screws.

Ferrant and Syd went quietly about their business. They spoke seldom and in low voices but they generated a floating sense of urgency and at times seemed to argue. He began to long for the moment to come when they would have to release whatever it was that bound and cut into his ankles. If he were to walk between them down to the boat, that was what they would have to do. And where would the Cid be, then? Watching with Br'er Fox from the window in Ricky's

room? Unable to do anything because if he did—
Would the Cid ever get the message? Where was he?
Now? Now, when Ricky wanted him so badly. It's too
much, he thought. Yesterday and the thunder and
lightning and the sea and blacking my eye and now all
this: face, jaw, mouth, ankle. No, it's too much. The
wall poured upwards, his eyes closed, and he fainted.

The boy Louis did not follow the path down to the
front but turned off it to his right and slithered,
darkling, along tortuous passages that ran uphill and
down, behind the backs of cottages, some occupied
and some deserted.

The moon had not yet risen and the going was tricky
but he was surefooted and knew his ground. He was
excited and thought of himself in terms of his favorite
comic strip as a Miracle Kid.

He came out of his labyrinth at the top of the lane
that ran down to the police station.

Here he crouched for a moment in the blackest of
the shadows. There was no need to crouch—the lane
was deserted—but he enjoyed doing it and then
flattening himself against a wall and edging downhill.

The blue lamp was on but the station windows were
dark, while those in the living quarters glowed. He
could hear music, radio or telly, with the fuzz family
watching it and the Miracle Kid, all on his own, out in
the dark.

"Whee-ee!!"

Across the lane like the Black Shadow. Envelope.
Under the door. Stuck. Push. Bell. Push. "Zing!!!"

In by the back door with Maman waiting. Hands in
pockets. Cool. Slouch in wagging the hips.

"Eh bien?" said Mrs. Ferrant, nodding her head up
and down. *"Tu es fort satisfait de ta petite personne,
n'est-ce pas?"*

Around the corner in the police station, Mrs. Plank,
peering up and down the lane, told herself it was too
late for a runaway knock. Unless, she thought, it was

that young Louis from around the corner who was allowed to wait up until all hours and was not a nice type of child. Then she noticed the envelope at her feet. She picked it up. Addressed to the Super and sealed. She shut the front door, went into the kitchen, and turned the envelope over and over in her hands.

There was no telling how late it might be when they returned, all of them. Joe had been very quiet when he came in but she knew he was gratified by the way the corners of his mouth twitched. He had told her they were going to search Syd Jones's premises but it was not to be mentioned. He knew, thought Mrs. Plank, that he could trust her.

It had been a most irregular way of delivering the note, if it was a note. Suppose it was important? Suppose Mr. Alleyn should know of it at once and suppose that by leaving it until he came in, if he did come in and not drive straight back to Montjoy, some irreparable damage was done? On the other hand, Joe and Mr. Alleyn and Mr. Fox might be greatly displeased if she butted in at that place with a note that turned out to be some silly prank.

She worried it over, this way and that. She examined the envelope again and again, particularly the direction, written in capital letters with some sort of crayon, it looked like: "MR. ALLEN." Someone who didn't know how to spell his name.

The flap was not all that securely gummed down. "Well I don't care, I will," she thought.

She maneuvered it open and read the message.

II

Before they set out for Syd's Pad, Alleyn had held a short briefing at the station with Fox, Plank, and the two constables from Montjoy: Cribbage and Moss.

"We're going into the place," he had told them, "because I think we've sufficient grounds to justify a search for illicit drugs. It will have to be an exhaustive search and as always in these cases it may bring us no joy. The two men we're interested in are known to have been in Saint Pierre yesterday and as far as we've been able to find out, haven't returned to the island. Certainly not by air. There has been no official passage to the Cove by sea and your chaps"—he looked at the two constables—"checked the ferry at Montjoy. This doesn't take in the possibility that they came back during the night in a French chum's craft and were transshipped somewhere near the heads into Ferrant's dinghy and brought ashore. We've no evidence—" he hesitated for a moment and caught Fox's eye—"no evidence," he repeated, "to support any such theory: it is pure speculation. If, however, it had so happened, it might mean that Ferrant as well as Jones is up at the Pad and they might turn naughty. Mr. Fox and Sergeant Plank are carrying handcuffs." He looked around at the four impassive faces. "Well," he said, "that's it. Shall we push off? Got your lamps?"

Plank had produced two acetylene lamps in addition to five powerful hand torches because, as he said, they didn't know but what the power might be off. He had also provided himself with a small torch with a blue light.

They had driven along the front, past the Cod-and-Bottle, and parked their car near Fisherman's Steps.

Ricky had described his visit to Syd's pad so vividly that Alleyn felt as if he himself had been there before. They didn't say much to each other as they climbed the steps. Plank, who in the course of duty beats had become familiar with the ground, led the way and used his torch to show awkward patches.

"We don't want to advertise ourselves," Alleyn had said. "On the other hand, we're making a routine search, not scaling the cliffs of Abraham in blackface.

If there's somebody at home who won't answer the door we effect an entrance. If nobody's there we still effect an entrance. And that's it."

They were about halfway up the steps and had passed the last of the cottages, when Plank said: "The place is up on the right, sir. If there was lights in the front windows we'd see them from here."

"I can just make out the roof."

"Somebody might be in a back room," said Fox.

"Of course. We'll take it quietly from here. Plank, you're familiar with the lie of the land. When we get there you take a man with you and move round to the back door as quietly as you can. We three will go to the front door. *If* there's anybody at home he might try a break. From now on, softly's the word. Don't rush it and don't use your torch unless you've got to and then keep it close to the ground."

They moved on slowly. The going became increasingly difficult, their feet slipped, they breathed hard, and once the larger of the Montjoy men fell heavily, swore, and said, "Pardon." Plank administered a stern rebuke. They continued uphill still led by Plank who turned every now and then to make sure they were all together.

On the last of these occasions he put out his hand and touched Alleyn.

"Sir," Plank breathed, "has someone fallen back?"

No, they were all there.

"What is it?"

"We're being followed."

Alleyn turned. Some way below them a torchlight darted momentarily about the steps, blacked out and reappeared, nearer.

"One of the locals? Coming home?" Fox speculated.

"Wait."

No. It showed again for a fraction of a second and was much nearer. They could hear uneven footfalls and labored breathing. Whoever it was must be scrambling, almost running up the steps.

"Christ!" Plank broke out. "It's the Missus."

It was Mrs. Plank, so out of breath that she clung to Alleyn with one hand and with the other shoved the paper at him.

"Sh-sh!" she panted. "Don't speak. Don't say anything. Read it."

Alleyn opened his jacket as a shield to her torch and read.

Fox, who was at his elbow, saw the paper quiver in his hand. The little group was very still. Voices of patrons leaving the Cod-and-Bottle broke the silence and even the slap of the incoming tide along the front. Alleyn motioned with his head. The others closed about him, bent over and formed a sort of massive huddle around the torchlit paper. Fox was the first to break the silence.

"Signed P.A.D.?" Fox said. "Why?"

"It's his writing. Weak. But his. It's a tip-off. 'Pad.' They didn't drop to it or they'd have cut it out."

"Practical," said Fox unevenly. And then: "What do we do?"

Alleyn read the message again, folded it, and put it in his pocket. Mrs. Plank switched off her torch. The others waited.

"Mrs. Plank," Alleyn said, "you don't know how grateful I am to you. How did this reach you?"

She told him. "I got the notion," she ended, "that it might be that young Louis Ferrant. I suppose because he's a one for runaway knocks."

"Is he, indeed? Now, please, you must go back. Go carefully and thank you."

"Will it—they won't?—will it be all right?"

"You cut along, Mother," said her husband. "'Course it will."

"Goodnight, then," she said and was gone.

Fox said: "She's not using her torch."

"She's good on her feet," said Plank.

Throughout, they had spoken just above a whisper. When Alleyn talked now it was more slowly and unevenly than was his custom but in a level voice.

"It's a question, I think, of whether we declare ourselves and talk to them from outside the house or risk an unheard approach and a break-in. I don't think," he stopped for a moment, "I don't think I dare do that."

"No," said Fox. "No. Not that way. Too risky."

"Yes. It seems clear that already they've ... given him a bad time—the writing's very shaky."

"It does say 'OK,' though. Meaning he is."

"It says that. There's a third possibility. He says 'till they've gone' and I can't think of them making a getaway by any means other than the way we discussed, Fox. If so they'll come out at some time during the night, carrying their stuff. With Rick between them. They've worked it out that we won't try anything because of the threat to Rick. We carry on now, with the old plan. We don't know which door they'll use so we'll have two at the back and three at the front. And wait for them to emerge."

"And jump them?"

"Yes," Alleyn said. "And jump them."

"Hard and quick?"

"Yes. They'll be armed."

"It's good enough," Fox said and there were satisfied noises from the other three men.

"I think it's the best we can do. It may be—" for the first time Alleyn's voice faltered, "a long wait. That won't—be easy."

It was not easy. As they drew near the house they could make it out in a faint diffusion of light from the village below. They moved very slowly now, over soft, uneven ground, Plank leading them. He would stop and put back a warning hand when they drew near an obstacle, such as the bramble bush where Miss Harkness had tethered her horse and Ricky had so

ostentatiously lit his pipe. No chink of light showed
from window or door.

They inched forward with frequent stops to listen
and grope about them. A breeze had sprung up. There
were rustlings, small indeterminate sounds and from
the pinegrove further up the hill, a vague soughing.
This favored their approach.

It was always possible, Alleyn thought, that they
were being watched, that the lights had been put out
and a chink opened at one of the windows. What would
the men inside do then? And there was, he supposed,
another possibility—that Ricky was being held
somewhere else, in one of the deserted cottages, for
instance, or even gagged and out in the open. But no.
Why "Pad" in the message? Unless they'd moved after
sending the message. Should Fox return and try to
screw a statement out of Mrs. Ferrant? But then the
emergence from the Pad might happen and they would
be a man short.

They had come to the place where a rough path
branched off, leading around to the back of the house.
Plank breathed this information in Alleyn's ear: "We'll
get back to you double quick, sir, if it's the front. Can
you make out the door?" Alleyn squeezed his elbow
and sensed rather than saw Plank's withdrawal with
P.C. Moss.

There was the door. They crept up to it, Alleyn and
Fox on either side with P.C. Cribbage behind Fox.
There was a sharp crackle as Cribbage fell foul of some
bush or dry stick. They froze and waited. The breeze
carried a moisture with it that tasted salt on Alleyn's
lips. Nothing untoward happened.

Alleyn began to explore with his fingers the wall, the
door and a step leading up to it. He sensed that Fox, on
his side, was doing much the same thing.

The door was weatherworn and opened inward. The
handle was on Alleyn's side. He found the keyhole,
knelt and put his eye to it, but could see nothing. The

key was in the lock, evidently. Or hadn't Ricky, describing the Pad, talked about a heavy curtain masking the door? Alleyn thought he had.

He explored the bottom of the door. There was very little gap between it and the floor, but as he stared fixedly at the place where his finger rested he became aware of a lesser darkness, of the faintest possible thinning out of nonvisibility that increased, infinitesimally, when he withdrew his hand.

Light, as faint as light could be, filtered through the gap between the door and the floor.

He slid his finger away from him along the gap and ran into something alive. Fox's finger. Alleyn closed his hand around Fox's and then traced on its hairy back the word *light*. Fox reversed the process. *Yes*.

Alleyn knelt. He laid his right ear to the door and stopped up the left one.

There was sound. Something being moved. The thud of stockinged or soft-shod feet and then, only just perceptibly, voices.

He listened and listened, unconscious of aching knees, as if all his other faculties had been absorbed by the sense of hearing. The sounds continued. Once, one of the voices was raised. Of one thing he was certain—neither of them belonged to Ricky.

To Ricky, on the other side of the door. Quite close? Or locked up in some back room? Gagged? What had they done to him to turn his incisive Italianate script into the writing of an old man?

Monstrous it was, to wait and to do nothing. Should he, after all, have decided to break in? Suppose they shot him and Fox before the others could jump on them, what would they do to Ricky?

The sounds were so faint that the men must be at the end of the room farthest from the door. He wondered if Fox had heard them, or Cribbage.

He got to his feet surprised to find how stiff he was. He waited for a minute or two and then eased across until he found Fox who was leaning with his back to the wall and whispered:

"Hear them?"

"Yes."

"At least we've come to the right place."

"Yes."

Alleyn returned to his side of the door.

The minutes dragged into an hour. The noises continued intermittently and, after a time, became more distant, as if the men had moved to another room. They changed in character. There was a scraping metallic sound, only just detectable, and then silence.

It was no longer pitch dark. Shapes had begun to appear, shadows of definite form and patches of light. The moon, in its last quarter, had risen behind the pine grove and soon would shine full upon them. Already he could see Fox and beyond him P.C. Cribbage, propped against the wall, his head drooping, his helmet inclined forward above his nose. He was asleep.

Even as Alleyn reached out to draw Fox's attention to his neighbor, Cribbage's knees bent. He slid down the wall and fell heavily to the ground, kicking the acetylene lamp. Wakened, he began to scramble to his feet and was kicked by Fox. He rose with abject caution.

Absolute silence had fallen inside the house.

Alleyn motioned to Fox and Fox, with awful grandeur, motioned to the stricken Cribbage. They cat-walked across to Alleyn's side of the door and stood behind him, all three of them pressed back against the wall.

"*If*—" Alleyn breathed. "We act."

"Right."

They moved a little apart and waited. Alleyn with his ear to the door. The light that had shown so faintly across the threshold went out. He drew back and signaled to Fox. After a further eternal interval they all heard a rustle and clink as of a curtain being drawn.

The key was turned in the lock.

The deep framework surrounding the door prevented Alleyn from seeing it open but he knew it *had* opened, very slightly. He knew that the man inside now looked out and saw nothing untoward where Fox and Cribbage had been. To see them, he would have to open up wide enough to push his head through and look to his right.

The door creaked.

In slow motion a black beret began to appear. An ear, a temple, the flat of a cheek, and then, suddenly, the point of a jaw and an eye. The eye looked into his. It opened wide and Alleyn drove his fist hard at the jaw.

Ferrant pitched forward. Fox caught him under the arms and Cribbage took him by the knees. Alleyn closed the door.

Ferrant's right hand opened and Alleyn caught the gun that fell from it. "Lose him. Quick," he said. Fox and Cribbage carried Ferrant, head lolling and arms dangling, around the corner of the house. The operation had been virtually soundless and had taken a matter of seconds.

Alleyn moved back to his place by the door. There was still no sound from inside the house. Fox and Cribbage returned.

"Still out," Fox muttered and intimated that Ferrant was handcuffed to a small tree with his mouth stopped.

They took up their former positions, Alleyn with Ferrant's gun—a French army automatic—in his hand. This one, he thought, was going to be simpler.

Two loud thumps came from within the house followed by an exclamation that sounded like an oath. Then, soft but unmistakable, approaching footsteps and again the creak of the opening door.

"Gil!" Syd Jones whispered into the night. "What's up? Where are you? Are you there, Gil?"

Like Ferrant, he widened the door opening and, like

Ferrant, thrust his head out.

They used their high-powered torches. Syd's face, a bearded mask, started up, blinking and expressionless. He found himself looking into the barrel of the automatic, "Hands up and into the room," Alleyn said. Fox kicked the door wide open, entered the house, and switched on the light. Alleyn followed Syd with Cribbage behind him.

At the far end of the room, face to wall, gagged and bound in his chair, was Ricky.

"Fox," Alleyn said. Fox took the automatic and began the obligatory chant—"Sydney Jones, I arrest—" Plank arrived and put on the handcuffs.

Alleyn, stooping over his son, was saying: "It's me, old boy. You'll be all right. It's me." He removed the bloodied gag. Ricky's mouth hung open. His tongue moved and he made a sound. Alleyn took his head carefully between his hands.

Ricky contrived to speak. "Oh, golly, Cid," he said. "Oh, *golly*!"

"I know. Never mind. Won't be long, now. Hold on."

He unstrapped the arms and they fell forward. He knelt to release the ankles.

Ricky's white socks were bloodied and overhung his shoes. Alleyn turned the socks back and exposed wet ridges that had closed over the bonds.

From between the ridges protruded a twist of wire and two venomous little prongs.

III

Ricky lay on the bed. In the filthy little kitchen, P.C. Moss boiled up a saucepan of water and tore a sheet into strips. Sergeant Plank was at the station, telephoning for a doctor and ambulance.

Ferrant and Syd Jones, handcuffed together, sat

side by side facing the table. Opposite them Alleyn stood with Fox beside him and Cribbage modestly in the background. The angled lamp had been directed to shine full in the prisoners' faces.

On the table, stretched out to its full length on a sheet of paper, lay the wire that had bound Ricky's ankles and cut into them. It left a trace of red on the paper.

To Ricky himself, lying in the shadow, his injuries thrumming through his nerves like music, the scene was familiar. It was an interrogation scene with obviously dramatic lighting, barked questions, mulish answers, suggested threats. It looked like a standard offering from a police story on television.

But it didn't sound like one. His father and Fox did not bark their questions. Nor did they threaten but were quiet and deadly cold and must, Ricky thought, be frightening indeed.

"This wire," Alleyn was saying to Syd, "it's yours, is it?"

Syd's reply, if he made one, was inaudible.

"Is it off the back of the picture frame there? It is? Where did you get it? There?" A pause. "Lying about? Where?"

"I don't remember."

"At Leathers?"

"S'right."

"When?"

"I wouldn't know."

"You know very well. When?"

"I don't remember. It was some old junk. He didn't want it."

"Was it before the accident?"

"Yes. No. After."

"Where?"

"In the stables."

"Where, exactly?"

"I don't know."

"You know. Where?"

"Hanging up. With a lot more."

"Did you cut if off?"

"No. It was on its own. A separate bit. What's the idea?" Syd broke out with a miserable show of indignation. "So it's a bit of old wire. So I took it to hang a picture. So what?"

Ferrant, on a jet of obscenities, French and English, told him to hold his tongue.

"I didn't tie him up," Syd said. "You did."

"*Merde.*"

Alleyn said: "You will both be taken to the police station in Montjoy and charged with assault. Anything you say now—and then—will be taken down and may be used in evidence. For the moment, that's all."

"Get up," said Fox.

Cribbage got them to their feet. He and Fox marshaled them toward the far end of the room. As they were about to pass the bed, looking straight before them, Fox laid massive hands upon their shoulders and turned them to confront it.

Ricky, from out of the mess they had made of his face, looked at them. Ferrant produced the blank indifference of the dock. Syd, whose face, as always, resembled the interior of an old-fashioned mattress, showed the whites of his eyes.

Fox shoved them around again and they were taken, under Cribbage's surveillance, to the far end of the room.

Constable Moss emerged from the kitchen with a saucepan containing boiled strips of sheet and presented it before Alleyn.

Alleyn said: "Thank you, Moss. I don't know that we should do anything before the doctor's seen him. Perhaps clean him up a bit."

"They're sterile, sir," said Moss. "Boiled for ten minutes."

"Splendid."

Alleyn went into the kitchen. Boiled water had been poured into a basin. He scrubbed his hands with soap that Syd evidently used on his brushes if not on himself. Alleyn returned to his son. Moss held the saucepan for him and he very cautiously swabbed Ricky's mouth and eyes.

"Better," said Ricky.

Alleyn looked again at the ankles. The wire had driven fibers from Ricky's socks into the cuts.

"I'd better not meddle," Alleyn said. "We'll get on with the search, Fox." He bent over Ricky. "We're getting the quack to have a look at you, old boy."

"I'll be OK."

"Of course you will. But you're bloody uncomfortable, I'm afraid."

Ricky tried to speak, failed, and then with an enormous effort said: "Try some of the dope," and managed to wink.

Alleyn winked back using the seriocomic family version with one corner of the mouth drawn down and the opposite eyebrow raised, a grimace beyond his son's achievement at the moment. He hesitated and then said: "Rick, it's important or I wouldn't nag. How did you get here?"

With an enormous effort Ricky said: "Went for a walk."

"I see: you went for a walk? Past this pad? Is that it?"

"Thought I'd case the joint."

"Dear God," Alleyn said quietly.

"They copped me."

"That," said Alleyn, "is all I wanted to know. Sorry you've been troubled."

"Don't mention it," said Ricky faintly.

"Fox," Alleyn said. "We search. All of us."

"What about them?" Fox asked with a jerk of his head and an edge in his voice that Alleyn had never heard before: "Should we wire them up?"

"No," Alleyn said. "We shouldn't." And he

instructed Cribbage to double-handcuff Ferrant and
Syd, using the second pair of bracelets to link their free
hands together behind their backs. They were sat on
the floor with their shoulders to the wall. The search
began.

At the end of half an hour they had opened the
bottom ends of thirty tubes of paint and found capsules
in eighteen of them. Dollops of squeezed-out paint
neatly ornamented the table. Alleyn withdrew Fox into
the kitchen.

"Fair enough," he said. "We've got the corpus
delicti. What we don't know yet is the exact procedure.
Jones collected the paints in Saint Pierre but were they
already doctored or was he supplied with the capsules
and drugs and left to do the job himself? If the latter,
there must be evidence of it here."

"Stuff left over?"

"Yes. They were about to do a bolt, probably under
orders to hide any stuff they couldn't carry. And along
came my enterprising son, 'casing' as he puts it, 'the
joint.'"

"That," Fox murmured, "would put them about a
bit."

"Yes. What to do with him? Pull him in, which they
did. But if they held him, sooner or later we'd set up a
search. I imagine that they were in touch with Madame
F. through that nefarious kid. Well, in their fluster,
they hit on the not uningenious idea of using Rick as a
screen for their getaway. And if Mrs. Plank had not
been the golden lady she undoubtedly is, they might
well have brought it off. I wish to hell that bloody
quack would show up."

"I'm sure he'll be all right," said Fox, meaning
Ricky.

The meticulous search went on, inch by inch
through the littered room, under the bed, stereo table,
in the shelves and cupboards, and through heaps of

occulted junk. They were about to move into an unspeakable little bedroom at the back when Alleyn said: "While we were outside, before Ferrant came to the door, I heard a metallic sound. Very faint."

"In the house?"

"Yes. Did you?"

"I didn't catch it. No," said Fox.

"Let's try the kitchen. You two," he said to Cribbage and Moss, "carry on here." He took off his jacket and rolled up his sleeves.

The kitchen was in the same state of squalor as the rest of the Pad. Its most conspicuous feature was a large and decrepit coal range of an ancient make with a boiler and tap on one side of the grate and an oven on the other. It looked as if it were never used. On top of it was a small modern electric stove. Alleyn removed this to the table and started on the range. He lifted the iron rings and probed inside with a bent poker, listening to the sound. He opened the oven, played his torch around the interior, and tapped the lining. He had let down the front of the grate and lifted the top when Fox gave a grunt.

"What?" Alleyn asked.

"His personal supply. Syringe. Dope. It's 'horse' all right," said Fox, meaning heroin. "There's one tablet left."

"Where?"

"Top shelf of the dresser. Behind an old cookbook. Rather appropriate."

A siren sounded down on the front. "This'll be the ambulance," said Fox. "And the doctor. We hope."

When Alleyn didn't answer Fox turned and found him face down in the open top of the range. "There should be a cavity over the oven," he said, "and th isn't and—Yes. Surprise, surprise."

He began pulling. A flat object was edged into view. The siren sounded again and nearer.

"It *is* the ambulance," Alleyn said. "You get this lot out, Br'er Fox and no reward for guessing what's the prize."

He was back with Ricky before Fox had collected himself or anything else.

Ricky took a bleary look at his father and begged him in a stifled voice not to make him laugh.

"Why should you laugh?"

"When did you join the Black and White Minstrels? Your face. Oh God, I mustn't laugh."

Alleyn returned to the kitchen and looked at it in a cracked glass on the wall. The nose was black. He swabbed it with an unused bandage and again washed his hands. Fox had extracted a black attaché case from the stove and had forced the lock and opened it. "What's that lot worth on the street market?" he asked.

"Two thousand quid if a penny," said Alleyn and returned to his son. "We've got Jones's very own dope," he said, "and we've got the consignment in transit." He walked down the room to Ferrant and Jones seated in discomfort on the floor. "You heard that, I suppose," he said.

Ferrant, in his sharp suit and pink floral shirt, spat inaccurately at Alleyn. He had not spoken since his passage with Syd.

But Syd gazed up at Alleyn. He shivered and yawned and his nose ran. "Look," he said, "give me a fix. Just one. Look, I need it. I got to have it. Look—for God's sake." He suddenly screamed. "Give it to me. I'll tell you the lot. Get me a fix."

IV

Ricky was in the Montjoy hospital, having managed a fuller account of his misadventures before being given something to settle him down for the night.

At half-past two in the morning, the relentlessly lit charge room at Montjoy police station smelled of stale bodies, breath, and tobacco, with an elusive background of Jeyes fluid.

Ferrant, who had refused to talk without the advice of a solicitor, had been taken to the cells while the station sergeant tried to raise one. Syd Jones whimpered, suffered onsets of cramp, had to be taken to the lavatory, yawned, ran at the nose, and repeatedly pleaded for a fix. Dr. Carey, called in to watch, said that no harm would be done if the drug was withheld for the time being.

Everything that Jones said confirmed their guesswork. He even showed signs of a miserable sort of complacence over his ingenuity in the matter of the paint tubes. He admitted, as if it were of little account, that it was he who tried to drown Ricky at Saint Pierre.

On one point only he was obdurate: he could not or would not say anything about Louis Pharamond, contriving, when questioned, to recover something of his old intransigence.

"Him," he said. "Don't give me him!" and then looked frightened and would say no more about Louis Pharamond.

Alleyn said: "Why didn't you take the sorrel mare to the smith as you were told to? After you got back with the horse feed?"

Syd drove his fingers through his thicket of hair. "What are you on about now?" he moaned. "What's that got to do with anything? OK, OK, so I biked back to my pad, didn't I? So what?"

"To get yourself a fix?"

"Yeah. OK. Yeah."

For the twentieth time he got up and shambled about the room, stamping and grabbing at the calf of his leg. "I got cramp," he said. He fetched up in front of Fox. "I'll have it in for you lot the way you're treating me. Sadists. Fascist pigs."

"Don't be silly," said Fox.

Syd appealed to Dr. Carey. "Doc," he said. "You'll look after me. Won't you, doc? You got to, haven't you? For Christ's sake, doc."

"You'll have to hang on a bit longer," said Dr. Carey and glanced at Alleyn. Syd broke down completely and wept.

Alleyn said: "Give him what he needs."

"Really?"

"Yes. Really."

Doctor Carey went out of the room.

Syd, fingering his beard and biting his dirty fingers, let out a kind of laugh. "I couldn't help it, could I?" he gabbled and looked sideways at Alleyn who had turned away from him and didn't reply.

"It was Gil used the wire on him, not me," Syd said to Alleyn's back.

Fox walked over to Plank who throughout the long hours had taken notes. Fox leaned over him and turned the pages back.

"Is this correct?" he asked Syd. "What you've deposed about the wire? Where you got it and what you wanted it for?"

"I've said so, haven't I? Yes. Yes. Yes. For the picture."

"Why won't you talk about Mr. Louis Pharamond?"

"There's nothing to say."

"Who's the next above Ferrant? Who gives the orders?"

"I don't know. I've told you. Where's the doc? Where's he gone?"

"He'll be here," said Fox. "You'll get your fix if you'll talk about your boss. And I don't mean Harkness. I mean who gives the orders. Is it Louis Pharamond?"

"I can't. I can't. They'd knock me off. I would if I could. They'd get me. Honest. I can't." Syd returned to his chair and wept.

Without turning around Alleyn said: "Let it be, Fox."

Doctor Carey came back with a prepared syringe and a swab. Syd with a trembling hand pushed up his sleeve.

"Good God," said the doctor, "you've been making a mess of yourself, haven't you?" He gave the injection.

The reaction was instantaneous. It was a metamorphosis—as if Syd's entire person thawed and re-formed into a blissful transfiguration of itself. He lolled back in his chair and giggled. "Fantastic," he said.

Doctor Carey watched him for a moment and then joined Alleyn at the far end of the room.

"He's well away," he said. "He's had ten milligrams and he's full of well-being: the classic euphoria. You've seen for yourselves what the withdrawal symptoms can be like."

Alleyn said: "May I put a hypothetical case to you? There may be no answer to it. It may be just plain silly."

"We can give it a go," said Dr. Carey.

"Suppose, on the afternoon of Dulcie Harkness's death, having taken himself off to his Pad he treated himself to an injection of heroin. Is it within the bounds of possibility that he could return on his motorbike to Leathers, help himself to a length of wire from the stables, rig it across the gap in the fence, wait until Dulcie Harkness was dying or dead, remove the wire, and return to his Pad? To reappear on his bike, apparently in full control of himself, later on in the evening?"

Doctor Carey was silent for some time. Syd Jones had begun to hum, tunelessly, under his breath.

Carey said at last, "Frankly I don't know how to answer you. Since my time in the casualty ward at Saint Luke's I've had no experience of drug addiction. I know symptoms vary widely from case to case. You'd do better to consult a specialist."

"You wouldn't rule it out altogether?"

"For what it's worth—I don't think I'd do that. Quite."

"I'll get that bugger," Syd Jones announced happily. "I'll bloody well get him."

"What bugger?" Fox asked.

"That'd be telling. Think I'd let you in? You got to be joking, Big Fuzz."

"About my son?" Alleyn asked Dr. Carey.

"Ah yes, of course. He's settled down nicely."

"Yes?"

"He'll be all right. There's been quite a bit of pain and considerable shock. He's had something that'll help him sleep. And routine injections against tetanus and so on. The cuts around the ankles were nasty. We'd like to keep him under observation."

"Thank you," Alleyn said. "I'll tell his mother."

"Of course I'm completely in the dark," said Dr. Carey. "Or nearly so. But, damn it all, I *am* supposed to be the police surgeon round here. And there *is* an adjourned inquest coming up."

"My dear chap," said Alleyn, "I know, and I'm sorry. You shall hear all. In the meantime what shall we do with this specimen?"

Syd Jones, gloomily surveyed by Fox, laughed, talked incomprehensibly, and drifted into song.

"You won't get any sense out of him. I'd put him in the cells and have him supervised. He'll go to sleep sooner or later," said Dr. Carey.

Syd was removed, laughing heartily as he went. Fox went out to arrange for a constable to sit in his cell until he fell asleep, and Alleyn, who now felt as if he'd been hauled through a mangle, pulled himself together and gave Dr. Carey a succinct account of the case as it had developed. They sat on the hideously uncomfortable wall bench. It was now ten minutes past three in the morning. The station sergeant came in with cups of strong tea: the third brew since they'd arrived, five hours ago.

Doctor Carey said: "No thanks, I'm for my bed." He stood up, stretched, held out his hand, and was professionally alerted. "You look done up," he said. "Not surprising. Will you get off now?"

"Oh yes. Yes, I expect so."

"Where are you staying?"

"At the Montjoy."

"Like anything to help you sleep?"

"Lord, no," said Alleyn, "I'd drop off in a gravel pit. Nice of you to offer, though. Good night."

He went to bed at his hotel, fell instantly and profoundly asleep and, having ordered breakfast in his room at seven-thirty and arranged with himself to wake at seven, did so and put in a call to his wife. It went through at once.

"That's your waking-up voice," he said.

"Never mind. Is anything the matter?"

"There was but it's all right now."

"Ricky?"

"Need you ask? But darling, repeat, it's all right now. I promise."

"Tell me."

He told her.

"When's the first plane?" Troy asked.

"Nine-twenty from Heathrow. You transfer at Saint Pierre-des-Roches."

"Right."

"Hotel Montjoy and George VI Hospital."

"Rory, say if you'd rather I didn't. You will, won't you?"

"I'd rather you did but God knows where I'll be when you get here. We may well blow up for a crisis."

"Could you book a room?"

"I could. This one."

"Right. I'll be in it."

Troy hung up. Alleyn rang up the hospital and was told Ricky had enjoyed a fairly comfortable night and was improving. He bathed, dressed, ate his breakfast, and was about to call the hotel office when the telephone rang again. He expected it would be Fox and was surprised and not overjoyed to hear Julia Pharamond's voice.

"Good morning," said Julia. She spoke very quietly and sounded harried and unlike herself. "I'm very sorry indeed to bother you and at such a ghastly hour. I wouldn't have, only we're in trouble and I—well, Jasper and I—thought we'd better."

"What's the matter?"

"And Carlotta agrees."

"Carlotta does?"

"Yes. I don't want," Julia whispered piercingly into the mouthpiece, "to talk down the telephone. *A cause des domestiques*. Damn, I'd forgotten they speak French."

"Can you give me an inkling?"

After a slight pause Julia said in a painstakingly casual voice. "Louis."

"I'll come at once," said Alleyn.

He called Fox up. On his way out, while Fox rang Plank, Alleyn left the L'Esperance number at the hotel office, ordered a taxi to meet Troy's plane, and booked her in. "And you might get flowers for the room. Lilies of the valley if you can."

"How many?" asked the grand lady at Reception.

"Lots," said Alleyn. "Any amount."

The lady smiled indulgently and handed him a letter. It had just been sent in from the police station, she said. It was addressed to him. The writing was erratic. There was much crossing out and some omissions, but on the whole he thought it rather more coherent than might have been expected. It was written on printed note paper with a horse's head printed in one corner.

Sir.

I am in possession of certain facts—in re slaying of
my niece—and been guided to make All Known
Before The People since they sit heavy on my
conscience. Therefore on Sunday next (please see
enclosure) I will proclaim All to the multitude the
Lord of Hosts sitteth on my tongue and He Will
Repay. The Sinner will be called an Abomination
before the Lord and before His People. Amen. I
will be greatly obliged if you will be kind enough
to attend.

> With compliments
> Yrs. etc. etc.
> C. Harkness
> (Brother Cuth)

He showed the letter together with the enclosure, a new
pamphlet, to Fox, who read it when they had set off in
Superintendent Curie's car.

"He doesn't half go on, does he?" said Fox. "Do you
make out he thinks he knows who chummy is?"

"That's how I read it."

"What'll we do about this service affair?"

"Attend in strength."

They drove on in silence. The morning was clear and
warm; the channel sparkled and the Normandy coast
looked as if it were half its actual distance away.

"What do you reckon Mr. L. Pharamond's been up
to?" asked Fox.

"I'll give you one guess."

"Skedaddled?"

"Skedaddled. And if we'd known, how could we have
stopped him?"

"We could have kept him under obbo," Fox mused.

"But couldn't have prevented him lighting out.
Well, could we? Under what pretext? Seen conversing
with G. Ferrant at one o'clock in the morning?

Query—involved in drug running? Dropped a sleeve
button in the horse paddock at Leathers. Had
previously denied going into horse paddock. Now says
he forgot. End of information. Query—murderer
Dulcie Harkness? He wouldn't be able to keep a
straight face over that lot, Br'er Fox."

Up at L'Esperance they found Jasper waiting on the
terrace. Alleyn introduced Fox. Jasper, though clearly
surprised that he had come, was charming. He led them
to a table and a group of chairs, canopied and
overlooking the sea.

"Julia's coming down in a minute," he said. "We
thought we'd like to see you first. Will you have coffee?
And things? We're going to. It's our breakfast."

It was already set out, with croissants and brioches
on the table. It smelled superb. When Alleyn accepted,
Fox did too.

"It really is extemely odd," Jasper continued,
heaping butter and honey on a croissant. "And very
worrying. Louis has completely vanished. Here comes
Julia."

Out of the house she hurried in a white trouser suit
and ran down the steps to them with her hands
extended. Fox was drinking coffee. He rose to his feet
and was slightly confused.

"How terribly kind of you both to come," said Julia.
"No, *too* kind. When one knows you're being so active
and fussed. How's Ricky?"

"In hospital," said Alleyn, shaking hands.

"*No!* Because of his black eye?"

"Partly. Could we hear about Louis?"

"Hasn't Jasper said? He's vanished. Into thin air."

"Since when?"

Jasper, whose mouth was full, waved his wife on.

"Since yesterday," said Julia. "You remember
yesterday morning when he was as large as life in his
zoot suit and talked to you on the front? In the Cove?"

"I remember," Alleyn said.

"Yes. Well, we drove back here for luncheon. And when we got here, he sort of clapped his hand to his brow and said he'd forgotten to send a business cable to Lima and it was important and he'd have to attend to it. Louis has—what does one call them?—in Peru."

Jasper said: "Business interests. We came originally from Peru. But he's the only one of us to have any business links. He's jolly rich, old Louis is."

"Well, then," said Julia. "He often has to ring up Lima or cable to it. They're not very clever at the Cove about cables in Spanish or long distance calls to Peru. So he goes into Montjoy. At first we thought he'd probably lunched there."

"Did you see him again before he left?"

"No. We were at luncheon," said Julia.

"We heard him come downstairs and start his car. Now I come to think of it," said Jasper, "it was some little time after we'd sat down."

"Have you looked to see if he's taken anything with him—an overnight bag for instance?"

"Yes," said Julia, "but not a penny the wiser are we. Louis has so many zoot suits and silken undies and pajamas and terribly doggy pieces of luggage that one couldn't tell. Even Carlotta couldn't. She's still looking."

"What else have you done about it?" asked Alleyn. He thought of his own gnawing anxieties during Ricky's disappearance and wondered if Carlotta, for example, suffered anything comparable; Jasper and Julia, though worried, clearly did not.

"Well," Julia was saying, "for a long time we didn't do anything. We'd expected him simply to whiz into Montjoy, send his cable, and whiz back. Then when he didn't we supposed he'd decided to lunch at the Montjoy and perhaps stay the night. He often does that when the little girls get too much for him. But he *always* rings up to tell us. When he didn't ring and didn't come back for dinner Carlotta telephoned the hotel and he

hadn't been there at all. And still we haven't had sniff
nor sight of him."

"I even rang the pub at Belle Vue," said Jasper.

"What about his car?"

"We rang the park where he always leaves it and it's
there. He clocked in about twenty minutes after he left
here."

"The thing that really is pretty bothering," Julia
said, "is that he was in a peculiar sort of state yesterday
morning. After we left you. We wondered if you
noticed anything."

Alleyn gave himself a moment's respite. He thought
of Louis: overelegant, overfacetious, giving his
performance on the front. "How do you mean:
'peculiar'?" he asked.

"For him, very quiet, and at the same time, *I* felt he
was in a rage. You mustn't mind my asking, but did you
have words, the two of you?"

"No."

"I only wondered. He wouldn't say anything about
being grilled by you and didn't seem to enjoy my calling
it that—I was just being funnyman. You know? But he
didn't relish it. So I wondered."

"Was that why you asked me to come?"

Jasper said: "What we really hoped you'd do is give
us some advice about what action we could take. One
doesn't want to make a sort of public display but at the
same time one can't just loll about in the sun supposing
that he'll come bouncing back."

"Has he ever done anything of this sort before?"

Julia and Jasper spoke simultaneously. "Not like
this," said Jasper. "Not exactly," said Julia.

They looked at Fox and away.

Fox said: "I wonder if I could be excused, Mrs.
Pharamond? We started a slow puncture on the way
up. If I'm not required at the moment, sir, perhaps, I
should change the wheel?"

"Would you, Fox? We'll call out if we need you."

Fox rose. "A very enjoyable cup of coffee," he said with a slight bow in Julia's direction and descended the steps to the lower terrace where the car was parked. It was just as well, thought Alleyn, that it was out of sight.

"Not true!" said Julia with wide-open eyes. "My dear! The tact! Have you many like that?"

"We have a finishing school," said Alleyn, "at the C.I.D."

Jasper said: "Answering your question. No, Louis, as Julia said, always lets us know if he's going to be away unexpectedly."

"Is he often away? 'Unexpectedly'?"

"Well—"

Julia burst out. "Oh let's not be cagey and difficult, darling. After all we asked the poor man to come so why shuffle and snuffle when he wants to know about things? Yes, Louis does quite often leave us for reasons undisclosed and probably not very respectable. He can't keep his hands off the ladies."

"Julia! *Darling!*"

"And *what* ladies some of them are. But then, it appears that Louis bowls them over like ninepins and has only to show himself at a casino in Lima for them to swarm. This we find puzzling. Perhaps he's been hijacked and taken away for a sort of gentlemanly white-slave trade, to be offered to sex-starved senoritas. Which would really suit him very well as he could combine their pleasure with his business."

"No, honestly," Jasper protested and giggled.

"Darling, admit. You're not all that keen on him yourself. But we do love Carlotta, *very* dearly," said Julia, "and we've got sort of inoculated to Louis like one does with sandflies, blood being thicker than water as far as Jasper is concerned."

Jasper said: "What steps *do* you think we should take?"

Alleyn found it odd to repeat the advice that he and Fox had offered each other yesterday. He said they could report Louis's disappearance to the police now or wait a little longer. He thought he would advise the latter course.

"Have you," he said, "looked to see if his papers—passport and medical certificates and so on—are in his room? You say he often makes business trips to Peru. Isn't it just possible that something cropped up—say a cable—calling him there on urgent business and that you'll get a radiogram to this effect?"

Jasper and Julia looked at each other and shook their heads. Alleyn was trying to remember in which South American countries extradition orders could be operated.

"Speaking as a policeman," said Julia, "which it's so difficult to remember you are, would the Force be very bored if asked to take a hand? I mean, busy as you all seem to be over the Harness affair? Wouldn't they think Louis's ongoings of no account?"

"No," Alleyn said. "They wouldn't think that."

A stillness came over the three. Jasper, who had reached out to the coffeepot, withdrew his hand. He looked very hard at Alleyn and then at his wife.

Julia said: "Is there something you know and we don't? About Louis?"

Carlotta came out of the house and down the steps. She was very pale, even for a Pharamond. She came to the table and sat down as if she needed to.

"I've made a discovery," she said. "Louis's passport and his attaché case and the file he always takes when he goes to Lima are missing. I forced open the drawer in his desk. So I imagine, don't you," said Carlotta, "that he's walked out on me?"

"You sound as if you're not surprised," said Julia.

"Nor am I. He's been precarious for quite a time. You've seen it, haven't you? You must have." They were silent. "I always knew, of course," Carlotta said, "that by and large you thought him pretty ghastly. But there you are. I have a theory that quite a lot of women require a touch of the bounder in their man. I'm one of them. So, true to type, he's bounded away."

Jasper said: "Carla, darling, aren't you rushing your fences a bit? After all, we don't know why he's gone. If he's gone."

Julia said: "I've got a feeling that Roderick, if we're still allowed to call him that, knows. And I don't believe he thinks it's anything to do with you, Carla." She turned to Alleyn. "Am I right?" she asked.

Alleyn said slowly: "If you mean do I know definitely he's gone, I don't. I've no information at all as to his recent movements."

"He's in trouble, though. Isn't he? It's best we should all realize. Really."

"What's he done?" Carlotta demanded. "He has done something, hasn't he? I've known he was up to something. I can always tell."

Jasper said with an unfamiliar note in his voice: "I think we'd better remember, girls, that we are talking, however much we may like him, to a policeman."

"Oh dear. I suppose we should," Julia agreed and sounded vexed rather than alarmed. "I suppose we must turn cagey and evasive and he'll set traps for us and when we fall into them he'll say things like 'I didn't know but you've just told me.' They always do that. Don't you?" she asked Alleyn.

"I don't fancy it's going to be my morning for aphorisms," he said.

"Somehow," Julia mused, "I've always thought—you won't mind my saying, Carla darling? I prefer to be open—I've always thought Louis was a tiny bit the absconding type."

Carlotta looked thoughtfully at her. "Have you?" she said as if her attention had been momentarily caught. "Well, it looks as though you're right. Or doesn't it?" she added turning to Alleyn.

He stood up. The three of them contemplated him with an air of—what? Polite interest? Concern? One would have said no more than that, if it had not been for Carlotta's pallor, the slightest tremor in Jasper's hand as he put down his coffee cup, and—in Julia?— the disappearance, as if by magic, of her immense vitality.

"I think," Alleyn said, "that in a situation which for me, if not for you, poses a problem, I'll have to spill the beans. The not very delicious beans. As you say, I'm a policeman. I'm what is known as an 'investigating officer' and if something dubious crops up I've got to investigate it. That is why I'm here, on the island. Now, such is the nature of the investigation that anybody doing a bolt for no discernible reason becomes somebody the police want to see. Your cousin is now somebody I want to see."

After a long silence Jasper said: "I don't like your chances."

"Nor do I, much."

"I suppose we aren't to know what you want to see him about?"

"I've gone further than I should already."

Carlotta said: "It's not about that girl, is it? Oh God, it's not about her?"

"It's no good, Carla," Julia said and put her arm round Carlotta. "Obviously, he's not going to tell you." She looked at Alleyn and the ghost of her dottiness revisited her. "And we actually asked you to come and help us," she said. "It's like the flies asking the spider to walk into their parlor, isn't it?"

"Alas!" said Alleyn. "It is, a bit. I'm sorry."

The child Selina appeared on the steps from the house. She descended them in jumps with her feet together.

"Run away, darling," her parents said in unison.

Selina continued to jump.

"Selina," said her father. "What did we tell you?"

She accomplished the final jump. "I can't," she said.

"Nonsense," said her mother. "Why can't you?"

"I got a message."

"A message? What message? Tell us later and run away now."

"It's on the telephone. I answered it."

"Why on earth couldn't you say so?"

"For him," said Selina. She pointed at Alleyn and made a face.

Julia said automatically: "Don't do that and don't point at people. It's for you," she said to Alleyn.

"Thank you, Selina," he said. "Will you show me the way?"

"Okey-dokey-pokey," said Selina, and seized him by the wrist.

"You see?" Julia appealed to Alleyn. "Quite awful!"

"One is helpless," said Jasper.

As they ascended the steps Selina repeated her jumping technique, retaining her hold on Alleyn's wrist. When they were halfway up she said: "Cousin Louis is a dirty old man."

Alleyn, nonplussed, gazed down at her. In her baleful way Selina was a pretty child.

"Why do you talk like that?" he temporized.

"What *is* a dirty old man?" asked Selina.

"Father Christmas in a chimney."

"You're cuckoo." She slid her hand into his and adopted a normal manner of ascent. "Anyway," she said, "Louis says he is."

"What do you mean?"

"Louis Ferrant says his mother says Cousin Louis is a D.O.M."

"Do you know Louis Ferrant?"

"Nanny knows his mother. We meet them in the village. 'Ie's bigger than me. He says things."

"What sort of things?"

"I forget," said Selina and looked uncomfortable. "I don't think Louis Ferrant's an awfully good idea," Alleyn said. He hoisted Selina up to his shoulder. She gave a shriek of pleasure and they entered the house.

It was Plank on the telephone.

"I thought you'd like to know, sir," he said. "They've rung through from Montjoy. Jones wants to bargain."

"He does? What's he offering?"

"As far as we can make out, info on Dulcie. He won't talk to anyone but you. He's drying out and in a funny mood."

"I'll come."

"One other thing, Mr. Alleyn. Mr. Harkness rang up. He's on about this service affair tomorrow. He's very keen on everybody attending it. There was a lot of stuff about Vengeance Is Mine Saith the Lord and the book of Leviticus. He said he's been guided to make known before the multitude the sinner in Israel."

"Oh, yes?"

"Yes. Something about it being revealed to him in a dream. He sounded very wild."

"Drunk?"

"Damn near DTs, I reckon."

"Do you suppose there'll be a large attendance?"

"Yes," said Plank, "I do. There's a lot of talk about it. He's sent some dirty big announcements to the pub and the shop."

"Sent them? By whom?"

"The delivery boy from the Cod-and-Bottle. Mr. Harkness was very upset when I told him Jones and Ferrant wouldn't be able to be present. He said the Lord would smite the police hip and thigh and cast them into eternal fires if Jones and Ferrant didn't attend the meeting. Particularly Jones. He's far gone, sir."

"So it would seem. We'll have to go to his party, of course. But first things first, Plank, and that means Jones. Is there anything to keep you in the Cove?"

"No, sir. I've informed Mrs. Ferrant her husband's

in custody and will come before the court on Monday."

"How did she take that?"

"She never said a word but, my oath, she looked at me old-fashioned."

"I daresay. I'll get down as soon as I can," said Alleyn and hung up.

When he came out of the house he found the Pharamonds still sitting around the table. They were not speaking and looked as if they had been that way ever since he left.

He went over to them. Jasper stood up.

"That was Sergeant Plank," Alleyn said. "I'm wanted. I wish I could tell you how sorry I am that things have fallen out as they have."

"Not your fault," said Julia. "Or ours if it comes to that. We're what's called victims of circumstance. Why's Ricky in hospital?"

"He was beaten up."

"Not—?" Carlotta broke out.

"No, no. By Gil Ferrant and Syd Jones. They come up before the beak tomorrow. Rick's all right."

Julia said: "Poorest Ricky, what a time he's having! Give him our love."

"I will, indeed," said Alleyn.

"Of course, if Louis should turn up, the Pharamonds, however boring the exercise, will close their ranks."

"Of course."

"And I with them. Because it behooves me so to do." She reached out her hand to Carlotta who took it. "But then again," she said, "I'm not a Pharamond. I'm a Lamprey. I think, ages ago, you met some of my relations."

"I believe I did," said Alleyn.

9

Storm Over

I

"BACK TO SQUARE ONE," Alleyn thought when they
brought Sydney Jones before him, once again
exhibiting all the unlovely symptoms of the deprived
addict. Doctor Carey had evidently not been overgen-
erous with the dosage.

He began at once to say he would only talk to Alleyn
and wouldn't have any witnesses in the room.

"It won't make any difference, you silly chap," Fox
said with a low degree of accuracy. But Syd knew a
thing worth two of that, and stuck to it.

In the end Fox and Alleyn exchanged glances and
Fox went away.

Syd said: "You going to fix me up?"

"Not without the doctor's approval."

"I've got something I can tell you. About Dulce. It'd make a difference."

"What is it?"

"Oh, no!" said Syd. "Oh dear me no! Fair's fair."

"If you can give me information that will lead substantially to a charge, the fact that you did so and did it of your own accord would be taken into consideration. If it turns out to be something that we could get from another source—Ferrant, for instance—"

Syd with a kind of febrile intensity let fling a stream of obscenities. It emerged that Syd now laid all his woes at Ferrant's door. It was Ferrant who had introduced him to hard-line drugs, Ferrant who established Syd's link with Jerome et Cie, Ferrant who egged him on to follow Ricky about the streets in Saint Pierre-des-Roches, Ferrant who kidnapped Ricky and brought him into the Pad.

"And this information you say you have, is about Ferrant, is it?" Alleyn asked.

"If they got on to it I'd shopped him, they'd get me."

"Who would?"

"Them. Him. Up there."

"Are you talking about Mr. Louis Pharamond?"

"*Mister. Mister* Philistine. *Mister* Bloody Fascist Sod Pharamond. You don't know," Syd said, "why I wanted that wire. Well? Do you?"

"To hang a picture."

"That's right. Because she said it gave her a feeling that I've got a strong sense of rhythm. That's what she said."

"This," Alleyn thought, "is the unfairest thing that has ever happened to me."

He said: "Get back to what you can tell me. Is it about Ferrant?"

"More or less that's what she said," Syd mumbled.

"Ferrant!" Alleyn insisted and could have shouted it. "What about Ferrant?"

"What'll I get for it? For assault?"

"It depends on the magistrates. You can have a solicitor and a barrister to defend you."

"Will *he* get longer? Seeing he laid it all on? Gil?"

"Possibly. If you can satisfy the court that he did."

Syd wiped the back of his hand across his face. "Not like that," he said, "not in front of him. In court. Not on your Nelly."

"Why not?"

"They'd get me," he said.

"Who would?"

"Them. The organization. That lot."

Alleyn moved away from him. "Make up your mind," he said and looked at his watch. "I can't give you much longer."

"I never wanted to do him over. I never meant to make it tough. You know? Tying him up with the wire and that. It was Gil."

"For the last time: if you have something to say about Ferrant, say it."

"I want a fix."

"Say it."

Syd bit his fingers, wiped his nose, blinked, and with a travesty of pulling himself together cleared his throat and whispered:

"Gil did it."

"Did what?"

"Did her. Dulce."

And then as if he'd turned himself on like a tap he poured out his story.

Dulcie Harkness, he said, had found out about the capsules in the paint tubes. It had happened one night when she was "going with" Syd. It might have been the night he took Ricky to the Pad. Yes—it was that night. Before they arrived she had taken it into her head to tidy up the paint table and had come across a tube that

was open at the wrong end. When Ricky had gone she
had pointed it out to Syd. Alleyn gathered that this
rattled Syd. He told her it was because the cap had
jammed. Dulcie had unscrewed the cap with ease and
"got nosey." Syd had lost his temper—he was, he said,
by that time high on grass. There was a fine old scene
between them and she'd left the Pad saying she
expected to be made an honest woman by him. Or else.

After that she kept on at him both before and after
his trip to London. Her uncle was giving her hell and
she wanted to cut loose and the shortest route to that
desired end, she argued, was a visit to the registry office
with Syd. By this time, it emerged, she was "going with
somebody else" and threatened to talk.

"Do you mean to Louis Pharamond?"

Never mind who. She got Syd so worried he'd
confided in Gil Ferrant and Gil had gone crook, Syd
said, revealing his antipodean origin. Gil had taken it
very seriously indeed. He'd tackled Dulcie, trying to
scare her with threats about what would happen to her
if she talked, but she laughed at him and said two could
play at that game.

That was the situation on the morning before the
accident. When he returned from his trip to the corn
chandler Syd found Ferrant lurking around the
stables. He had driven up in his car. Alleyn heard with
surprise that Mrs. Ferrant had been with him. It
appeared that she did the fine laundering for
L'Esperance and they had called there to deliver it.
Ferrant said that within the next few days he was going
over to Saint Pierre under orders from above and Syd
was to hold himself in readiness to follow. To collect a
consignment. Ferrant wanted to know how Dulcie was
behaving herself. Syd gave him an account of the fence-
jumping incident, her threat to try it herself, and the
subsequent row with her uncle.

Ferrant had asked where she was and Syd had said
up in her room but that wouldn't be for long. She'd

broken out before and she would again and if he knew anything about her she'd take the mare over the jump.

"Where," Alleyn asked, "was her uncle at this time?"

In his office, writing hellfire pamphlets, Syd supposed. And where was the sorrel mare? In her loose-box. And Mrs. Ferrant? She remained in the car.

"Go on."

Well, Ferrant supplied Syd with dope, and he'd brought a packet, and he said why didn't Syd doss down somewhere and do himself a favor. He was friendlier than Syd had known him since the row over Dulcie. They were in the old coach house at the time and Syd noticed how Ferrant looked around at everything.

Well. So Syd had said he didn't mind if he did. He went into one of the unoccupied loose-boxes where he settled himself down on the clean straw and shot up.

The next thing he could be sure about was that it was quite a lot later in the afternoon. He pulled himself together and went into the coach house where he had parked his bike. It was then that he noticed the length of wire that had been newly cut from the main coil. He thought it would do for hanging pictures and he took it. He then remembered he was supposed to take the sorrel mare to the smith. He looked in her loose-box but she wasn't there. It was too late to do anything about it now so he biked down to the cliffs. After a time he got around to wondering what had gone on at Leathers. He returned there and met Ricky and Jasper Pharamond who told him about Dulcie.

Here Syd came to a stop. He gazed at Alleyn and pulled at his beard.

"Well," Alleyn said, "is that all?"

"All! God, it's everything. He did it. I know. I could tell, the way he carried on afterward when I talked about it. He was pleased with himself. You could tell."

At this point Syd became hysterical. He swore that if they put him in the witness-box he wouldn't say a

word about heroin or against Ferrant because if he did
he'd "be in for it." It was for Alleyn to follow up the
information he'd given him but he, Syd, wasn't going
to be made a monkey of. It was remarkable that
however frantic he became he never mentioned
Ferrant's name or alluded to him in any way without
lowering his voice, as if Ferrant might overhear him.
But when he pleaded for his fix he became vociferous
and at last began to scream.

Alleyn said he'd ask Dr. Carey to look at Syd and
saw him taken back to his cell.

Fox came back into the room. "What d'you make of
all that, Mr. Alleyn?" he asked. "Cooked up, would
you say, to incriminate Ferrant?"

"Hard to tell, but I wouldn't think entirely cooked
up."

"All this stuff about Ferrant being *nicer* to him?"

"He would be nicer, Br'er Fox, if he needed Syd to
pick up a consignment. He wouldn't want to goad him
to a point where he refused to cooperate."

"I suppose not," Fox grunted, discontentedly.

He and Alleyn then called on Gil Ferrant and were
received with a great show of insolence. Ferrant
lounged on his bed. He still wore his sharp French suit
and pink shirt but they were greatly disheveled and he
had an overnight beard. He chewed gum with his
mouth open and looked them up and down through
half-shut eyes. Almost, Alleyn thought, he preferred
Syd.

"Good morning," he said.

Ferrant raised his eyebrows, stretched elaborately,
and yawned.

"No doubt," Alleyn said, "it's been explained to you
that you haven't much hope of avoiding a conviction
and the maximum sentence. If you plead guilty you
may get off with less. Do you want to make a
statement?"

Ferrant shook his head slowly from side to side and

made a great thing of shifting the wad of gum.

"Advised not to," he drawled.

Alleyn said: "We've found enough heroin at Jones's place to send you up for years."

Ferrant said, "That's his affair."

"And yours. Believe me, yours."

"No comment," he said and shut his eyes.

"You're out on a limb," said Alleyn. "Your master's cleared off. Did you know that?"

Ferrant didn't open his eyes but the lids quivered.

"You'd do better to cooperate," Fox advised.

Ferrant, still lolling on the bed, opened his eyes and looked at Alleyn. "And how's Daddy's Baby Boy this morning?" he asked and smiled as he chewed.

In the silence that followed this quip Alleyn, as if desire could actually change place with action, saw—almost felt—his fist drive into the bristled chin. His fingernails bit into his palm. He looked at Fox, whose neck seemed to have swollen and whose face was red.

A long-forgotten phrase from *Little Dorrit* came into Alleyn's mind: "Count five-and-twenty, Tattycoram." He had actually begun to count the seconds in his head when Plank came in to say he was wanted on the telephone by Mrs. Pharamond. In the passage he said to Plank, "Ferrant won't talk. Mr. Fox is having a go. Take your notebook."

Plank, after a startled glance at him, went off.

When Alleyn spoke to Julia she sounded much more like her usual self.

"What luck!" said Julia. "I rang the Cove station and a nice lady said you might be where you are. It's to tell you Carlotta's had a message from Louis. Are you pleased? We are."

"Am I to hear what it is?"

"It's a picture postcard of the Montjoy hotel. Someone has written in a teeny-weeny hand: 'Picked up in street' and it's very grubby. It says 'Everything

OK. Writing. L.,' and it's addressed, of course, to Carla: Would you like to know how we interpret it?"

"Very much."

"We think Louis has flown to Peru. I, for one, hope he stays there and so I bet, between you and me and the gatepost, does Carlotta. He was becoming altogether too *difficile*. But *wasn't* it kind of whoever it was to fish the card out of some gutter and pop it in the post?"

"Very kind. Can you read the postmark? The time?"

"Wait a sec. No, I can't. There's muddy smudge all over it."

"Will you let me see it?"

"Not," said Julia promptly, "if it'll help you haul him back. But we thought it only fair to let you know about it."

"Thank you," Alleyn said.

"So we're all feeling relieved and in good heart for Mr. Harkness's party tomorrow. I suppose poorest Ricky won't attend, will he? How boring for him to be in hospital. We're going to see him. After the party so as to tell him all about it. He's allowed visitors, I hope?"

"Oh yes. His mother's arriving today."

"Troy! But how too exciting! *Jasper*," screamed Julia. "Troy's coming to see Ricky." Alleyn heard Jasper exclaiming buoyantly in the background.

"I must go, I'm afraid," Alleyn said into the receiver. "Thank you for telling me about the postcard."

"You aren't at all huffy, I suppose? You sound like Ricky when he's huffy."

"A fat lot of good it would do me if I was. Oh, by the way, does Mrs. Ferrant do your laundry?"

"The fine things. Tarty blouses. Frills and pleats. Special undies. She's a wizard with the iron. Like Mrs. Tiggywinkle. Why?"

"Does she collect and deliver?"

"We usually drop and collect. Why?"

"I must fly. Thank you so much."

"Wait a bit. Do you suppose Louis dropped the postcard on purpose so that we wouldn't get it until he'd skedaddled?"

"The idea does occur, doesn't it? Goodbye."

On the way to the cove he reflected that a great many people in the Pharamonds' boots would be secretly enchanted to get rid of Louis but only the Pharamonds would loudly say so.

II

"First stop, Madame Ferrant," said Alleyn as they drove into Deep Cove. "I want you both to come in with me. I don't fancy the lady is easily unseated but we'll give it a go."

She opened the door to them. Her head was neatly tied up in a black handkerchief. She was implacably aproned and her sleeves were rolled up. Her face, normally sallow, was perhaps more so than usual and this circumstance lent emphasis to her eyes.

"Good morning," she said.

Alleyn introduced Fox and produced the ostensible reason for the call. He would pack up his son's effects and, of course, settle his bill. Perhaps she would be kind enough to make it out.

"It is already prepared," said Mrs. Ferrant and showed them into the parlor. She opened a drawer in a small bureau and produced her account. Alleyn paid and she receipted it.

"Madame will understand," Alleyn said in French, "that under the circumstances it would regrettably be unsuitable for my son to remain."

"*Parfaitement*," said Mrs. Ferrant.

"Especially since the injuries from which he suffers were inflicted by madame's husband."

Not a muscle of her face moved.

"You have, of course," Alleyn went on, changing to English, "been informed of his arrest. You will probably be required to come before the court on Monday."

"I have nothing to say."

"Nevertheless, madame, you will be required to attend."

She slightly inclined her head.

"In the meantime, if you wish to see your husband you will be permitted to do so."

"I have no desire to see him."

"No?"

"No."

"I should perhaps explain that although he has been arrested on a charge of assault there may well follow a much graver accusation: trading in illicit drugs."

"As to that, it appears to me to be absurd," said Mrs. Ferrant.

"Oh, madame, I think not. May I remind you of your son's errands last night? To and from the premises occupied by Sydney Jones? Where your husband and Jones handled a consignment of heroin and where, with your connivance, they planned their escape?"

"I know nothing of all this. Nothing. My boy is a mere child."

"In years, no doubt," said Alleyn politely.

She remained stony.

"Tell me," Alleyn said, "how long have you known the real object of your husband's trips to Marseilles and the Côte d'Azur?"

"I don't know what you mean."

"Are they for pleasure? Do you accompany him?"

She gave a slight snort.

"A little romance, perhaps?"

She looked disgusted.

"To take a job?"

She was silent.

"Plumbing?" Alleyn hinted, and after another

fruitless pause: "Ah, well, at least he sends postcards. To let you know where he is to be found if anything urgent crops up, no doubt."

She began to count the money he had put on the table.

"There is another small matter," he said, "on which I think you can help us. Will you be so kind as to carry your memory back to the day on which Dulcie Harkness was murdered."

She put her hands behind her back—suddenly, as if to hide them—and made to adjust her apron strings. "Murdered?" she said. "There has been no talk of murder."

"There has, however, been talk. On that day, late in the morning, did you and your husband visit Leathers?"

Her mouth was a tight line, locked across her face.

"Madame," said Alleyn, "why are you so unwilling to speak? It may be I should not have used the word you object to. It may be that the 'accident' *was* an accident. In order to settle it, either way, we welcome any information, however trivial, about the situation at Leathers on that morning. We understand you and your husband called there. Why should you make such a great matter of this visit? Was it connected with your husband's business activities abroad?"

A metaphysician might, however fancifully, have said of Mrs. Ferrant that her body, at this moment, "thought," so still did she hold it and so deeply did it breathe. Alleyn saw the pulse beating at the base of her neck. He wondered if there was to be a sudden rage.

But no: she unlocked her mouth and achieved composure.

"I am sorry," she said. "You will understand that I have had a shock and am, perhaps, not quite myself. It is a matter of distress to me that my husband is in trouble."

"But of course."

"As for this other affair: yes, we called at Leathers on the morning you speak of. My husband had been asked to do a job there—a leaking pipe I think he said it was, and had called to say that he could not undertake it at that time."

"You saw Mr. Harkness?"

"I remained in the car. My husband may have seen him. But I think not."

"Did you see Sydney Jones?"

"Him! *He* was there. There was some talk about a quarrel between Harkness and the girl." Her eyes slid around at him. "Perhaps it is Harkness to whom you should speak."

"Do you remember if there were any horses in the stables?"

"I did not see. I did not notice the stables."

"Or in the horse paddock? Or on the distant hillside?"

"I didn't notice."

"What time was it?"

"Possibly about ten-thirty. Perhaps later."

"Had you been anywhere else that morning?"

"To L'Esperance."

"Indeed?"

"I do *la blanchisserie de fin* for the ladies. I deliver it there."

"Is that the usual procedure?"

"No," she said composedly. "Usually one of their staff picks it up. As we were driving in that direction and the washing was ready, I delivered it."

"Speaking of deliveries, you do know, don't you, that young Louis—to distinguish him," said Alleyn, "from the elder Louis—delivered a note from your husband addressed to me. At the police station? Here very late last night? He pushed it under the door, rang the bell, and ran away."

"That's a bloody lie," said Mrs. Ferrant. In English.

The conversation so far had been conducted in a lofty mixture of French and English and, in both languages, at a high level of decorum. It was startling to hear Mrs. Ferrant come out strongly in basic British fishwife.

"But it isn't, you know," Alleyn said mildly. "It's what happened."

"No! I swear it. The boy has done nothing. Nothing. He was in bed and asleep by nine o'clock."

The front door banged.

"Maman! Maman!" cried a treble voice, "Where are you?"

Mrs. Ferrant's hand went to her mouth.

They heard young Louis run down the passage and in and out of the kitchen.

"Maman! Are you upstairs? Where are you?"

"Ferme ton bec," she let out in the standard maternal screech. "I am busy. Stop that noise."

But he returned, running up the passage, and burst into the parlor.

"Maman," he said, "they have nicked papa. The boys are saying it. They nicked him last night at the house where he gave me the letter." He stared at Alleyn. "Him," he said, and pointed. "The fuzz. He's nicked papa."

Mrs. Ferrant raised her formidable right arm in what no doubt was a familiar gesture.

Louis said, "No, *Maman!*" and cringed.

Alleyn said: "Do you often give Louis a *coup* for speaking the truth, Mrs. Ferrant?"

She thrust the receipted bill at him. "Take it and remove yourself," she said. "I have nothing more to say to you."

"I shall do so. With the fondest remembrances of your sole *à la Dieppoise*."

Upstairs, in Ricky's room Fox said: "What do we get out of that lot?"

"Apart from confirmation of various bits of surmise and conjecture I should say damnall, or very nearly so. If it's of interest, I think she's jealous of her husband and completely under his thumb. I think she hates his guts and would go to almost any length to obey his orders. Otherwise, damnall."

They packed up Ricky's belongings. The morning had turned sunny and the view from the window, described with affection in his letters, was at its best. The harbor was spangled, seagulls swooped and coasted, and down on the front, a covey of small boys frisked and skittered. Louis was not among them.

Alleyn laid his hand on the stack of paper that was Ricky's manuscript and wondered how long the view from the window would remain vivid in his son's memory. All his life, perhaps, if anything came of the book. He covered the pile with a sheet of plain paper and put it into an attaché case, together with a quantity of loose notes. Fox packed the clothes. In a drawer of the wardrobe he found letters Ricky had received from his parents.

"Mrs. F. will have enjoyed a good read," said Alleyn grimly.

When everything was ready and the room had taken on that blank, unoccupied look, they put Ricky's baggage in the car. Alleyn, for motives he would have found hard to define but suspected to be less than noble, left five pounds on the dressing table.

Before they shut the front door they heard her cross the passage and mount the stairs.

"She'll chuck it after you," predicted Fox.

"What's the betting? Give her a chance."

They waited. Mrs. Ferrant did not throw the five pounds after them. She snapped the window curtains across the upstairs room. A faint tremor seemed to suggest that she watched them through the crack.

They returned to Montjoy after a brief visit to Syd's Pad, where they found Moss and Cribbage, who had

completed an exhaustive search and had assembled the
fruits of it on the work table: a tidy haul, Alleyn said.
He pressed his thumb down on tubes of paint and felt
the presence of buried capsules. He looked at the
collection, still nestling under protective rows of flake
white: capsules waiting to be inserted. And at a chair
the legs of which were scored with wire and smudged
with blood.

"You've done very well," he said and turned to
Plank. "Normally," he said, "I'd have sent for
Detective-Sergeant Thompson who's my particular
chap at the Yard, but seeing you're an expert, Plank, I
think we'll ask you to take the photographs of this area
for us. How do you feel about tackling the job?"

Scarlet with gratification, Plank intimated that he
felt fine and was dropped at his station to collect
photographic gear. Moss and Cribbage were to take
alternate watches at the Pad until such time as the
exhibits were removed. Fox and Alleyn returned to
Montjoy.

As their car climbed up the steep lane to the main
road, Alleyn looked down on the Cove and wondered
whether or not he would have occasion to return to it.

When he walked into his room at the Hotel
Montjoy, he found Troy there waiting for him.

III

Sunday came in to the promise of halcyon weather.
A clear sky and a light breeze brought an air of
expectation to the island.

Ricky's progress was satisfactory, and though his
face resembled, in Troy's words, one of Turner's more
intemperate sunsets, no bones were broken and no
permanent disfigurement need be expected. His ankles
were still very swollen and painful but there was no sign

of infection and with the aid of sticks he hoped to be able to hobble out of hospital tomorrow.

In the morning Alleyn and Fox had a session on the balcony outside the Alleyns' room. They trudged through the body of evidence point by point in familiar pursuit of an overall pattern.

"You know," Fox said, pushing his spectacles up his forehead when they paused for Alleyn to light his pipe, "the unusual feature of this case, as I see it, is its lack of definition. Take the homicide aspect, now. As a general rule we know who we're after. There's no mystery. It's a matter of finding enough material to justify an arrest. It's not *like* that, this time," Fox said vexedly. "You may have your ideas and so may I, Mr. Alleyn. We may even think there's only the one possibility that doesn't present an unanswerable objection, but there's not what I'd call a hard *case* to be made out. We've got the drug scene on the one hand and this poor girl on the other. Are they connected? Well, *are* they? *Was* she knocked off because she threatened to shop them on account of requiring a husband? And if so, which would she shop? Or all? We've got three names that might, as you might say, qualify—but only one available for the purpose of marriage."

"The miserable Syd."

"Quite so. Then there's this uncle. There were all these scenes with him. Threats and all the rest of it. Motive, you might think. But he wasn't drinking at that time and you can't imagine him risking his own horseflesh. The mare he's so keen on just as likely to be killed as the girl. And in any case he'd threatened to give her what for if she had a go. *And* he ordered Jones to remove the mare so's she couldn't try. No, I reckon we've got to boil it down to those three unless—by cripey, I wonder."

"What?"

"What was it you quoted yesterday about a female

informant in France? I've got it," said Fox and repeated it. He thought it over, became restless, shook his head, and broke out again. "We've no nice, firm *times* for anything," he lamented. "Mr. and Mrs. Ferrant, S. Jones, Mr. Louis Pharamond all flitting about the premises, in and out and roundabout and Mr. Harkness locking the girl up. The girl getting out and getting herself killed. Mr. Harkness writing these silly pamphlets. *I* don't know," Fox said and readjusted his glasses. "It's mad."

"It's half-past eleven," said Alleyn. "Have a drink."

Fox looked surprised. "Really?" he said. "This is unusual, Mr. Alleyn. Well, since you've suggested it I'll take a light ale."

Alleyn joined with him. They sat on the hotel balcony and looked not toward France but westward across the Golfe to the Atlantic. They saw that battlements of cloud had built up on the horizon.

"What does that mean?" wondered Troy, who had come out to join them. "Is that the weather quarter?"

"There's no wind to speak of," Alleyn said.

"Very sultry," said Fox. "Humid."

"The cloud's massing while you look at it," Troy said. "Swelling up over the edge of the ocean as fast as fast can be."

"Perhaps it's getting ready for Mr. Harkness's service. Flashes of lightning," said Alleyn, "an enormous beard lolloping over the top of the biggest cloud, and a gigantic hand chucking thunderbolts. Very alarming."

"They say it's the season on the island for that class of weather," Fox observed.

"And in Saint Pierre-des-Roches judging by Rick's experience."

"Oppressive," sighed Fox.

The western sky slowly darkened. By the time they had finished work on the file, cloud overhung the Channel and threatened the island. After luncheon it

almost filled the heavens and was so low that the
church spire on the hill above Montjoy looked as if it
would prick it and bring down a deluge. But still it
didn't rain. Alleyn and Troy walked to the hospital and
Fox paid a routine visit to the police station.

By teatime the afternoon had so darkened that it
might have been evening.

At five o'clock Julia rang up, asking Troy if they
would like to be collected for what she persisted in
calling "Cuth's party." Troy explained that she would
not be attending it and that Alleyn and Fox had a car.
Jasper shouted greetings down the telephone. They
both seemed to be in the best of spirits. Even Carlotta
joined in the fun.

Troy said to Alleyn: "You'd say they rejoiced over
the bolting of egregious Louis."

"They've good cause to."

"Is he in deep trouble, Rory?"

"Might well be. We don't really know and it's even
money that we'll never find out."

The telephone rang again and Alleyn answered it.
He held the receiver away from his ear and Troy could
hear the most remarkable noises coming through, as of
a voice being violently tuned in and out on a
loudspeaker. Every now and then words would belch
out in a roar: "Retribution" was one and "Judgment"
another. Alleyn listened with his face screwed up.

"I'm coming," he said when he got the chance. "We
are all coming. It has been arranged."

"Jones!" the voice boomed, *"Jones!"*

"That may be a bit difficult, but I think so."

Expostulations rent the air.

"This is too much," Alleyn said to Troy. He laid the
receiver down and let it perform. When an opportunity
presented itself he snatched it up and said: "Mr.
Harkness, I am coming to your service. In the
meantime, goodbye," and hung up.

"Was that really Mr. Harkness?" asked Troy, "or

was it an elemental on the rampage?"

"The former. Wait a jiffy."

He called the office and said there seemed to be a lunatic on the line and would they be kind enough to cut him off if he rang again.

"How can he possibly hold a service?" Troy asked.

"He's hell-bent on it. Whether he's in a purely alcoholic frenzy or whether he really has taken leave of his senses or whether in fact he has something of moment to reveal is impossible to say."

"But what's he *want*?"

"He wants a full house. He wants Ferrant and Jones, particularly."

"Why?"

"Because he's going to tell us who killed his niece."

"For crying out loud!" said Troy.

"That," said Alleyn, "is exactly what he intends to do."

The service was to be at six o'clock. Alleyn and Fox left Montjoy at a quarter to the hour under a pall of cloud and absolute stillness. Local sounds had become isolated and clearly defined: voices, a car engine starting up, desultory footfalls. And still it did not rain.

After a minute or two on the road a police van overtook them and sailed ahead.

"Plank," said Alleyn, "with his boys in blue and their charges. Only they're not in blue."

"I suppose it's OK," Fox said rather apprehensively.

"It'd better be," said Alleyn.

As they passed L'Esperance, the Pharamond's largest car could be seen coming down the drive. And on the avenue to Leathers they passed little groups of pedestrians and fell in behind a procession of three cars.

"Looks like capacity all right," said Fox.

Two more cars were parked in front of the house and the police van was in the stable yard. Out in the horse paddock the sorrel mare flung up her head and stared at them. The loose-boxes were empty.

"Is he looking after all this himself?" Fox wondered. "You'd hardly fancy he was up to it, would you?"

Mr. Blacker, the vet, got out of one of the cars and came to meet them.

"This is a rum go and no mistake," he said. "I got a most peculiar letter from Cuth. Insisting I come. Not my sort of Sunday afternoon at all. Apparently he's been canvassing the district. Are you chaps mixed up in it, or what?"

Alleyn was spared the necessity of answering by the arrival of the Pharamonds.

They collected around Alleyn and Fox, gaily chattering as if they had met in the foyer of the Paris Opéra. Julia and Carlotta wore black linen suits with white lawn blouses, exquisite tributes to Mrs. Ferrant's art as a *blanchisseuse de fin*.

"Shall we go in?" Julia asked as if the bells had rung for Curtain-Up. "We mustn't miss anything, must we?" She laid her gloved hand on Alleyn's arm. "The baskets!" she said. "Should we take them in or leave them in the car?"

"Baskets!"

"You must remember! 'Ladies a Basket.' Carlotta and I have brought langouste and mayonnaise sandwiches. Do you think—suitable?"

"I'm not sure if the basket arises this time."

"We must wait and see. If unsuitable we shall wolf them up when we get home. As a kind of hors d'oeuvre. You're dining, aren't you? You and Troy? And Mr. Fox, *of course*?"

"Julia," Alleyn said, "Fox and I are policemen and we're on duty and however delicious your langouste sandwiches I doubt if we can accept your kind invitation. And now, like a dear creature, go and assemble your party in the front stalls and don't blame me for what you are about to receive. It's through there on your right."

"Oh dear!" said Julia. "Yes. I see. Sorry."

He watched them go off and then looked into the police van. Plank and Moss were in the front, Cribbage and a very young constable in the back with Ferrant and Syd Jones attached to them. The police were in civilian dress.

Alleyn said: "Wait until everyone else has gone in and then sit at the back. OK? If there aren't any seats left, stand."

"Yes, sir," said Plank.

"Where are your other chaps?"

"They went in, Mr. Alleyn. As far front as possible. And there's an extra copper from the mainland like you said. Outside the back door."

"How are your two treasures in there?"

"Ferrant's a right monkey, Mr. Alleyn. Very uncooperative. He doesn't talk except to Jones and then it's only the odd curse. The doctor came in to see Jones before we left and gave him a reduced fix. The doctor's here."

"Good."

"He says Mr. Harkness called him in to give him something to steady him up but he reckons he'd already taken something on his own account."

"Where is Doctor Carey?"

"In the audience. He's just gone in. He said to tell you Mr. Harkness is in a very unstable condition but not incapable."

"Thank you. We'll get moving. Come on, Fox."

They joined the little stream of people who walked around the stables and along the path to the old barn.

A man with a collection plate stood inside the door. Alleyn, fishing out his contribution, asked if he could by any chance have a word with Mr. Harkness and was told that Brother Cuth was at prayer in the back room and could see nobody. "Alleluia," he added, apparently in acknowledgment of Alleyn's donation.

Alleyn and Fox found seats halfway down the barn.
Extra chairs and boxes were being brought in,
presumably from the house. The congregation appeared to be a cross section of Cove and countryside in
its Sunday clothes with a smattering of rather more
stylish persons who might hail from Montjoy or even
be tourists come out of curiosity. Alleyn recognized
one or two faces he had seen at the Cod-and-Bottle.
And there, stony in the fourth row, with Louis beside
her, sat Mrs. Ferrant.

A little farther forward from Alleyn and Fox were
the Pharamonds, looking like a stand of orchids in a
cabbage patch and behaving beautifully.

In the front three rows sat, or so Alleyn concluded,
the hardcore Brethren. They had an air of proprietor-
ship and kept a smug eye on their books.

The curtains were closed to exclude the stage.

An audience, big or small, as actors know, generates
its own flavor and exudes it like a pervasive scent. This
one gave out the heady smell of suspense.

The tension increased when a thin lady with a white
face seated herself at the harmonium and released
strangely disturbing strains of unparalleled vulgarity.

"Shall we gather at the River?" invited the harmonium.

"The Beautiful
The Beautiful
The Ree-iv-a?"

Under cover of this prelude Plank and his support
brought in their charges. Alleyn and Fox could see
them reflected in a glazed and framed scroll that hung
from a beam: "The Chosen Brethren," it was headed,
and it set out the professions of the sect.

Plank's party settled themselves on a bench against
the back wall.

The harmonium achieved its ultimate fortissimo
and the curtains opened jerkily to reveal six men seated

behind a table on either side of a more important but
empty chair. The congregation, prompted by the elect,
rose.

In the commonplace light of early evening that filled
the hall and in a total silence that followed a last
deafening roulade on the organ, Mr. Harkness entered
from the inner room at the back of the platform.

One would have said that conditions were not
propitious for dramatic climax: it had, however, been
achieved.

He was dressed in a black suit and wore a black shirt
and tie. He had shaved and his hair, cut to regimental
length, was brushed. His eyes were bloodshot, his
complexion was blotched, and his hands unsteady, but
he seemed to be more in command of himself than he
had been on the occasions when Alleyn encountered
him. It was a star entrance and if Mr. Harkness had
been an actor he would have been accorded a round of
applause.

As it was he sat in the central chair. There he
remained motionless throughout the ensuing hymn
and prayers. These latter were extemporaneous and of
a highly emotional character and were given out in turn
by each of the six supporting Brethren, later referred to
by Plank as "Cuth's sidekicks."

With these preliminaries accomplished and all being
seated, Cuthbert Harkness rose to deliver his address.
For at least a minute and in complete silence he stood
with head bent and eyes closed while his lips moved,
presumably in silent prayer. The wait was hard to bear.

From the moment he began to speak he generated
an almost intolerable tension. At first he was quiet but
it would have come as a relief if he had spoken at the
top of his voice.

He said: "Brethren: This is the Day of Reckoning.
We are sinners in the sight of the Great Master. Black
as hell are our sins and only the Blood of Sacrifice can
wash us clean. We have committed abominations. Our

unrighteousness stinks in the nostrils of the All-Seeing Host. Uncleanliness, lechery, and defilement stalk through our ranks. And Murder."

It was as if a communal nerve had been touched, causing each member of his audience to stiffen. He himself actually "came to attention" like a soldier. He squared his shoulders, lifted his chin, inflated his chest, and directed his bloodshot gaze over the heads of his listeners. He might have been addressing a parade.

"Murder," roared Mr. Harkness. "You have Murder here in your midst, Brethren, here in the very temple of righteousness. And I shall reveal its Name unto you. I have nursed the awful knowledge like a viper in my bosom, I have wrestled with the Angel of Darkness. I have suffered the torments of the Damned but now the Voice of Eternal Judgment has spoken unto me and all shall be made known."

He stopped dead and looked wildly around his audience. His gaze alighted on the row against the back wall and became fixed. He raised his right arm and pointed.

"Guilt!" he shouted. "Guilt encompasseth us on every hand. The Serpent is coiled in divers bosoms. I accuse! Sydney Jones—"

"You lay off me," Syd screamed out, "you shut up."

Heads were turned. Sergeant Plank could be heard expostulating. Harkness, raising his voice, roared out a sequence of anathemas, but no specific accusation. The accusing finger shifted.

"Gilbert Ferrant! Woe unto you Gilbert Ferrant—"

By now half the audience had turned in their seats. Gilbert Ferrant, tallow-faced, stared at Harkness.

"Woe unto you, Gilbert Ferrant. Adulterer! Trader in forbidden fruits!"

It went on. Now, only the Inner Brethren maintained an eyes-front demeanor. Consternation mounted in the rest of the congregation. Mr. Harkness now pointed at Mrs. Ferrant. He accused her of stonyheartedness and avarice. He moved on to Bob Maistre (wine-bibbing) and several fishermen unknown to Alleyn (blasphemy).

He paused. His roving and ensanguined gaze alighted on the Pharamonds. He pointed: "And ye," he apostrophized them: "Wallowers in the fleshpots..."

He rambled on at the top of his voice. They were motionless throughout. At last he stopped, glared, and seemed to prepare himself for some final and stupendous effort. Into the silence desultory sounds intruded. It was as if somebody outside the barn had begun to pepper the iron roof with pellets, only a few at first but increasing. At last the clouds had broken and it had begun to rain.

One might be forgiven, Alleyn thought afterwards, for supposing that some celestial stage manager had taken charge, decided to give Mr. Harkness the full treatment, and grossly overdone it. Mr. Harkness himself seemed to be unaware of the mounting fusillade on the roof. As the din increased he broke out anew. He stepped up his parade-ground delivery. He shouted anathemas: on his niece and her sins, citing predictable biblical comparisons, notably Jezebel and the Whore of Babylon. He referred to Leviticus 20:6 and to the Cities of the Plains. He began to describe the circumstances of her death. He was now very difficult to hear, for the downpour on the iron roof was all-obliterating.

"And the Sinner..." could be made out, "... Mark of Cain... before you all... now proclaim... Behold the man..."

He raised his right arm to the all-too-appropriate accompaniment of a stupendous thunderclap and turned himself into a latterday Lear. He beat his bosom and seemed at last to become aware of the storm.

An expression of bewilderment and frustration appeared. He stared wildly about him, gestured incomprehensively, clasped his hands, and looked beseechingly around his audience.

Then he covered his face with his hands and bolted into the inner room. The door shut behind him with such violence that the framed legend above it crashed to the floor. Still the rain hammered on the iron roof.

Alleyn and Fox were on the stage with Plank hard at their heels. Nothing they said could be heard. Alleyn was at the door. It was locked. He and Fox stood back from it, collected themselves and shoulder-charged it. It resisted but Plank was there and joined in the next assault. It burst open and they plunged into the room.

Brother Cuth hung from a beam above the chair he had kicked away. His confession was pinned to his coat. He had used a length of wire from the coil in the old coach house.

IV

Alleyn pushed the confession across the table at Fox. "It's all there," he said. "He may have written it days ago or whenever he first made up his mind.

"He was determined to destroy the author of his damnation, as he saw her, and then himself. The method only presented itself after their row about Dulcie jumping the gap. He seems to have found some sort of satisfaction, some sense of justice in the act of her disobedience being the cause of her death. He must have . . . made his final preparations . . . during the time he was locked up in the back room before the service began. If we'd broken in the door on the first charge we might just have saved him. He wouldn't have thanked us for it."

"I don't get it, sir," Plank said. "Him risking the sorrel mare. It seems all out of character."

"He didn't think he was risking the mare. He'd

ordered Jones to take her to the smith and he counted on Dulcie trying the jump with Mungo, the outlaw, the horse he wanted to destroy. In the verbal battle they exchanged, he told her the mare had gone to the smith and she said she'd do it on Mungo. It's there, in the confession. He's been very thorough."

"When did he rig the wire in the gap?" Fox asked. He was reading the confession. "Oh yes. I see. As soon as Jones went to the corn chandlers, believing that on his return he would remove the sorrel mare to the blacksmith's."

"And unrigged it after the Ferrants left, when Jones was sleeping off his drugs in the loose-box."

Fox said: "And that girl lying in full view there in the ditch, looking the way she did! You can't wonder he went off the rails." He read on.

Plank said: "And yet, Mr. Alleyn, by all accounts he used to be fond of her, too. She was his niece. He'd adopted her."

"What's all this he's on about? Leviticus twenty, verse six," Fox asked.

"Look it up in the Bible they so thoughtfully provide in your room, Br'er Fox. I did. It says:*'None of you shall approach to any that is near of kin to him to uncover their nakedness.'*"

Fox thought it over and was scandalized. "I see," he said. "Yes, I see."

"To him," Alleyn said, "she was the eternal temptress. The Scarlet Woman. The cause of his undoing. In a way, I suppose, he thought he was handing over the outcome to the Almighty. If she obeyed him and stayed in her room, nothing would happen. If she defied him, everthing would. Either way the decision came from on High."

"Not my idea of Christianity," Plank muttered. "The Missus and I are C of E," he added.

"You know," Alleyn said to Fox, "one might almost say Harkness was a sort of cross between Adam and the Ancient Mariner. 'The woman tempted me,' you know. And the subsequent revulsion followed by the awful necessity to talk about it, to make a proclamation before all the world and then to die."

They said nothing for some time. At last Fox cleared his throat.

"What about the button?" he asked.

"In the absence of its owner, my guess would be that he went into the horse paddock out of curiosity to inspect Bruno's jump and saw dead Dulcie. Dulcie who'd been threatening to shop her drug-running boyfriends. That, true to his practice as a strictly background figure of considerable importance, Louis decided to have seen nothing and removed himself from the terrain. Too bad he dropped a button."

"Well," Fox said after a further pause. "We haven't had what you'd call a resounding success. Missed out with our homicide by seconds, lost a big fish on the drug scene, and ended up with a couple of tiddlers. *And* we've seen the young chap turn into a casualty on the way. How is he, Mr. Alleyn?"

"We've finished for the time being. Come and see," said Alleyn.

Ricky had been discharged from hospital and was receiving in his bedroom at the hotel. Julia, Jasper, and Troy were all in attendance. The Pharamonds had brought grapes, books, champagne, and some more langouste sandwiches because the others had been a success. They had been describing, from their point of view, Cuth's party as Julia only just continued not to call it.

"Darling," she said to Ricky, "your papa was quite wonderful." And to Troy, "No, but I promise. Superb." She appealed to Fox. "You'll bear me out, Mr. Fox." Rather to his relief she did not wait for Fox to do so. "There we all were," Julia continued at large. "I can't tell you—the noise! And poor, poorest Cuth, trying with all his might to compete, rather, one couldn't help thinking, like Mr. Noah in the deluge. I don't mean to be funny but it did come into one's head at the time. And really, you know, it was rather impressive. Especially when he pointed us out and said we were wallowers in the fleshpots of Egypt, though why Egypt, one asks oneself. And then all those—'effects,' don't they call them?—and—and—"

Julia stopped short. "Would you agree," she said, appealing to Alleyn, "that when something really awful happens it's terribly important not to work up a sort of phony reaction? You know? Making out you're more upset than you really are. Would you say that?"

Alleyn said: "In terms of self-respect I think I would."

"Exactly," said Julia. "It's like using a special sort of pious voice about somebody who's dead when you don't really mind all that much." She turned to Ricky and presented him with one of her most dazzling smiles. "But then you see," she said, "thanks to your papa we only saw the storm scene, as I expect it would be called in Shakespeare. Because after they broke in the door a large man pulled the stage curtains across and then your papa came through like men in dinner jackets do in the theater and asked for a doctor and told us there'd been an accident and would we leave quietly. So we did. Of course if we'd—" Julia stopped. Her face had gone blank. "If we'd seen," she said rapidly, "it would have been different."

Ricky remembered what she had been like after she had seen Dulcie Harkness. And then he remembered Jasper saying: "The full shock and horror of a death is only experienced when it has been seen."

Julia and Jasper said they must go and Alleyn went down with them to their car. Jasper touched Alleyn's arm and they let Julia go ahead and get into the driver's seat.

"About Louis," Jasper said. "Is it to do with drugs?"

"We think it may be."

"I've thought from time to time that something like that might be going on. But it all seemed unreal. We've never known anybody who was hooked."

Alleyn echoed Julia. "If you had," he said, "it would have been different."

When he returned, it was to find Fox and Troy and Ricky quietly contented with each other's company.

Alleyn put his arm round Troy.

"'And so we say farewell,'" he said, "'to the Pharamonds and their Wonderful Island.' Pack up your bags, chaps. We're going home."